FLIPSIDE EROTICA
both sides of the story

flip book over ↻

Darren Michaels

ISBN: 978-0-615-27210-8

Printed in USA

www.flipside-erotica.com

This book is dedicated to those who are
smart enough to *dream*, brave enough to *act*,
and confident enough to know that life is all about the
experiences you have along the way.

A special thank you to HyperDonkey.com
for the technical assistance on this book project and the
www.flipside-erotica.com website. Without your help,
this project would not have been possible.

Table of Contents — Her Eyes

	Page
Introduction	
Leslie	9
Ashleigh	17
Jillian	23
Laura	31
Katie	39
Gina	47
Andrea	59
Lindsay	67
Nicole	75
Stacy	83
Katherine	91
Ashleigh & Hannah	99

Introduction

I hope you enjoy the unique twist this book presents. I have written each and every story; I do "research" with some of the people in the stories, and have certainly asked questions regarding thoughts and feelings to gain a better understanding of both sides of the story. These stories are a mixture of experiences I have had. All are based on fact, at least concerning the person(s) involved. Some are true to the letter, some are the way I wished things worked out, and some of them are total fabrications built around someone I've met. As the reader, you will have to decide which is which.

If you are looking for a romance novel, put this book back where you found it. This is a book about classy adults doing erotic things. Take it for what it is worth, pure entertainment. As an advocate for safe sex, I strongly encourage you to take the necessary precautions in your own adventures. Although I do not make reference to the use of condoms in every story, I assure you I do my part to protect myself and my partner. You should be sure to do the same.

Please log onto my website at www.flipside-erotica.com and let me know what you think of this project. Enjoy the free preview of the audio downloads that is offered. Some of the voices in the audio files are the actual people in the stories; some are just friends of mine. Again, you will have to decide for yourself who's who. ☺

Leslie

"Hey, what are you doing tonight" I ask. He does his usual thing, hesitating before answering me. "Hmm, I don't know, what do you have in mind?" he asks in his non committal voice. "Let's go for a swim…see you around 8pm" I say. I like to play the role of choosing when we get together, and I know he likes it when I initiate things.

He is a little younger than I am; a former athlete who is still in great shape. He can certainly handle my appetite for sex. Nothing makes the stresses of the week melt away like a good hard pounding after a glass or two of wine. He is a little taller than I am, and loves to play rough. I can feel the sting of his hand already, and I shudder just a little in anticipation. His shaved head and goatee seem to fit his bad-boy demeanor perfectly. I'm sure no one at work would ever guess that I have my own beckon call boy, but it's really how I want it. I like my space, my time, but once in a while I need to feel the weight of a man on top of me.

I hear his car pull up out front and I reach into the garage, pushing the button to raise the door for him to pull in. I prefer to not have the neighbors know I get company once in a while. I chug the last half glass of wine I poured for myself, and meet him at the door in my latest acquisition from Victoria's Secret; a lovely sheer teddy that leaves nothing to the imagination yet somehow still manages to look a touch classy. God I am looking forward to this. I take one look and want him right there in the kitchen; but part of me wants to make it last. That voice speaks a little louder, and I settle for a long, deep kiss against the door. I let him know I am hungry for it, kissing him hard before pulling away and walking towards the back door. I drop the teddy to the floor as if leaving him a trail for him to follow. Walking into the backyard, I am surprised at just how bright the moon is tonight. The warm air hits my naked body and I can feel my nipples surge forward. I walk over to the diving board, take one big hop and dive into the water. It is the perfect temperature, warm on my skin and yet still invigorating.

I am already tired of waiting, and he is taking longer than I want. I swim over to his side of the pool, and express my distaste for taking his sweet time by sending the biggest splash I can muster in his direction.

Her Eyes

He has his sandals off, but I want him naked. He starts to protest, so I do it again. "Alright, alright...I'm coming!" he exclaims. He tears off his shirt and tosses it aside, and then come the shorts. He is already getting hard, and his body looks amazing in the moonlight. He starts for the stairs and I swim his direction, meeting him on the steps. I take his cock in my mouth right away. "This is why you are here, and I am done playing around" I think to myself. While I still can, I jam his cock all the way into my throat. Soon he will be too hard for that, so since I still can I smash my nose against his hard stomach. He is getting harder by the second, and I am already struggling to take it all in. I put my hand around the base and slowly began to jerk it while I run my tongue all over him. He owns the hardest cock I have ever had, and I love every inch of it.

I am squatting on the stairs, knee deep in the warm water. I lean forward and put my free hand on the rough surface of the deck, settling in for a good, long session. Nothing gets me hotter than sucking this man's cock. I love the feeling of it in my mouth; the hardness against my tongue, the heat and the taste of him. He is rewarded for being shaved and trimmed in all the right places by getting extra time in my mouth. I am so focused on my task that I barely notice the shadows we are casting against the water's surface. It is a blending of the two of our forms; the distinct shape of my head disappearing into his body's shadow. I slide his cock out of my mouth and run my tongue over his balls; I look up to see nothing but the bottom of his chin as he throws his head back in ecstasy.

I feel him put his hand on the back of my head, and as I brace myself for his excitement to get the better of him and push me forcefully onto him. Instead he pulls my hair firmly and takes it from me. I sit there staring at his wet cock glistening in the moonlight for a second before I realize what has just happened. I want it back in my mouth, and I lean forward to get it. He pulls my hair firmly and laughs, looking down at me. "What the Hell is he doing?" the thought flashes through my mind. I look up at him, only to find him smiling down at me. "You arrogant fuck!" I scream inside. I reach back and let him have it, whacking him hard on the ass. The echo of skin on skin resonates in the back yard and I know that hurt. "Say it!" he commands. I have never been with a man who has as much self control as he does, and I know I'd have to surrender at some point. I wasn't going to give in that easily; I try a different tactic. I run through my standard protests, feigned sadness and then anger. Nothing. He is a rock and I know it. I hate him for it; and yet I love the fact that he knows me so well that he understands on some deep level that this turns me on more than anything anyone has ever done. To break me down, to truly be taken control of is my deepest desire and he owns me because of it.

"Say it and you can have it" he states in a firm voice. "Oh come on...don't do this to me." I plead. "You know the rules, and who makes the rules?" he reminds. "Me" I say firmly. He yanks the handful of hair he had in his hand, and I wince a little. "Who makes the rules?" he asks again. "Fuck you!" I snarl, trying to mask a smile with contempt. I'm not in the mood to try every trick in the book to win this little exchange, so I am skipping right to being angry. I am going to have to give in anyway, so I might as well get what I want sooner. "Do you want to suck my cock or not?" he asks firmly. "Yes" I reply, giving in. "Please?" I add sheepishly. "That wasn't so bad, was it?" he laughs. With that he let go of my hair and I attack his cock. I am so turned on by his power play, of denying me what I want even at his own expense, I am crazy with desire. I moan and whimper as I go after it. I jam his cock into the back of my throat, wanting all of it in my mouth even though I know it will be too much. I fight the urge to gag and ram it into me again, sucking hard as I withdraw all the way. I begin jerking him furiously, my hand gliding over the entire length of his slobbered cock. I feel like I am going to burst, burned by a fire from within.

Just when I think I can't take any more, I feel his hands on my breasts. He smashes them up against me and starts pinching my nipples. They are so hard and I am so hot I think I may come just from that. I shiver under his touch, aching for more. He brushes the back of his fingers over my nipples that are hard enough to cut glass. The sensation is amazing and I become lost in a blinding swirl of pleasure. I keep sucking him the best I can, but the feeling welling up inside of me is becoming almost unbearable. He pinches them and I think I might explode, pain and pleasure battle for control within my body. I can't take it any more and his cock pops out of my mouth as I cry out. I bury my face into his thigh, trying to muffle the animal noises I can hear myself making. He leans forward and I know where he is heading. "Oh

11

God…yes…touch me!" I beg. He makes small wet circles around my clit which is straining with excitement. I lean into him, and he buries what feels like two fingers deep into my throbbing wet pussy as I feel the explosion from deep inside me release. He shoves his fingers back into me and I nearly scream as I come again and again. One blends into another as I ride the waves of pleasure, shaking under his intruding fingers inside me. I look up at him, lost in the feeling and totally surrendered to the moment.

"Oh fuck that was so good!" I say to him. "Only the beginning, sweetheart…only the beginning" he states. And I believe him; since the very first time we were together the sex has been bone charring to say the least. I am still in my orgasm-induced haze when I hear a splash at the other end of the pool. I didn't even realize that he had walked away from me, let alone to the other side of the pool. He jumps onto the mattress sized raft that is floating in the deep end, and is heading my direction. I just smile, knowing that he is going to fulfill his earlier promise of us truly just getting started. I want him in my mouth again, and also want him to return the favor to my now hyper-sensitive pussy. I join him, climbing onto the raft and settling my hips down over his face. I grab his cock again, desperately wanting my mouth on it.

It springs to life instantly under my touch, and once again he is rock hard and ready for battle. He wastes no time going to work on me; putting his hands on my hips, he reaches up to meet my most sensitive area. I arch my back to connect with his mouth, aching to feel his silky tongue on my clit. He catches me off guard by going right for it, shoving his tongue into my slippery hole. I would have gasped aloud again if not for his cock wedged in my throat blocking the noise. He does it again and again, forcing his tongue inside me. The feeling is exquisite, and the vibrations from my moans reverberate down the shaft of his cock. God do I love this position; I can get him deeper into my mouth and he is stroking his tongue all over me. We float all around the pool, adrift on a sea of pleasure in mutual exchange and free of any inhibitions. The raft acts as our own private island, away from the rest of the world, and I am safe to truly let go, unfettered to revel in our ecstasy.

We continue on until I have two more brain melting orgasms under his command. I can tell he is growing close to his own, and I feel the dirty urge to swallow his load. I haven't done that in years, but I want his. I am so caught up in the moment; I want to tear down my own walls. "You're going to have to quit that soon" he informs me. "I don't want to quit...give it to me" I tell him. I continue jerking the base and sucking hard on the rest of his cock. I can tell he is getting close; I can feel him swelling in my mouth, and I find myself moaning in anticipation of his release. "God I can be a dirty whore when I want to be" I think to myself. He takes a couple of labored breaths, and mutters through gritted teeth "Oh fuck, here it comes." That is my cue, and I lunge at him, burying his cock into my throat. I can feel it spasm, expanding over and over as he shoots his load down my throat. He arches into me, grabbing the back of my head and holding me there; I am not going anywhere even if I wanted to. It is so fucking hot, once again being under his control and almost forced to do what he wants me to. His orgasm subsides, and he slumps back against the raft, totally spent. "Too bad...it's my turn now" I think to myself.

I spin around on him, facing him for the first time in who knows how many minutes. I lean forward and whisper in my desire-laden voice "I want you inside me." I know he will meet the challenge, and I don't even bother to wait for him. I climb on top of it, impaling myself on his cock. I slowly settle all the way down on it, taking it to the hilt. He touches me deep inside; I love the pressure of him against my insides. I slowly ride him, grinding and twisting against his body. I place my hands on his chest and dig my nails into his flesh. He runs his hands all over my body, tracing my curves and finally settling on my breasts which are once again aching for his touch. My nipples jump to attention. I love the way his strong hands squeeze my breasts and press them into my ribcage. The pressure is exquisite. I ride him faster, and he joins my rhythm.

The surface of the water reacts accordingly, and becomes choppy as our force increases. I can feel yet another one building inside me. He can sense it too, reading the signs he has seen so many times. He grabs my hips and forces me downward as he thrusts up into me. The penetration is even deeper than before, pushing against me inside. I feel him arching and lifting us both off the raft. My eyes widen in pleasure, and I am on autopilot. Desire takes over, and I find speed and rhythm I barely knew I had. I ride him like a wild stallion, grinding and slapping

Her Eyes

down onto him. I am delirious with pleasure as I throw my head back and cry out in another explosion. I'm not even sure if I had one really long one or several back to back orgasms, but the intense feeling reverberates through my body and I lose sense of time and control. I finally I can take no more and I collapse, slumping forward onto him in a heap of quivering flesh.

As my senses start to restore, I am vaguely aware of the fact that we are no longer moving. The next thing I know, I am in a bear hug and getting rolled into the water. I am instantly sober, and struggle to the surface. "You bastard!" I yell as I reach the surface. I splash wave after wave of water in his direction, but he is already swimming for the other side of the pool. I am so mad that he broke me out of my haze, but I also sense we are not finished either. I chase after him, barreling towards him at the shallow end of the pool. I get to the steps and stand up, taking a playful swing at him for dunking me. He grabs my wrist and spins me around. My arm is pinned between us, and he clamps his teeth down on my neck. His hands are all over my tits again, pressing them against me. I arch my back to feel his cock pushing against my aching pussy; I can't believe that I want more, but I just can't get enough of him. His hand leaves my breast, and finds its way to my mouth. I open and let him in; sucking feverishly on his fingers like it is his cock. He pulls his fingers out of my mouth and goes directly between my legs with them. His fingers are wet from my saliva, and easily enter me. He moves away from me, and now uses his other hand to attack me from behind. I am frozen with delight. I look towards the bright moon as once again I feel a surge of desire welling up inside me. He works me with both hands, front and back as I begin to moan aloud once again.

Suddenly he stops, and shoves me forward onto the towels he had placed on the deck. In one swift move he is all the way in me, burying himself to the hilt. The suddenness and force of the move catches me totally off guard, and I am so deep under his spell once again that I forget all about trying to curb the noises emanating from my mouth. I cry out at his every impact into me. The water splashes around us as my thighs get rammed into the side with each thrust. My arms are pinned behind my back, and he is pressing my body into the pool deck padded only by the towels. He has one foot on the deck and is splitting me in half with his hardness. He grabs a handful of my wet hair and yanks my head back. It

14

is too much, and I let go with a loud cry of ecstasy. I start before him, reaching the crest of my orgasm as he starts his. I buck and push back into him, wanting more even though there is no room for it. He fucks me hard, taking what he wants until he explodes inside of me. He pumps me until I have every last drop of it. He releases his hold on me and we both collapse forward, unable to support our spent bodies any longer. "Holy shit that was hot" he mutters. After a moment he climbs off of me and falls back into the pool.

I am instantly brought back to full attention as I realize the applause coming from the neighbor's house is for us. I am sure that they could hear us going at it, and decided to let us know they appreciated the show. So much for my plan of keeping his visit a secret. When I lift my face from my hands, he is just standing there smiling at me, with that arrogant grin on his face. Again.

Ashleigh

I called Darren to see if he wanted to go for a hike like we used to. I need to get away and get some space between my thoughts for a change. We have drifted apart since I started seeing someone else; seemingly unable to become just friends after all we had been through together. It seems as though I have found someone that I am very compatible with, but the spark of attraction is missing. Darren and I were unable to find a common ground as a couple, but the chemistry was never a question.

We meet at the designated spot, and ride together to our destination. Traffic is light and we make good time, arriving early in the morning in the northern Arizona mountains. I find myself shooting glances at him; my body seems to recognize his proximity. We hit the trail, passing a few hikers that must have turned back early in the trek. We see some fishermen, and ask if anyone else has passed by recently. They said no, and we are likely to be by ourselves deep in the mountains. I ache at the memory of some of the times spent alone deep in the mountains with him.

He suggests we take a short cut and find a secluded part of the stream. I agree, and we leave the trail and climb through the rough terrain to the top of the ridge. We can see for miles around, and the creek stretches out below us, far away from the trail where anyone else would be. We begin our decent through the trees to the bottom of the canyon. He arrives first, tearing off his shirt and shoes, cannon-balling into the middle of the large pool. I follow close behind, removing my shoes before diving in. He surfaces just as I leave the rock, and our eyes meet on my way down. He starts to say something, but it is too late. I hit the surface and the shock of the cold water knocks the breath from me. I fight to the surface, gasping for air. He is laughing at me from the side of the stream. I laugh too, realizing the irony in that once again I have jumped without checking where I am landing.

After a short time in the cool water, we both grow used to the temperature. Darren swims to a big rock in the middle of the pool, and sits back enjoying the sun on his face. God he looks beautiful sitting there. I find myself staring at him, drawn to him. As if pulled by an unseen force, I find myself swimming to him. I quietly sit next to him, waiting, hoping he will know what I am thinking. He opens his eyes to find me looking at him. "What do you think you are doing on my rock?" he questions in a playful tone. I am caught off guard, but delighted when I realize he still reads me like a book. "But I like your rock, don't you want to share?" I ask, growing nervous with anticipation. "It's been so long since he has touched me" I think to myself. He informs me there will be some sort of toll to pay. "I have wanted to suck your cock all day" I blurt out. "Oh that was subtle" I thought to myself. My only response to his question about the boyfriend is "He doesn't do it right." At this point I figure Darren is grandfather-claused in.

The heat coming from my thighs is winning the battle against the cold water; I am no longer fighting to stay warm. The thought of having him in my mouth once again is sublime; the mountain air, the cold water, and on a rock in the middle of a stream is something right out of a cheesy romance novel. I reach over and pull the drawstring on his shorts. I am on my knees in front of him, looking up like I have done so many times before. Memories and sensations flood my mind as I pull his shorts down and out of my way. I engulf it immediately, unable to contain my excitement any longer. I ram it into the back of my throat, proving the heights of my desire. I become aware that I am practically whimpering and moaning with desire as I bob up and down on his cock. Despite the water washing him clean, I can quickly sense the familiar taste of his skin, and I savor every moment.

After a moment or two he manages to wrestle my shirt off me with only a minor interruption. My tits are free; exposed to the sun, warming them. I am totally engrossed in my task, unconsciously clamping my thighs together in desire. He sees my frustration building, my desire burning through me. He reaches down and grabs my hand, lifting me to my feet. He yanks my shorts down to my ankles, and I am fully exposed to him atop the rock we are claiming as our own. He kneels before me, facing my throbbing pussy. He grabs one of my legs and throws it over his shoulder, and I do my best to balance on one leg. His face is in between my thighs before I can draw in a breath. His tongue shoots in and out of me like silken fire, caressing every inch of my aching sex. I throw my head back in ecstasy, almost throwing myself off balance. I dig my nails into his shoulder to hold myself in place.

He continues to run his tongue all over me, focusing a little more on my sensitive clit now than before. Alternating between long and short strokes, he draws a long, deep orgasm from its hiding place within me. It is exquisite, intense, and perfect. I am lost in it, aware of the hard rock under my foot yet floating on a cloud of pleasure, suspended above the Earth. My body arches to meet his mouth, wanting more…not wanting this moment to ever end. Finally I can give no more and I almost collapse on top of him. He holds me in place while I try to regain my composure.

After a moment, I am ready for more. No one has ever made me feel the way he does, and I long for whatever he has in mind next. "God do I miss this" I tell him. He bends down and puts his hands behind me knees, lifting me up. I throw my arms around his neck, bracing myself for what he wants. I realize his intent is to hold me up and fuck me right here; and I squeal in delight. The position is amazing, allowing deep penetration into me. But more than that, the underlying feeling of protection and security of being in his arms like this just adds to it. It is an odd combination of feelings, but a perfect package nonetheless.

I reach down behind me and find his hard cock, guiding it into my waiting pussy. My body envelops him as he pushes it deep into me. I start bucking my hips against him, traveling up and down his length. He touches me so deep inside, filling me completely. His strong hands cup my ass, helping me move faster against him. Waves of pleasure radiate through me as I start a series of orgasms in his arms. My cries fuel his strength, and he fucks me harder and harder. Soon the echoes of my voice can be heard throughout the canyon. I couldn't care less; I am free from inhibition in his arms, lost in the most exquisite moment I have ever known.

He lowers my feet into the water again, arms shaking from holding me in that position. The cool water renews my clarity, and I am now aware of my exposed condition. I don't want to get back in the cold water, but I have no choice if I want to hide from the world. I dive in, rushing for the cover of the rocks on the side of the creek. I arrive, and race for my backpack. I find my towel, and quickly dry off a little. I fold the towel and lay it on the rock, assuming position on top of it. He comes to me, dripping wet, staring down at me. I have grown shy, and close my legs in front of him. He is still rock hard, and is not interested in my personal dilemma. He spreads my legs open, shoving his cock into me. It is cold from the water, but quickly warms inside me. I moan in delight as he pushes in and out of me. He grabs my ankles, impacting my body over and over with his. Our bodies slap together, and I am trapped between him and the rock beneath me. He pounds me into oblivion once again.

I can tell he is nearing the end, and I have the dirty desire to have him come all over my tits. He asks me where I want it, and I share my thought with him: "Right here" I say, pushing them together. He pulls out of me and I slide down the rock right in front of him. He jerks his cock for me, and quickly is ready to burst. He groans, gritting his teeth as he shoots it all over my chest. The look in his eyes is deep and burning as he finishes. I lean forward, taking it in my mouth, running my tongue over his length. He shudders at the sensation of it.

We jump back into the water, and then get dressed for the hike back. We have a long way to go, and my legs are heavy and weak from our session in the wild. We find the trail and walk slowly towards the truck, as if to prolong our time together.

Ashleigh

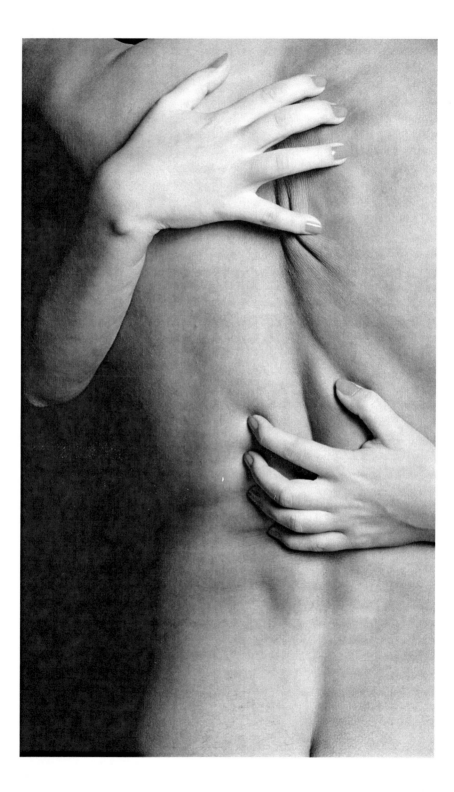

Jillian

Well, it's happened again; I am back in the cycle of working all the time. No wonder I am such a bitch at work; my hair was a lot shorter the last time I got laid. And no more bartenders; Mike is a good guy but barely 28, and I do not need that whole drama again. How am I going to meet someone if all I do is work? Hmm, I did like the guy who is running the big event at the club coming up next month. I wonder if he noticed me. He is a little shorter than most of the guys I have dated; I wonder if he'd be up to the task.

I hear his voice in the reception area, and for some reason I am suddenly nervous to see him. "He has no idea what I've been thinking, so why should seeing him now change?" I ask myself. Here they come...I busy myself with papers on my desk. "Anything else?" my assistant asks. "No" I respond firmly, and she shuts the door behind her. We speak about the project, pouring over the minutia of details for the pending event. We have met several times now, and the time is drawing near. I grimace at the thought of not having an excuse to see him any more. We finish, stand at the same time, and shake hands. I look deep into his eyes, but he doesn't seem to notice. I watch him leave, his tight jeans highlighting his fit build.

The event is less than a week away, and we have met once a week to make sure we are on track. We didn't need to; I just suggested it to see him regularly. I am doing my best to show interest while still being professional, but he does not notice. God, I swear you have to flash your boobs to get some guys to catch on. He walks out, and I figure that was about my last chance to get his attention. I need a drink.

I walk into the bar in the hotel, despite the fact that Mike is working tonight. He sees me coming and pours me a glass of my favorite wine. I may have to settle for him tonight, blaming it on a wine-induced momentary lapse of reason tomorrow. That always sounds better than I was so horny I hooked up with an ex just to get laid. I look around the bar; not too many candidates in here anyway...wait; he's here. I don't believe it. I wave to him, and he waves back. I signal with a motion of my head to join me at the table behind where I am seated, and he grabs

23

his beer and heads my way. Poor Mike; so close and he never even knew it.

He sits across from me, explaining he was supposed to meet someone, but appears they will not be making it. We chat more comfortably than before, but another glass of wine would not hurt. He offers to buy the next round, but I tell I'll buy since I never pay for anything here. "I used to date that bartender" I reveal in a whispered voice. "Really! Isn't he a lot younger than you?" he inquires aloud. I laugh internally as I watch him mentally back peddle from that statement. I do my best not to even change expressions, but finally can't help it and let him off the hook with a big smile. "Yes, I like younger guys. They are the only ones who can keep up with me" I tell him. I thought his jaw was going to hit the table. Now I have really flustered him. "I'm sorry; I shouldn't have said that. I am going to scare you off" I tell him, laughing.

He leans forward, admitting to me that he was intimidated by me when we met, but he is glad to see another side of me tonight. "I leave the bitch mask on the door handle at work" I confess. It is obvious he had no clue that I was checking him out all the times we had met in my office. I would drift off at times, thinking about taking him right there on my desk, fucking him until I've had my fill and then send him on his way. I've had enough to drink now that I am probably telling him too much, but I am enjoying the time with him more than I expected. His athletic background is only one facet of him, and he keeps pace with me on every topic I throw at him. He is very funny, and has me laughing until I am in tears at times. In fact, things are going so well I kind of lose track of time. He glances at his watch; "It's about that time, isn't it?" I blurt out. He has no idea what I mean, once again. He lays a twenty down on the table as a tip; "Classy" I thought to myself. I am running out of time and ideas…"Oh, I need something from my office, would you mind walking over there with me?" I am sure the old "damsel in distress" routine would do the trick. "Sure" he replies, not having any idea what is in store for him.

I open the door to my office, turning on the lights as we enter. I walk into my office, expecting to find him following me. I turn, and it appears he has stopped in the reception area. Actually, maybe this will be better, I thought. I am going to fuck him right here on my desk, just like I day dreamed. The words echo through my mind as I quickly strip off the jacket and skirt I have on. I am standing in my office in just my bra and panties, and my heels of course. I call his name, striking a pose in the center of the room. He comes in, quickly coming to a halt when finding me waiting for him. "I want to suck your cock and then fuck you on my desk. Any problems with that?" I feel my commanding office attitude return in a surge. He shakes his head in agreement, still trying to process what is going on, I'm sure. "Shut the door" I instruct.

I slip off my heels and walk over to him. I am the one in charge; dictating the place and the pace at which we will go. I want it fast and hard, and then I am going home. I walk to him, spinning him around and backing him towards the front of my desk. I can see he is growing excited at my proposition, the bulge rising in his pants. I grab his shirt, tearing it off of him. I want his mouth on mine, and I take it. I grab him and kiss him forcibly, glad to finally be on my way to getting what I need. The taste of the Altoid in my mouth is overwhelming the beer he was drinking. His body is firm, and I enjoy pressing my flesh into his. I run my nails across his chest, following them with my tongue. I reach down to feel his cock through his pants.

I fall to my knees in front of him, for the first time looking up to meet his eyes. Grabbing his belt, I pull it through the loops and toss it aside. I undo the buttons and pull the zipper on his pants, his cock plopping out in front of my face. I devour it, swallowing it all. I can feel him growing harder in response to my mouth on him, and soon he is at full capacity. I smash my nose into his stomach, letting him know I can handle anything he has to offer me. I run my tongue all over it, jamming it into my cheek and then back into my throat. I love to choke myself on it just a little, and rub it on the back of my throat to fight my own reflex. God I am so into this! I find myself moaning as I explore every inch of him. I can tell he is getting close, and I certainly hope he can recover quickly if I let him come right now. But I am feeling especially naughty, so I want to taste it. I increase my pace and really start going after it. He moans and groans, trying to hold it off. I feel his hand on the back of my head, and I am ready for the pending shove, but just at the last second he pulls away from me. "Not yet, my dear. I am far from done with you" he tells me, looking down at me.

Her Eyes

I stand, and inform him "My turn" as I walk to the other side of the desk. I sit on the edge of the desk, and point to the chair. He sits in front of me, looking like his is awaiting my next command. I reach down and grab the side of my sopping wet panties, pulling them aside. "Go to work" I say, enjoying the power of being in charge. He hesitates for a second, making me wait before he dives in. He reaches up to pull my panties aside a little farther, exposing me even more. Instead, he rips them off me in one forceful move. The tearing sound stuns me, and I am frozen in confusion. He puts his hand in the middle of my chest, and shoves me back on the desk. His hands find my breasts, and he unclips the hook on my bra, freeing them. He presses his hands into my breasts, smashing them against me. His roughness comes out of nowhere and I am in total shock. His mouth is on my nipple, biting it hard. "What the fuck is going on?" shoots through my mind. A minute ago this guy was taking orders and now this? Oh God that feels good, though. The sudden turn of events has intrigued me.

I can feel his cock poking my wet pussy as he stretches to reach my nipples. I want it in me, and I arch my back to give him entry. "Oh, God, yes...put it in me" I cry inside. He pushes it inside just a little, teasing me. I want it all, and try to scoot forward into him. He withdraws, pulling out of me. I reach around, grabbing his ass, trying desperately to get more of what he just gave me a taste of. He stands up, and looking down at me states in a very firm voice "You will get fucked when I am good and ready." "Who the fuck does he think he is?" I ask myself. He is kissing his way down my stomach and towards my aching pussy, and I am willing to relinquish a little control to get what I want. Suddenly his finger is deep inside me without warning; I gasp in surprise. I am so wet from his teasing me with his cock it glides right in. Now his tongue is on me, and I am ready to explode. He works me over, replacing one finger for two and stroking his tongue all over me. He is eating my pussy like a pro, and I am going crazy on top of the desk in my office. I am so close, ready to come when he finally shoves his fingers deep into me. I come so hard; shuddering and flailing around, knocking the phone off the desk. He keeps at it, never letting up, timing my every move. I am turning to jello as he laps me into submission. I come again and again, knocking everything off the surface I am laying on. "Holy Fuck" is all I can say.

26

"I'm ready to fuck you now, Jillian. How do you want it?" he asks. I stammer for a response, my brain numb with pleasure. He shoves his cock deep into me before I can answer. My eyes widen in surprise. He has me hang my legs down over the desk, and the angle is perfect. He places his hands on my thighs, and tries to hold me in place as I find myself thrashing around on my desk again. He is hitting my G-spot with each stroke, and I am on the verge of another already. I look up at him, my eyes hazy with desire. He stares down at me, his eyes burning into me as he sticks out his tongue and licks his thumb. I know what is coming, and can't wait for it. He touches it to my clit, and I feel the pressure all through me. I am so close once again, and he can sense it. He grabs my hips with his free hand and bangs into me with three or four hard strokes. I put my elbows under me so I can watch him penetrate me. My eyes are half open as I brace myself for another orgasm…and he stops. No more thumb, no cock…nothing.

I am in a frenzy; so close, right on the edge. I reach down to do it myself, and he grabs my wrist and pulls my hand away from myself. "No!" he scolds me. "Not until I say so." I am so angry I instinctively reach back with my other hand and take a swing at his face. He blocks it, and pulls away from me. I am crazy with desire, willing to do anything to get what I want. "Please!?!" I beg in a desperate voice. "That's better" he says and plants his cock deep inside me once again. He grabs my shoulder and thrusts into me as hard as he can. He fucks me as hard as anyone ever has. "OH God, OH FFFFUUUUUCCCCKKKKK!!!!!" He keeps fucking me as my cries echo through the empty office. Finally he pulls away once again and sits down on my office chair. I am helpless on the desk as I recover from the pounding I just received.

After a few moments, I am ready for more. I sit up on the desk, finding him still sitting in my big leather office chair. I walk over to him, straddling him by throwing a leg over each arm of the chair. I grab the top of the chair, his hands clasp around my lower back. My breasts are in his face, and he wastes no time sucking them once again. I grind my hips into him, rotating side to side and back and forth. I love fucking him this way, my sweat-slick body gliding over his. I fuck him for a few minutes like this, and I am ready once again. It rises within, and he puts his hands on my hips. "Ready?" he asks. "Oh yes!" whatever he has in mind, I want it. He takes over, jerking me back and forth on his stiff rod.

Her Eyes

The feeling is amazing, and I explode into yet another amazing orgasm. I felt my nails puncture the leather on the top of my chair. I melt in his arms, my juices running out of me onto the leather.

He gives me a moment to recover, but then I have to stand to relieve the pressure in my legs. I walk towards the desk, and he tells me to bend over it. I jump to follow his command, and then realize what I am doing. He is controlling me...and for some reason...I like it. "That's better, be a good little slut for me." I stick my ass in the air for him, as if to say do what you will to me. His hand is in the middle of my lower back, and he eases his cock into me once again. He starts pounding me right away, slamming me into the desk, putting his foot on the surface next to me. I hear a loud smack, and then feel the welt on my ass start to rise. I gasp in surprise, and then moan in approval. Now he has a handful of my hair and is yanking my head back so far I am staring at the ceiling. He is fucking me like he owns me, and I am beyond turned on because of it. I can feel him growing inside me, and I think I have one left to bring out. I focus on his point of entry, picturing it sliding in and out of me. Another slap of his hand to the same spot, and I wince a little at the sting of his hand. I feel his thumb on my most private spot, and I want him to have it. I feel his thumb invade me, pushing just inside. My own motion increases in response, as if I am trying to driving back into him even though I am basically trapped between him and the desk. He finds a burst of speed and hammers me, inching me to the edge of another orgasm. I plant my hands on the desk, trying to find the traction to fuck him back. I am groaning and begging for more, begging him to take me there one more time.

I feel the stretching sensation of his thumb in my ass, having buried his thumb and his cock deep into me at the same time. The sensation is incredible, and I let loose once more. I spasm and contract, crying out loudly. His hand slaps my ass once more time before he stiffens and explodes inside me. He pumps it into me, jamming me into the desk. I can feel each flex of his cock inside as he finishes his task. He collapses on top of me. "Wow!" are his only words. He pulls away from me, sitting back on the chair. After a moment I stand up and turn, looking back at him. I can't believe what he just did to me. I feel...surprised. I thought this was going to be my show, and he turned the tables on me. I sit on the floor in front of him, laying my head on his lap as if I am his pet. I can't believe I just thought that, but it is exactly how I feel. He brushes the hair out of my eyes, looking down at me. I am trembling from the experience, but even happier that I found someone who can handle me.

Find audio downloads and more fun stuff at:
www.flipside-erotica.com

Laura

"Tonight's the night" I tell Misty. "I am finally going to do it. I am boyfriend free and horny as hell, and I am going to do it." "What are you talking about?" Misty inquires. "I am going to call Darren and get what I have wanted for all these years". "Oh, God!....you can't be serious!" is her response. "He doesn't want to, don't you get it?" she reminds me. We have talked this to death, but nothing she says can change my mind. Since the first time I saw him, I have wanted him. I wasn't even sure what that meant back then, but I have learned what two people can do together, and I want to share that with him. "For the last time, forget it!" she states. "No, I have a plan..."

We finish getting ready and headed out for the night. "Can't believe I am almost 19 years old and I still have to lie to get out of the house over night" I think to myself. I tell mom that we have softball practice in the morning, and I am staying at Misty's house overnight. We have to be at the field at 7:30AM, so we won't be out long tonight. "Have fun" she yells as I close the door behind us. Free at last. I check my purse to make sure I have my sister's ID, and off we go.

My watch read 12:53AM, and it is time to put my plan into action. Misty's boyfriend met up with us, and we head back to his place. Misty told her mom that we are staying at my house so she could spend the night at his place. I was going to crash on the couch, but I had a better idea. I think one carefully placed phone call will do the trick. I dial his number....ring, ring, ring...c'mon...answer, I am pleading to myself. "Who is this?" he yells into the phone. "It's me, Laura, I need your help." "Oh, hey." He says, softening his voice in recognition. "Misty met this guy and we are at his place and his friend won't leave me alone and I got scared so I just left. Can you come and pick me up?" I rattle my rehearsed speech into the phone. "Start walking, I will pick you up in 20 minutes" he says. I hang up the phone, and the internal conflict begins. Can I really do this? Am I ready? My head is flooded with self doubt as I sit down on the couch. Too late now, I guess. God...the lengths I go to get what I want.

Ten minutes later I walk out the door to the corner. There is a convenience store right across the street, and I am going to wait there for

31

him. He pulls up after a few minutes, and my stomach is in knots at the mere sight of his car. "Oh my God am I glad to see you!" I tell him, climbing into his car. Our eyes meet and I can see the concern on his face. "Okay, so now what?" he asks. "I can't go home, Misty and I are supposed to be somewhere at 7:30 in the morning, and that is the excuse I used to get out tonight. Can we go to your place?" I ask in hopes of a positive response. "Sure" he replies. We drive off, and I begin to wonder just what I have gotten myself into. He asks how I have been, and from there the conversation flowed. I always liked that about him, he genuinely listens to me. We talk the whole way back to his place, and most of my tension melts away. I knew this connection is not one sided, I could feel it. It is like we are right back where we left off six months ago before my latest train wreck of a relationship started. I am glad to be away from that ex, but even happier to be here, right now, with Darren.

We get to the door, and he opens it for me; always the gentleman, I thought. "Where do you want to sleep?" he asks. "Right on top of you" flashes through my head, but I manage to quell the urge to blurt it out. "With you, I guess", sounding as unsure as I could manage. He walks into the bedroom and returns with a big t-shirt and a pair of shorts. He hands them to me and turns away, walking into the bedroom. I go to the bathroom and "change" and gather my composure as the nerves begin to creep in again. I open the bathroom door, and it is nearly dark in the house. I wait for my eyes to adjust; the light from the front room barely illuminates my path to the bedroom. I feel my way down the wall, finding the doorway and walk through into the place of my dreams for the past few years. Even when I had a boyfriend I would find myself thinking of him instead. I couldn't believe my fantasy is about to come true.

I find the foot of the bed, and crawl into the sheets next to him. I am trembling with excitement and nerves as I pull the covers over us. I decided to forego the clothes he gave me, and let him know what I really want. I snuggle up against him, his body already warm from being under the covers a few minutes ahead of me. He quickly realized that I am naked, and rolls over to meet me. I can't see his face, but I can feel his breath on me. I reach out and find him in the darkness, pulling his mouth toward mine. My stomach is so tense I feel like I might be sick, but I want this…I know I want this. I push forward, trying to relax into his kisses. He rolls me over, and is now on top of me, the weight of his body pressing me into the mattress. He takes my hands and pushes them above my head, binding them together with his hand, holding me there. I can feel his hardness through his shorts, and his breath quickening as his excitement grows.

His hands begin to explore me; and finally caress my breasts; my nipples are so hard they practically hurt. He pinches them gently, tugging at them as his kisses grow harder. He breaks our kiss, and I feel his hot mouth on my nipple. His tongue flicks and flutters as he sucks it. His hands are squeezing my breasts, pressing them into me. I love his touch; firm and masculine and yet still gentle. He is taking his time, easing his way into it like I thought he would. He is not like the boys I have dated; he is a man, and he knows what he is doing. He slides his arm around me, pulling me to meet his mouth. I arch myself into him, wanting him to take everything that I am offering him. His tongue travels from one breast to another, and then slowly down my ribs. I am aching to have him inside of me, but I don't dare ask. I wait for him, dealing with the frustration in exchange for the pleasure of him tasting me. I can feel my excitement begin to run down my leg, his mouth getting closer and closer to his target. He teases me, avoiding my hot mound for the moment. He bites the inside of my thigh, sending shivers of anticipation all through me. "Dear God...PLEASE!" I am screaming on the inside.

I move to try to meet his mouth, only to have him dodge me. He is driving me crazy, and I feel like I am going to explode. I gasp half in relief and half in pleasure as his tongue finally hits my swollen clit. It is like touching an electrical socket; the jolt of pleasure hitting directly in the core of my being. It only takes a few flicks of his tongue and I am ready to explode; I reach down and grab the back of his head, pulling his face into my pussy. Before I know what hits me, he has two fingers deep inside me; his mouth mauling the rest of me. I arch my back, bending to meet his mouth. "Oh, fuck Darren...FUCK!!!!!" I scream. Barely cognizant, my hips buck involuntarily into his face, adding even more to what he is already doing to me. He grabs my legs in effort to hold me still. I can't hold back the flood any longer, and I release the wave of my first orgasm under his touch. Wave after wave crash through me as I become lost in a sea of pleasure. Before long he wins the battle, and I am pinned to the bed. He continues to flick and suck my tender clit as I slowly float back to Earth.

After a moment to regain my senses, I want to return the favor and satisfy a goal I have had for a long time. I want his cock in my mouth. I reach down and grab it; God, it is so hard. I spin around, and take it in my mouth. "I have always wanted to do this to you" I tell him. He moans as I slowly stroke the top half of his cock with my tongue. I work my mouth around it, feeling and tasting as I go. I can taste the testosterone oozing out of his pores; he tastes so…manly. I grab his cock at the base, my hand barely closing around its girth. I jerk it slowly, keeping my mouth on the top half as I grip and jerk the bottom. He moans again in approval, loving everything I am doing to him. I can feel the head of his manhood swelling in my mouth and I know he is getting close. I want to swallow every drop of it, and I make sure he knows it. I slide my hand between his legs and grab his ass, pulling him into me. His cock jams into the back of my throat, but I fight the reflex to pull away. I am groaning in anticipation of it, and the moment arrives. He pumps stream after stream of it down my throat, and I swallow it like a dirty girl should. I keep going, sucking away at it until he can no longer take it and pushes me away.

He flops down on the bed beside me, spent from what I just did to him. What *I* did to him…the thought echoing through my mind brings a smile to my face. I am fully recovered from my first orgasm, and I want more. I want him inside me, and I want it now. I climb on top of him, and impale myself with his rock solid rod. I settle myself all the way down on it in one smooth stroke, pushing until I hit bottom. I wince a little; it is not really pain that I feel. He strikes my core with it, and I suddenly feel small sitting on top of him. I grind slowly into him, taking as much length as I can stand. I position myself so my clit is rubbing against his hard stomach, and slowly grind myself towards my goal. He reaches up and squeezes my tits again, pushing them together. He sits up, and I wrap my arms around his neck to hold him there.

His mouth is on my breasts again; his tongue battling my hard nipples into submission. His new position allows me more room for movement, and I increase the speed of my hips. I am fucking him now, in control of what I have wanted for so long. He jerks upwards, his cock ramming deep into me as he pushes both of us off the bed momentarily. I toss my head back in a delightful mix of pleasure and pain. The feeling jumpstarts my desire and I begin to ride him furiously. He lies back underneath me, and I unchain the animal within. The involuntary noises that escape me don't even sound human as I ride him for all I can. I feel his hands on my hips, helping me keep my rhythm intact and I go fucking crazy on top of him. He thrusts upwards again, and I come as if the dam burst. "Oh Jesus! That feels so fucking good!" I cry out. My pussy clamps down on him, and I spasm over and over in pure ecstasy. I ride him and ride him, until I am completely spent, and I collapse down on top of his body.

"God, that was amazing!" I mutter to him, my brain melted from the experience. "Not the same as the boys you're used to fooling around with, huh?" he says, I'm sure with that Cheshire grin on his face. "Arrogant bastard…justified, but arrogant" I think to myself. "Not even close" I admit begrudgingly. I am completely spent and so sensitive I am not sure I can take any more of this. I hold perfectly still on top of him, trying to recover my breath and my senses.

I feel him start to move inside me, slow, short strokes at first as if to test my resiliency. I moan automatically in approval, unable to help but wanting to make sure he doesn't stop. I try to sit up, only to have him pull me back down against him. I wasn't sure I could even make it to a sitting position, let alone move like that again; I am glad he has something else in mind. I feel his hand on my face; he brushes the hair out of his way and his lips find mine once again. Our tongues shoot in and out of one another's mouths as his movements grow longer and deeper. He puts his hands on my ass, grabbing me and pulling me forward, and then releasing me to slide back. His hands help me achieve a greater range, and I am once again getting his hardness deep inside me. My whole body feels like it is touching his in this position, and despite my weight on top of him, he moves under me with ease. Soon I find myself joining his rhythm, my body responding to his moves. I am not even sure which one of us is leading; it is as if we are moving as one. I am growing close again, and my moans of delight are a dead giveaway. He does it again, thrusting upward into my depths, filling me completely and setting off one more explosion inside me. I bury my face into his neck, trying to muffle the screams emitting from me. I am uncontrollable; he has brought me to that point again. I let go, and grind into him as hard and fast as I can, my lustful cries echoing through the house. Finally, my body gives in, and I go completely limp. I am a jellyfish on top of him once more.

I have no idea how much time had passed before he gently rolls me off of him down onto the bed. I lay on my stomach, unsure I can go on, but willing to muster the energy to try. I know what he wants; he wants to take me from behind. I want him to take me from behind. I arch my back, sticking my ass in the air, ready for the taking. He guides his cock into me, filling me up once more. His strokes are slow and controlled at first, and I can tell he is fighting back the urge to come. He leans forward, his desire-roughened voice echoing in my head "My turn". His speed and intensity builds, and soon he is slamming into me, his cock stretching my young pussy to its limits. It hurts, but I want more; I reach for the wall and place my palms flat against the cold surface. I push back into him, now bracing for impact. I feel like he is tearing me apart inside and yet somehow the pleasure outweighs the pain and I moan for more. He holds my hips, and pounds me even harder...I realize he is going to make me come one more time before he gives in to his own. I am growing closer, and he pushes me forward and lies on top of me.

His hand quickly finds my clit; despite the intensity of his thrusts, his touch is gentle. He expertly rubs my swollen pearl, and I am quickly standing on the precipice again. I squeeze my legs together, tightening around him more than ever. His moans are beginning to outpace mine, and I know that we are both close. I start to buck my hips, my desire overpowering his weight on top of me. I begin first, but he quickly follows. Both of us explode into a frenzy of pleasure, bucking and grinding and moaning. "Oh Jesus...I'm gonna come again!" is the last thing I remember crying out. He empties himself into me, growling through clenched teeth. I can feel it pulsing inside me as I climax again. My face is buried in the pillows, and he collapses on top of me. We lay in a sweaty heap on the sheets; absolutely spent in our efforts.

After a few moments pass, he looks at the clock. This was an absolute fantasy come true, and I don't care if I had to trick him into it the first time. I take solace in the fact there will be more to follow. I drift off to sleep in his arms, wondering what the next time together will bring. I hope this will lead somewhere, but I guess time will tell. After all these years, I am just glad I finally got to know what he was like, and it was even better than I pictured.

Katie

"Here he comes, relax...act casual" I tell myself. I fiddle with something on the reception desk to appear occupied when he walks into the office. "Good morning Darren." "Hello Katie" he replies, repeating the usual exchange we have each morning. "What are you doing this weekend?" I inquire, hoping to get an opportunity to spring my idea on him. "It's a three day weekend...got big plans? What do you do for fun, anyway?" I wonder aloud. "Everything but kiss on the mouth" he replies instantly. I laugh nervously and then so does he. "That's funny!" is all I can come up with. "Thanks, I stole that line from the movie Pretty Woman". He continues walking into the office, and as soon as he clears my desk I drink in a long, lingering look as he walks away. He leaves, and I feel like I blew my chance to talk to him about my opportunity this weekend.

I let him settle into his desk for a few minutes before I decide to try again. I ring his desk, and he picks up the phone. "It will be easier to do this when we're not face to face" I thought. "So, were you serious about what you said earlier?" I ask in as sexy a voice as I can muster. There is a long pause, and I panic and almost hang up the phone. Finally I can't take it any longer, and blurt out "I am going to be alone this weekend for the first time in quite a while, and I was wondering if you want to get together. I haven't been with a man in almost four years, and I was hoping you'd want to be the one to...well, I think you get the idea. Another long pause. My heart is racing; my pulse pounding in my ears as I wait what seems like an eternity for his answer. "Uh, yeah...sure", he finally responds. "Cool, come see me before you leave today". I hang up the phone, and exhale deeply. My palms are sweating from the mental ordeal of being so forward. "How am I going to be relaxed enough with him to really enjoy this? Calm down," I keep telling myself. I think of a solution, and it makes me feel a little better.

Five minutes before the getting off hour...the inside joke made me laugh to myself, Darren walks around the corner, beaming a huge smile at me. He is obviously looking forward to this as much as I am. I look him up and down again, slowly letting my eyes explore what I am about to see up close and personal. "I've been thinking about you all day. God, I am so turned on!" I confessed to him. "I hope you live close by, I

Her Eyes

want you right now" I say in my sexy voice. "As luck would have it, I do...right down the street. Follow me" he instructs. I leave the building soon after him, careful not to draw any attention to our plans. He pulls out of the parking area, and I follow him at a safe distance. I remember the solution for my nerves is sitting in the ash tray. I light the roach; inhaling the smoke into my lungs, holding it, and then blowing the smoke out the window. Almost instantly the buzz hits me, and the effect is exactly what I am hoping for. A soothing mellowness envelopes me, and my mind quiets. I reach for one of my clove cigarettes to cover the smell of the weed. I light it up, and draw the tasty smoke into my lungs.

We arrive at his house, and I am growing wet with anticipation. I have been waiting all day for this; let alone the time suffering through this attraction with no way to act on it. Finally, a window of opportunity, and I am going to make the most of it. He unlocks the door and we walk through. I follow close behind, and when he turns to shut the door behind us, I am right there. For the first time I am in his personal space, and a rush of heat flushes through me. I grab him, and kiss him hard before he even has a chance to think about what is happening. I catch him off guard, and back him against the wall. My mind is calm under the influence of the grass; I'm not sure I ever could be so bold without it. My hands find his hips, and I slide them around back for my first feel of that cute ass of his. It is firm, almost hard under his pants. Years of fitness have sculpted it into a candy apple, and I can't wait to take a bite. His hands begin to roam over my body as well. We make out like high-schoolers in the entry way of his house. "I will fuck him right here if he lets me" I thought. Suddenly I become aware of the pressure of his hand between my legs. I moan in pleasure, melting under his touch.

"I need a shower" he proclaims, and begins shedding clothing as he walks down the hallway. I wait for a second, collecting my thoughts as I lean against the wall. I follow soon after, and am stripping my own clothes off as I walk down the hall to the place I had coveted for quite some time. I walk through the bedroom, dropping my clothes on the floor. I look around, taking a mental picture for later use. I join him in the bathroom, eager to see him standing in the shower. I push the glass door back, soaking in his naked body standing under the water. He opens his eyes, and reaches for the door, sliding it shut behind me. God, his body is amazing. His clothes don't do his athletic build justice, he is

40

beautiful. He gives me a long, lingering look, and an approving smile. I can see his cock was growing already, and I want it now. "Come here" I tell him. "No" he says firmly, and turns away from me. I smack his ass hard in protest, hoping he will turn around and kiss me. He does, and he gently but firmly pushes me against the shower wall. My eyes widen in surprise at the sudden impact against the wall.

And so it begins; the real dance between us. Our mouths meet in another deep kiss. Our bodies press against one another, and I can feel him rubbing against my swollen clit. I wrap a leg around him, pulling him closer to me as if there was actually any room left. He must have other ideas; he reaches down and grabs my leg, pulling it up over his hip. It opens me to him, and his teasing continues as he rubs his stiff rod against me. I am aching to be penetrated. "Please, PLEASE!" I keep thinking as loudly as I can. He grabs the back of my head, pushing me into his waiting mouth. Our tongues shoot in and out of each other's mouths as he continues to rub me into a frenzy. I feel him grab a handful of my wet hair, and he yanks my head back as he begins to bite my neck. God, he is driving me crazy, I am dying for relief. I am midway through my thoughts when he finally quenches my desire.

I feel him enter me, penetrating my wet, aching depths. He goes deep into me, parting my walls as far up into me as he can go. I dig my nails into his arm as it feels like he is going to lift me off my feet with his thrusts. He presses me against the shower wall, his wet body slapping into mine. I am getting exactly what I need; a good, hard fuck...by a man. I love my girlfriend, but I desire the feel of a man once in a while. He is fucking me like she never could, and I explode in the first few strokes. His long strokes fill me completely, and I feel it well up from deep inside. I toss my head back, releasing the waiting orgasm from within. He never stops, plunging it in and out of me as I shudder with delight.

The first wave passes after a moment, and I begin to notice that my calf is cramping. I have been standing on one leg through the first round, and it seems he had no intentions of stopping now. I lay on him as much as I can, making him bear my weight. It brings enough relief to my leg to allow me to focus on the stiff rod being run in and out of me. My pussy is gripping him, making the friction between us even more intense.

41

The first one felt like an explosion inside me, but this one was going to be different. It starts deep inside, and my moans match his strokes. It keeps building and building, like a huge wave rising above me. Finally the wave crests, and I scream aloud as the pleasure crashes over me. He keeps pounding into me, just like I want. I am shuddering all over, partly from the deep, intense orgasm and partly from the fatigue of balancing on one leg. I hope that he can hold me up as I slump into his arms, my brain in a fog of delight.

I look up at him. "That was fucking amazing" I praise. I want my mouth on him, glad he quenched at least some of my desire for him. "Now it's your turn" I say. I find two wash clothes hanging on the rail in the shower, and decide to put them to good use. I throw both of them on the floor of the shower, and put one knee on each. I am planning on sucking his cock for a long time, and I do not want to be hindered by pain in my knees from the tile floor. It is right in front of me, and I stare at it for a moment, memorizing every ripple and vein. I put my hands on his hips, and in one move swallow him whole. I go all the way down on it, smashing my nose into his stomach. I hold it there, and then withdraw halfway, only to go all the way down again. I withdraw again, running my tongue over the length of it. I reach up and cup his balls in my hand as I continue to suck him from top to bottom. I love the taste of him, and the feeling of his hot member in my mouth. It is as hard as some of the toys I have, but the real thing is so much better.

I reach around with both hands, grabbing his ass and pulling him into my mouth. I take all his length, sucking it as hard as I can. I can tell he is getting close, and I want to taste his juice. I increase my speed; I hear his muffled groans as he grows closer to exploding in my mouth. He arches his whole body to meet my mouth as he mumbles "Oh God, Oh my God." He tenses, bracing for it. "Come in my mouth" I tell him, and I grab it and begin jerking it furiously. "Oh fuck here I come!" he warns, and I am ready. I open my mouth, burning to feel the streams of it hit my tongue. I catch as much of it as I can before wrapping my lips around it and sucking him dry. I swallow it all, loving every drop of it. I keep going until I have every bit of it, and he can take no more. I stand up, and shower off again. He turns the water off, and we reach for the towels to dry off. We leave the towels behind, and head to the bed for round two.

We climb into bed, eager to pick up where we left off. I climb on top of him, pressing my body into his. We kiss some more, a little slower this time. We build up speed as we go, and I can feel his hardness returning to full strength. I want it in me again, and I sit up on top of him. I reach down and guide it into me, pushing myself down on the hard length. I slowly begin to grind myself all over him. I put my hands on his chest, digging my nails into his flesh. I switch from grinding to moving up and down on it, and then swirling my hips. His hands lift my breasts, pushing them together. His fingers on my nipples send shivers down into my core, triggering the beginning of another orgasm. I start to build up speed, pressing down onto him and forcing his cock deeper into me. I am barely aware that my moans are growing louder and louder. I can feel it begin, and suddenly I am thrust upward, his hardness piercing my folds and driving deeper into me than before. I spasm; my rhythm breaking down as I convulse in pleasure. We sink back into the bed, and I fall forward onto his chest. I am breathing so hard I think I may pass out. "Fuck he is good" I thought to myself, and in a moment I am going to want more.

He rolls me over, never withdrawing from me. I lift my legs, giving myself over to him once more. I put my feet on his chest, and he begins to slide his swollen cock in and out of me. He starts slow at first, but before long is feeding my pussy with long, deep strokes. "Oh fuck yes...that's what I want...pound me" I groan. He slams into me extra hard once in a while, penetrating me even deeper than the other strokes. Hitting bottom sends jolts of electricity all through me, and my eyes widen, my mouth open in a silent scream.

He slides my feet off of his chest, and I now support some of his body weight with my knees against him. I am aching for more, but he keeps slowly fucking me. I enjoy the sensation, but I can get nice at home. "Fuck me harder" I snarl up at him. He gives me what I want, and starts slamming into me again. He straightens his legs, giving himself even more leverage to pound into me. I love it; taking all of it deep into me, stretching my pussy as he hammers me like a nail. I dig my fingernails into his arms while I thrash around underneath him. I have one more in me, and he is drawing it out. He begins to groan with each stroke, fighting off his own so I can come first. I focus inside, feeling him driving in and out of me. I start again, losing control and bucking my hips to meet his thrusts. He fucks me and fucks me, like no one has in a long, long time. He stands up, putting off his own release for just a little longer.

I roll over onto my stomach, finding him standing near the bed. I look up to find his manhood pointing right at me, and I can't resist putting my mouth on it one more time. I scoot forward on the bed and vacuum-seal my lips around the purple head. He groans in approval, and has to be so close from all the friction we'd created over the last hour. I focus on just the top for awhile, and then started to take it deeper and deeper into my mouth. Suddenly he pulls away, catching himself indulging a little too much I guess. Then he states "I want your ass before we're done." The words made me tremble to the core. It is so naughty, and I want to be so naughty today. "Oh, you nasty boy, you. Come and get it." I roll over and rise to my knees, anticipating the entry into my most private hole. "Go slow; it's been a long time" I caution.

He slides on a condom and removes a bottle of lube from the drawer by the bed. He squirts it directly on my opening, and it makes me jump. He rubs his shielded cock all over me, lubricating it for its journey. He puts one foot on the mattress, and I brace myself to be stretched to my limits. He guides the tip in, my body resisting entry at first. Finally the head pokes through, and he slowly pushes forward into my depths. I am towing the line between pleasure and pain, wanting more but not sure I should ask. He is careful, slowly sliding his dick in and out of my ass. God, just thinking it makes me feel so filthy and hot, I want to come already.

I feel his hand searching for my clit; it is rubbed raw and yet I still want his touch. I grab handfuls of the sheets, partly bracing myself for his increasing speed and partly to hold myself in place on the bed. I am now growling through my gritted teeth, feeling like an animal getting fucked from behind. "Put your fingers inside you" he commands me. I obey, under his spell, ready for anything. I am so wet I push three fingers into my pink folds with no problem. He grabs a handful of my hair again, the tension in my scalp only adding to my maddening desires. He is growing huge inside me, ready to burst. I fuck him back, meeting his thrusts by pushing backwards into him, driving him even deeper into me. It feels like he is burying all of it into me, and the thought of taking it all in my ass became too hot to contain myself any longer. My hand finds a mind of its own; I am finger-fucking myself with blinding speed. I start coming right before he does, and we ride out each other's orgasm while feeling the full impact of our own. "Fucking amazing" are the only words that come to mind. We slump forward onto the bed, exhausted from our efforts.

Finally, he gathers his strength and climbs off of me, heading for the shower. I can't move; it is as if he hit a nerve deep inside me and I am now paralyzed by my own pleasure. I am still face down on the bed when he returns to the room; the bed is a wreck from the afternoon's activities. He climbs into bed, laughing at what he has done to me. We drift off to sleep, lying next to one another, plotting our next encounter...

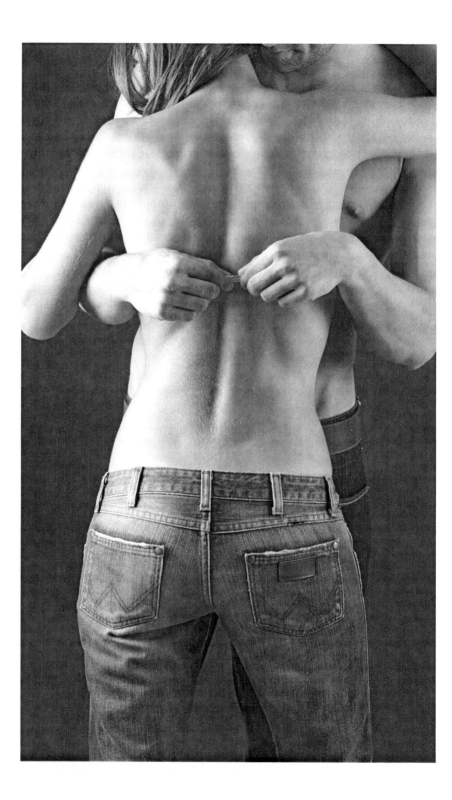

Gina

I am sitting in the airport reading my book, thinking about the week I just spent back home. I am so glad to have moved on; it seems I have lived a lot more now that I am away from the East Coast. I miss everyone, but am very happy leading the life I have now. My boarding group gets called and I stand to get on the plane. I can tell the guy behind me wants to start a conversation, but I keep my nose in my book. I work my way down the aisle and find a window seat. He follows me into the row, and jokes about me stealing the window seat. I look up at him, and realize that he is a lot more attractive than I first thought. I've got to learn to quit tuning people out so quickly.

He sits down, leaving the seat between us open. By the time the plane takes off I find myself very interested in our conversation. He is well read, well spoken and very funny. I had almost forgotten how much I hate to fly. I order a drink as soon as we reach cruising altitude, and he decides to join me. "I'd better be careful" reminding myself that I am quite the lightweight drinker. Our conversation continues, and he asks what month I was born in. "I was born on June 1st" I reply, wondering where he is headed with this line of questioning. "Oh no, not a Gemini!" he exclaims loudly. He teases me about my evil twin and the naturally bipolar astrological sign I was born under. I laugh, admitting that I can have a bit of a wild side at times. We are getting closer to our destination, and I begin to realize that this man is very intriguing. I really want to spend more time with him than this flight will allow. We'll see what happens in the next hour.

We shift topics of conversation to one of his hobbies, which is creative writing. Seems like an odd thing for a man, so I question him a little further. I laugh when he tells me he is an erotic fiction writer. "You don't believe me?" he says in a mockingly defensive voice. Ok pal, I'll bite…"What do you write about?" I certainly lobbed that one up for him. He looks at me for a second, staring deep into my eyes, fixing my gaze upon him. "Typically I take situations that I have actually been in, and add an erotic encounter to the story, like meeting someone on a plane, for example" he tells me. I knew it; he is totally picking up on me! I can't wait to bust him on this. "Ok, I am going to need some proof" I inform him. I am a little disappointed that he is resorting to such

47

a cheesy tactic. He reaches for his bag, pulling out a small laptop computer. He turns to me, and asks "tell me something that would turn you on, a scenario that you would like." I slap him on the arm, and reply "No way!…I'm not telling you anything like that!" I laugh at him; he's cute enough to win me back a little. "Ok, fine, then we'll go with one I like." He searches through his computer for a moment, and then slides the screen in front of me. "Here, read this one" he tells me.

Over the next few minutes, my mindset totally changes. I thought he had blown it, but it turns out he is not only serious about this, but good at it as well. I am instantly pulled into the story, entranced. His words flow and the scene develops; two strangers meet on a plane and end up spending the night together. The scene he describes is very erotic, and I feel myself flushing as I read about how this man makes love to the woman who was a stranger just a few hours ago. I can't help but wonder if he has actually done this or at the very least if he thinks it, he can also do it. My mind races as I finish the story. I look out the window, trying to muster the courage to tell him that I want to be the woman in the story. "So, what did you think of my story?" he inquires. I take a moment to answer, lost in thought. "Um, yeah, it was good" is my response. The silence is growing uncomfortable, and I blurt out "Can I buy you a drink when we land?" I wish I hadn't done that, wishing I could retract that statement but it was too late. We are playing poker, and I just showed my hand.

The plane touches down, and we both grab our cell phones to check for messages. I wasn't expecting any; it is more out of nervous fidgeting than anything. I hear him start laughing while listening to a message, and I wonder what that is about. He tells me that the meeting he is here for has been pushed back to tomorrow at one. His assistant has booked a room at the hotel nearby, so he'll be staying over and have time to kill. I offer to give him a lift to the hotel, not wanting to part company just yet. He whispers to me that he would love my company tonight, and I feel the heat rise in my face. "We'll see how things go" I tell him, now aware that the heat in my thighs is much higher than usual as well. We stand, collect our bags and head for my car in the parking lot.

We arrive at the hotel, and he invites me to join him for dinner. I agree, going with the flow of the day's events. He checks into the hotel and we head for the elevator. I realize that I have shown my hand again by bringing my bag with me, but decide I can cover by saying I want to change before dinner. We get into the elevator and the voice in my head tells me that this is too much too soon. I start to worry about what I am diving into here, when he looks at me and says "Don't worry, I am nervous about this too." I drop my bag on the floor. "Kiss me" I blurt out to him. "Kiss me before I change my mind". He reaches for me, gently placing his hand along side my face, pulling me towards him. He gives me a slow, deep kiss and about halfway through I finally relax and kiss him back. "That was perfect" I think to myself. "There, the first one is always the toughest" he says. "Smartass" I thought, while pushing him playfully.

We arrive on our floor and head for the room. I follow him closely into the room, and suddenly he stops and turns to face me. I look up at him, and instantly we kiss. I never hesitated, and I am glad to see my reservations about this are quickly melting away. We kiss with growing passion for a little bit, both of us growing more comfortable with one another by the second. After a moment we stop, looking at each other. We break into a laugh at the same time, knowing the night is going to hold much more for us. He picks up his bags and arranges them in the room. "You hungry?" he asks. "God yes...but you're buying me dinner first" I respond teasingly. I grab my bag and head to the bathroom to change into something a little more girly looking and date appropriate.

Over dinner we really get to know one another. I am glad to see that this guy is genuinely interested in me, and not just out for a quick hook up while he is in town. We order drinks before dinner, and then during dinner, and before long I am feeling rather warm and fuzzy. We are sitting side by side, and having a great time. We discuss our lives, and I learn that he travels frequently, but rarely to this side of the country. He likes his job, is successful and it has been a while since his last relationship. He asks how I managed to lose the accent; I tell him as much as I miss the family, I love my life here and blending in is a big priority for me. I confess I am not really due back at work until noon tomorrow, giving him the green light for tonight. I am loving every minute I spend with him, and the attraction grows deeper with each passing moment.

Her Eyes

The server brings our dessert, and he rudely grabs the spoon off of the plate before offering me a bite. He pushes me out of the way, pretending to hog the entire dessert for himself. He takes a huge bite, and looks intent on not letting me have any of the chocolate, sloppy mess on the plate. I protest, but having older brothers has taught me that rarely works. I jam my fingers into his ribcage, making him jump. I wrestle the spoon from him, and find myself very excited at the struggle between us. I shove the spoon into the whipped creamed gooey mess, and prepare for a huge victory bite, but he bumps my arm and I dump the entire spoonful down the front of my dress. "Damn! I was doing such a good job of being lady-like too" I scold myself, embarrassed.

He grabs the napkin from his lap and starts to try and clean up the mess, apparently feeling responsible for the chocolate disaster. He is trying frantically to rescue my dress from the chocolate, and about halfway through realizes that he is rubbing his hands all over my chest. I am flushing under his touch, when he looks up at me. All of the sudden it hit him, and he looked completely embarrassed and guilty. The look on his face is so funny I burst out laughing. He realizes how comical this must look, and joins me in the laughter. We are laughing loudly and are causing quite a scene in the middle of the restaurant. The server comes over and asks if he can help, trying to keep us from disturbing the other patrons.

The waiter sees the mess we have made and offers to bring us another dessert. "Yes, please, and extra whipped cream this time if you would be so kind. And can we get that to go?" I ask, trying to hold my composure. He looks at me, questioning, searching for confirmation of what he is hoping is true. I hope the wicked look in my eyes answers his question. The waiter returns and delivers my wishes, and bids us a good night. I didn't respond, but thought I am pretty sure it will be. He pays for dinner and we get up to leave.

On the way to the elevator I discover that I am a little more buzzed than I thought. I hold his arm as we walk, stabilizing myself. I keep randomly laughing, and verbally confess "Wow, I am toasted". "Me too" he adds as we step into the elevator. "I'm not sure I can feel my feet anymore" he adds A devilish thought flashes through my mind, and I drop to one knee. "Can you feel this?" and promptly bite him on the thigh. He jumps, yelling loudly in surprise. I hear the elevator ding and hop to my feet just as the doors open. I sway from the head rush, but try to stand still, not looking guilty to the people who just walked in. I am shaking in effort not to laugh aloud, luckily our floor is the next one. I am not sure I can make it out of the elevator before I explode in laughter. The door opens, and I stumble out, laughing my ass off as soon as my foot hits the floor. We are both laughing, hanging onto one another as we make our way down the hall. He grabs the key from his pocket and goes to open the door. I am in a hurry to be inside, and walk right into the door that he neglected to open in time. I hit my head on the door, and he hits the floor. He is laughing so hard tears are streaming down his face as I stand there rubbing the mark on my forehead.

The impact has snapped me out of my slightly drunken state, and I am slightly annoyed at him for laughing at me. I climb on top of him on the floor, and pin his arms down. He stops laughing, realizing that I am no longer joining in his delight at my expense. He lies still for a second, waiting to see what I have in mind. After a moment of us staring at one another, he bucks his hips, and rolls me over onto the floor. He rolls on top of me, his weight pressing me into the carpet. He now pins my hands above me, and kisses me hard. "Oh God...I was waiting for that" I think as my mouth explores his. After a moment we both seem to realize that we are in the hallway of the hotel. He stands, and then helps me to my feet.

He pins me against the door, kissing me deeply once again. His hands hold my face, and we kiss one another feverishly. He finds the door, and opens it without his mouth leaving mine. He leads me, backing me into the room, kicking the dessert bag I dropped earlier into the room. The door shuts with a loud bang, and we are now safe inside the confines of the hotel room. The pace of our kissing increases, and his hands travel downward over my body. I let out an impassioned whimper under the touch of his hands. He reaches behind me, feeling the buttons on the back of my dress. He undoes them, and then goes right to the straps on my shoulders. He steps back, and pulls the loops. The dress slides off of me, crumbling on the floor at my feet. I am standing in front of him in my underwear, shy and exposed, but wanting to continue. He looks me up and down, and melts my trepidation with an approving smile. Now it is my turn to see him, and I step forward, grabbing his shirt. I untuck it, and he pulls it over his head, tossing it on the floor. I put my hands on his chest, feeling the warmth of his skin. I kiss him briefly, and then begin the task of removing his belt. He helps again, pulling it free from his pants, tossing it towards the bed. He kicks off his shoes, and I remember to do the same. We are moving quickly, and I am ready.

He spins me around, pulling me against his body. His fingers run through my hair, and he keeps a handful of it. He exposes my neck, and begins to kiss the back of it. I can feel my skin prickle under his mouth, and my knees feel like they are going to buckle. I push into him to stabilize myself, wanting more of what he is doing. He opens wide and sinks his teeth into my neck, and I feel the breath leave my body. I instinctively grind my ass against him, wanting to feel his hardness. He continues to tease me; running his fingers through my hair, over my body, pausing at my breasts, gently squeezing them against me. The room is barely lit, and I can see about half of our reflection in the mirror across the room. It is so hot watching him devour me like this. He continues mauling my neck, moving from spot to delicious spot. His hands are on my breasts again, and he squeezes them more firmly this time. I let out a low moan as he unclips my bra. I push back into him, my desire for him growing.

He runs his fingers over my nipples, and the rhythm of it is delightful. My small breasts feel like they are swelling under his touch, and I lay my head back on his shoulder as he continues to work them over. He lifts and squeezes them and the fire between my thighs is reaching the point of aching. I grab the back of his head, and he moves up to nibble on my ear. His hot breath echoes in my head, and the sensation is wonderful. I can feel his bulge pressing into my back, and I want to touch it. I reach behind me, and feel it for the first time. It seems to be straining to break free of his pants; it wants to come out and play. I moan again, this time in anticipation of him inside me. He runs his hands down my stomach, and right into my red silk panties. I am drenched with excitement, and his finger explores my moist folds. He finds my clit, and pushes it up into me. It is pulsating in excitement, and he rubs me gently but firmly until I am ready to pass out. I don't want to come this soon, and I place my hand on top of his, slowing his pace. I look up in the mirror again, and the sight of his hand inside my panties is enough to make me almost explode. I have to stop or I am going to come right now.

I pull away, and he seems concerned and confused. "What's wrong?" he asks. "Not a thing" I reply, trying to reassure him. I look up to meet his eyes, and slowly kiss my way down kiss stomach until I am on my knees in front of him. I run my hand over it again, and am practically drooling at the thought of my mouth on him. I reach for the waistband, but he beats me to it, pulling the buttons apart. His cock is peaking out the top, and he rips open his pants to reveal it to me. I grab it, wanting to feel it in my hand. I jerk it slowly; it is so hard I can't make it relent under my grip. "This is going to be fucking good" I think to myself. I put it in my mouth, tasting his skin. "You are so hard". I go back for more, not wanting to leave it. "God I love how you taste" I say, running my tongue all over him. I love sucking his cock, and jerk it while I do. He tilts his head back in pleasure, and I hear a groan escape his lips. I take it deep into my mouth, holding it there as long as I can, and then withdrawing it completely. I do it over and over, feeling every inch of him travel over my tongue and into my throat. I am so into it I don't want to stop, increasing my speed and reaching around to grab his ass. He reaches down and pushes me away, apparently wanting to delay his release as I did.

I walk to the bed, and look back to see him grabbing the bag with the dessert in it from the floor. I am so ready to go I practically tear my own panties off of myself and pull the covers back, climbing into bed. He walks over to me, bag in hand. "What do you intend to do with that?" I ask, knowing the answer but wanting to hear him say it. "I am going to smear what's left of the whipped cream on your thighs and then lick it off of you" he states. "And I don't get any?" implying that I was more than happy to continue what I had started a few minutes ago. "We can share if you insist" he agrees, climbing into bed with me. He opens the bag, finding the dessert upside down in the plastic box. He digs two fingers into the whipped cream, getting a big glob of it. I get up on my elbows, aching to watch him eat the whipped cream off of me. He touches some to each nipple, and then pushes my legs apart, spreading the sticky white cream all over my thighs.

53

Her Eyes

He starts at the top, licking my nipples clean, running his tongue all over them. His tongue traces down my stomach, slowly working his way downtown. He lies between my legs, looking up at me with a dirty little grin on his face. I bite my lip in anticipation, waiting for him to...Oh God there it is! He dives in, smearing the whipped cream all over his face as he licks my pussy clean. His hot tongue flashes over me, and I fight to hold still and let him continue. I wrap my legs around his head, holding him there and bracing myself against him. I want to let go and just go crazy, bucking my hips wildly, but I fight the urge. I am so close, and I want this orgasm more than any other I ever have had. He reaches up and exposes me, pulling the skin back from my clit. He has complete access to it now, and I writhe under the pressure of his tongue, tearing the sheets from the corners of the bed.

He slides his finger into me, working it in and out of me while his tongue lashes my clit. I can feel it rising in me, and I begin to tense up in anticipation. I dig my heels into the mattress, arching to meet his mouth in a frenzy of passion. I am flying, sailing through the clouds towards the heavens. He slides another finger into me, and the added tension pushes me over the edge. I bridge myself off of the bed, exploding in the most intense orgasm I have ever experienced. He puts his hand under my lower back, holding me off the bed while he continues to work me over. I finally relax, collapsing on the bed in a sticky, spent mess.

I am numb with pleasure, unable to move for a moment. He comes to me, brushing the hair out of my eyes as he gently settles down on top of me. He kisses me gently, giving me time to recuperate from the impact. As I regain strength, I kiss him harder and harder. I can feel his cock pressing into the soft flesh between my thighs. My clit is so sensitive from what he just did to me, but I still want more. He is teasing me, waiting for me to give him a sign. I throw my arms around him, pulling him tight against me. I wrap my legs around him, the change in angle granting him access into my waiting folds. He penetrates me, driving it deep on the first stroke. I jump as he hits bottom, filling me completely. "Does that hurt?" he asks, surprised at my reaction. "Almost" I reply, loving the feeling of it, on the verge of pain. He starts with short strokes, rubbing his hard length in and out of my opening. We kiss one another firmly, and I feel his hand slide under my lower back. I moan again, knowing what is coming.

He lifts himself above me, and begins to pound me with long, deep strokes. I love each second of it, moaning loudly once again. Our bodies slap together, his impacting mine, smashing me into the bed. My eyes are shut tightly; I am lost inside my head, sensation and thoughts flood my mind. He slides my knees against his chest, and I hold his weight above me. The change in angle is exquisite, and I can feel myself clamping down on him with each thrust. Every time his body impacts mine I let out a loud groan. He fucks me hard for several more minutes before having to stop, holding it back once more. He lies down on the bed beside me.

I want the chance to ride him, and am taking the opportunity before it is too late. I climb on top of him, guiding it back inside me. He rests on his elbows, and I lean down to kiss him. I hold his face while I kiss and grind on top of him. I start slow, but soon find myself riding him faster and faster. I sit up on top of him, and put my hands on his chest. I turn it loose, and my hips take over. I grind my clit into his firm stomach as I slide back and forth on him. His hands are on my breasts, and I am growing very close to another one. He pinches my sensitive nipples, and I moan "Oh God that's good" in delight. He sits up, placing his hands behind him on the bed. His hands run through my hair, and he explores every inch of my body on top of him. It feels so good my body finds more strength to power on. I look down at him, lost in pleasure. I throw my arms around his neck, and grind myself into oblivion. "Oh God...you're gonna make me come again!" I cry out. He joins in the fray, bucking his hips up into me. "Oh my God, I'm coming...I'm coming" I repeat over and over. I dig my nails into his shoulder, and explode into another phenomenal orgasm. He slumps back on the bed, and I follow. I lie on top of him for a moment to catch my breath. "Don't worry, you're next" I inform him.

"Did you use all the whipped cream?" I ask, searching for the plastic lid. I find it on the floor, and am glad to see there is some left. I run my fingers along the textured plastic, digging the remaining whipped cream out. "Stand up" I tell him. He jumps up, ready for his turn. He stands on the bed, sitting on the headboard. I get on my knees in front of him, and smear the topping all over his swollen member. I grab the base again, and slowly proceed to remove the cream with my tongue. I can taste him, and myself in a delicious mixture added to the whipped cream. I moan as I take more and more of it in my mouth. I hear him moan as well, and his voice beckons me on. He is close, and I want it in my mouth. I feel him tense, and know it is time. "Yes….that's it" I tell him, opening my mouth for him. He shoots several streams of it into my waiting mouth, and I lick my lips to add cream to the mix. I suck and suck him, until he can't take any more and pushes me away. "Ok, ok...I surrender" he says, laughing.

We collapse on the bed, now both of us a sweet, sticky mess. I spend the night with him, so glad I took the chance to have this amazing encounter. Even if I never see him again, I will remember this night forever. I drift off into a deep sleep in his arms.

Andrea

God I hate this job! If it wasn't for the fact that I can schedule around my other job, I would drop it in a second. One more year and I'll be done with school, get a real job, and never push buttons on a blender in this stupid health club snack bar again! I think to myself. I really need something to take my mind off of the crap this week has shoveled my direction. I wonder if he's coming in today...

"So, how are you today, Andrea?" a familiar voice inquires. "Shitty!" I snap back. I break into a five minute rant about all the things pissing me off. Finally, I catch myself and laugh, realizing what I am doing. "I'm sorry, but boy did I need that!" I confess. "Hey, that's what I am here for" he replies. "How about if I do something to take your mind off of everything" he says, raising an eyebrow at me. I tilt my head a little, praying he says something halfway intelligent instead of the usual lines I hear stuck behind this counter. "Make it sexy and I'm yours" I plead inside. "Well you have your choice, we can go out for dinner and drinks, or we can skip dinner...and go right to the drinks" he offers, softening his directness a little. "Hhmmm, close enough" I thought. I want him, but I am still going to be particular about how this goes down. Men never have any clue just how fine a line they walk during these negotiations.

I laugh, and look him up and down. "I don't have time for dinner and drinks." The look on his face changes. Figuring I am shooting him down; he appears to be bracing himself for crossing the line. "Look, you've been coming here for how long now, and you're finally getting the balls to ask me out?" How about if we skip the formalities and just go back to your place and have pissed-off, dirty sex?" I look up at him, and try not to laugh at the stunned look on his face. He looks up to the task; his fit body honed under hours of training every week here at the gym in my direct line of sight. I watch him in the weight room, sweating and straining three days a week, and now I want to put him to the test. He's put in his time, spending a lot of time sitting across the counter from me. "Alright, let's go" he shoots back. I finish closing up and flip the CLOSED sign over, signaling the end of a long day.

Her Eyes

I follow him outside, parting ways with him at the door as soon as we leave the gym. I don't want word of this getting around; I spend enough time deflecting the onslaught of bad pick-up lines, posers and wannabe's. I hop into my Jeep and click on the lights, searching for his car. I fall in place behind him, and we head out of the parking lot. All of the sudden I am nervous about this; do I really know this guy well enough? Is this safe? Am I gonna end up on a missing person's list? My mind is flooding with every thought as to why this is a bad idea. I want to turn at the next light and bail out, but something keeps me going. Driven by a deep, primal desire, I continue to follow him. He's older than me; he'll make it ok, he'll make it comfortable I reassure myself. I wonder just how much older he is. I don't recall if he ever actually told me. I wonder if he is as nervous about this as I am.

He pulls into his driveway, and I pull in next to him. He is leaning against his car, seemingly deep in thought when I walk up to him. He stares at my shoes, and his eyes linger over me until they met mine. I stand frozen in front of him, my stomach suddenly in knots. I wait for him to make the first move; I offered and followed him here, I figure that is enough. I nervously bite my lip, waiting. "Well, do you want..." he never even finishes his sentence. He reaches for me, putting his arm around my waist and pulls me into him. He grabs my hair, pulling my head back, exposing me to his waiting mouth. I let out a moan of approval at his boldness, desiring to be taken. We kiss harder, and I press against him, feeling his taut body envelop mine. He releases my hair, and holds my face as we kiss some more. He seems to be auditioning his ability to be rough or gentle, depending what the situation calls for. I am melting like chocolate in his arms; my passion growing with each flutter of his tongue against mine. I let my hands explore that gym-hardened body of his, the one I have watched all these weeks; waiting...hoping.

I feel a yank on my hair, and open my eyes to find him looking at me. He is hungry for me, and I love it. Even though this is about my need for sex, I still want to be *desired*. He grabs my hand and leads me to the front door. He fumbles with the keys, and I am bursting inside. "Hurry up!" I shout, grabbing his waist. "Patience my dear, patience" he throws back, looking over his shoulder. He's revved my engine and now he is stalling...and it is driving me crazy. I am used to men who attack me, get what they want, and leave; but this is going to be different, I can tell. I want it now, but I had the feeling he is going to follow his plan, no matter what I do. We push the door open, and I blurt out "Quit stalling and kiss me". I shove him against the wall and lunge at him, my tongue shooting into his mouth, my lips grinding into his. For the moment, I have the upper hand, I am controlling the pace, and we are moving forward. "It's all I want; just give me what I want" echoes through my head.

Damn…he's doing it again! I think as he pulls away from me. He turns away and shuts the door behind us. He quickly turns around, telling me to follow him into the kitchen. I trail behind him, eager to see what is in store for me in the kitchen. He flicks on the lights in the hallway, but for some reason leaves the kitchen lights off. He grabs me in his strong hands again, and tugs at my work shirt, pulling it free from my shorts. I want to tear my shirt off and stand in front of him exposed, but he tells me to wait. He removes his shirt, baring his torso. I reach for his flesh, feeling the warmth trapped beneath his skin. I look up at him, smiling an approving grin. I lean forward, pressing my lips against his hard chest muscles. I kiss my way down to his abs, tracing the groove between his subtle six pack. I keep going down, working my way towards his manhood trapped beneath his dress pants. I can see it straining against the thin fabric, and I trace the outline with my fingers. It is so hard I think it might tear right through his pants. "May I?" I ask, dropping to my knees. He hesitates, and then grabs my hands, pulling me to my feet. "Not yet" he says, and turns away from me yet again.

He goes to the cupboard, grabbing a small glass. Next, he opens the freezer, and places several small ice cubes into the glass. "What are you doing with those?" I ask. "You'll see" is the only reply I get. He returns to me, grabbing the bottom of my shirt. He pulls it over my head, tossing it aside. Then he places his hands on my hips, lifting me up, and placing me on counter top. He kisses me again, and gently lays me back onto the marble surface. I am lying parallel to the floor, my bare back on the cold, hard surface. He stands over me, looking down at me in my bra and shorts. He gently runs his hands over me, starting at my neck, and on down from there. I am aching for his hands on me, all over me. He brushes his fingers over my nipples and I can feel them harden instantly. The sheer material is barely containing them as he begins to pinch my nipples between his fingers. I moan in delight, finally feeling some semblance of relief from the pressure inside my entire body. He leans forward and kisses my neck. He seems to be searching for the spots I like most, and I react when he finds one. He responds to my moans, focusing on the areas I like best. He keeps working over my nipples, and what was once bringing relief is now equating to some sort of inner frustration.

He reaches down between my breasts, and unclips my bra. He touches them immediately, kneading them together. His hands, rough from the gym, are still soft on my tender skin. He manages to be gentle despite his grip being strong and firm. He plays with my breasts as if he were worshiping them. I am growing dizzy with rising passion, wanting more, and faster than I am getting it. I am….ooooooohhhhh! I couldn't finish my thought; the ice cube is on my nipple without warning. It takes my breath away, and I arch my back in shock. He laughs at my reaction, seemingly to be exactly what he is looking for.

His mouth is on my breasts, reversing the affect of the ice. My nipples which became instantly hard under the ice cube now softened under his tongue. He tosses the ice aside; I hear it rattle around in the sink. He is pulling at my shorts, and I lift myself off the counter to ease his task. He pulls them off, slow and sexy, fitting the tempo of everything else he does. I lay on the counter in my panties, waiting, praying for him to go faster. I can feel a trickle of my own moisture run down my leg, my frustration grows by the second. I am drenched with excitement; he reaches down and peels the wet material off me. I'm completely naked in his kitchen. He moves to the end of the counter, and he stands there looking down at me. I am a little self conscious, and didn't realize that my legs are closed. He places his hands on my knees, and slowly pushes my legs apart. His eyes burn holes into me as he stares down from above. He watches me intently as his hands begin to explore my lower body. He seems to be avoiding my aching pussy on purpose. I squirm in anticipation of that first touch, silently begging him to do it. Finally I can't take it anymore, and I startle myself with my own voice, sounding like someone else. "Please, please touch me!" I growl at him. He finally complies, and buries a finger deep into my juicy hole. I can feel it squish as he enters me, and his thumb rubs my pulsating clit. I slam my hands down on the counter top, gasping for breath because his touch has stolen it from me. After what seems like only a moment of blurred frenzy, I arch my back and explode into a hard, almost violent orgasm. I buck my hips in response to his continuing pressure inside and on top of me. It is exquisite, and I feel any remnants of tension exit my body. I relax, and settle back onto the counter top.

I lay still, recovering my senses. I feel him start to kiss my knees, and slowly work his way towards my slick pussy. He works slowly upward towards his goal; my eyes are closed, my forearm over my face. I feel a finger slide into me, slowly pushing in and out of me. Holy shit this guy is driving me crazy! I thought I'd be on my way home by now, and we are just beginning. I am getting close again; I am twisting and writhing around from just one finger…and the anticipation of his mouth on me. All of the sudden he stops. I laugh, partly out of frustration and partly at his ability to catch me just as I am letting go. He looks up at me from between my legs, smiling that smile of a man getting exactly what he wants. "I think you are getting too hot" he says playfully. I search briefly for an explanation of his play on words, and then it happens. He shoves an ice cube inside me; the sudden cold deep inside me makes me cry out loud.

The mix of sensations is maddening; so hot from everything he is doing, and now so cold from the ice cube inside me. "Cold, huh?" he laughs aloud. "Sadistic bastard" I thought to myself. "Let's see if I can warm you back up." With that he dives in, sucking and licking my pussy at a frenzied pace. He works over my clit, flooding the area with heat once again. I can feel the melting ice trickling out of me onto the counter, and soon his tongue finds its way into my cold canal. I lift my hips off the counter, bucking them into his face, rubbing his nose into my clit in a convulsive pattern. I am going to explode again, and nothing is going to stop me. I grab the edge of the counter, stiffening into another blinding explosion of passion. I let out a loud yell, oblivious to anything but my own pleasure, completely lost in the moment. I fall back to Earth, landing on the counter top in his kitchen.

After a moment or two, I regain my equilibrium enough to realize that he must be dying for some relief of his own. I jump down off the counter, and go right to my knees in front of him. If he was hard before, I can't wait to feel him now. He removes his belt as my shaky hands undo his button in the top of his pants. I open the zipper, and slide his pants down to reveal his shaft. It is at full attention, and I want it. I grab it and squeeze. It is so hard I don't think it gives at all under my grip. I slide my hand up and down its length, feeling every inch of it. I reach under it and cup his balls, the skin tightening under my touch. I lean forward, taking as much of it as I can on the first try. I work my mouth back and forth over it, alternating my hand and my mouth in a rhythm I have done before. I hear him moan in pleasure as I devour his hard cock. I love it; having his cock in my mouth is returning the favor of all he has done to me so far, and all I imagine is to come. I extend my tongue, trying to take it deeper into my mouth. I increase my pace as I grow more and more in tune with him and what I am making him feel.

I feel him swelling in my mouth, and I don't want to stop. I keep going at it, until finally he grabs my hair and forcibly pulls me away from him. He helps me to my feet, and reaches under my knees, lifting me in his arms. Carrying me into the living room, he puts me to rest on the edge of a chair. He kneels in front of me, spreading my legs again. He teases me with it, rubbing on my clit and touching my opening without entering me. Oh God, he is giving me that look again, and I glare back at him. I can't believe that I have come twice already and I still am dying for more. "Dammit, FUCK ME NOW!" I say in a sex-roughened voice. My words free him, and he plunges himself deep into me. I am tight with tension, and the wet friction is incredible. He is working it into me slowly, an inch at a time. He pushes and withdraws, only to push a little deeper next time. My cries of ecstasy grow in proportion to his thrusts. Soon he is fucking me at a furious pace, burying all of it into me. I can feel a twinge of pain buried under a flood of pleasure as he fills me completely and then some. The impact of his body into mine is amazing, sending waves of pleasure through me. I am not even sure when one orgasm stops and another starts; I am lost in a deep well of delight, drowning in my own head.

He withdraws from me, and sits on the chair next to me. Despite my weakened state, I am powered on by my desire for more. I climb on top of him, guiding it into me again. My soaked pussy takes him in easily, and I sink it deep into me. "I love being on top" I think to myself. I arch my back, taking another inch of it into my folds. He grabs my hips, increasing my speed. "I love being on top!" I whisper. I find myself grinding into him faster than I ever have before, driven by absolute abandon, powered by my own unquenchable thirst for more. "Oh my God...I'm gonna come again!" I yell, my voice echoing through the house. Every fiber of my being blows apart all at once, and my frantic bucking slows into deep, grinding spasms of my body against his. Just as it starts he lifts up into me, and I scream again. He is ready as well, his cock swelling beyond containable limits. He explodes inside of me, and I can feel every pulse of his manhood as he empties himself into me. We ride it out as long as we can, and then crumble into the chair, reeling from the intensity of our session, breathless.

I look up at the clock, it reads 9:45. We had been at it for an hour and a half; far longer than I had planned for. I look back to him, and am searching for the polite and proper way to excuse myself. "I know...it's alright" he says before I find the words. We get up and dress again, and he follows me outside. He grabs me and kisses me long and deep once more. "That was incredible" I tell him, thanking him indirectly. "You feel better?" he asks, already knowing the answer. I laugh, realizing he is wondering if this was a one time thing. I smile, thinking he is crazy to think I wouldn't want another dose of that. "Yes, but next week looks pretty rough, too" I say, baiting him for an invite. His response: "Remember, that's what I'm here for!"

Lindsay

I can't believe it, stuck doing inventory again. Since the day I was hired Mr. Bryant has shown up late, left early, and sticks me with doing inventory of his formalwear shop every quarter I mumble to myself. Well, that's it; I am quitting this job the first chance I get. It's bad enough that I've have no social life what so ever since the break up, should I suffer in my work life as well? Sheila called about going out tonight, but now I have to cancel thanks to my boss.

I see the lights dim and hear the door shut; I head to the back room to fetch the bottle of wine I bought on my lunch hour for dinner at Mom's tomorrow night. It can be replaced; I am going to need it tonight for the long task ahead. I pour a tall glass, exhaling a deep, heavy sigh and head out to the front of the store to begin. I am startled to see someone in the store; there shouldn't be any customers left. He quickly begins explaining why he is here and that he is in a bind. "We are supposed to be closed for inventory tonight, but…I guess if you are going to make it quick it'll be ok" I inform him. Oh my God, that guy is so cute I think as I turn away. What are the odds a guy like that walks in here tonight? Oh my God, what am I going to do??? Settle down, first of all I instruct myself as I walk to the back office.

He has his back to me when I return to the front of the store. When he turns, he gives me a lingering smile, and compliments me on my perfume. I laugh shyly, flushing with both excitement and nervousness. He is wearing a black leather jacket, snug fitting jeans and a black t-shirt that clings to him like it is wet. The casual yet stylish shoes he is wearing compliment his look, and I wonder if that is by design or a tasteful coincidence. I have an almost overwhelming urge to run my tongue over every inch of him. He is a little taller than I am, with a slim yet powerful build. He is making me smile bigger than I have in quite some time. I notice he is looking at my left hand, and I ask "What did you expect to find, a ring?" I say smiling once again. "I was married once, to my high school sweetheart. We thought we knew it all, and eloped despite our family's opposition. We were just kids, and we couldn't cut it in the real world. We split up after a while, and went our separate ways". His interest in me only strengthens my desire for him.

67

Her Eyes

"No one likes to drink alone, would you like a glass of wine?" I query. Suddenly I don't care if I am here all night long. I am unsure if it's because I'm lonely or if we have a real connection, but we seem to be able to talk to one another so easily. He points out that we have not addressed the issue of getting him a tux. "Oh, piece of cake, the style is already chosen, all I have to do is take your measurements to see what size you are and we'll be all set" I inform him. I laugh at the sound of what I just said, wondering if he caught onto my unintentional play on words. God I wonder what he would think of me if I just kissed him right here in the store.

I tell him to follow me into the fitting room. I find a measuring tape and walk towards him. He removes his jacket, tossing it onto a nearby chair. I get my first real look at him, and am frozen in my tracks. His body looks like it is chiseled granite; I can even see the ripples in his abs through his shirt. I look up at him, meeting his gaze. I don't know what to do, so I move behind him so I can measure across his shoulders. God I am aching for him to turn around and kiss me; just take me in his arms and kiss me deeply. I fumble with the cloth tape, trying to focus on what I should be doing and not what I want. I scribble down a measurement for his shoulders, and then reach around his waist to measure again. I can feel the tautness of his body, and I lean into him to reach all the way around him. I am practically breathing down his neck as I strain to…oh my God I just brushed my mouth against him. "Did he notice?" flashes through my mind. What did I just do? I just crossed an invisible line following my desire instead of my brain into this uncharted territory. I stammer for something to say. He turns to look at me, and I am not sure what to do. He gives me a glance, an eyebrow raising in a curious look. I want this man, and I have the distinct feeling that I am going to have to take a chance and make it obvious before he would do anything.

I whisper in his ear "try to hold still" as I continue to work at getting his measurements recorded. I reach around his waist, and pull him towards me, pressing my body into his. I run my hands over his chest, caressing him like I long for him to do to me. I begin to lightly kiss the back of his neck, and he lets out a moan from deep inside. I can feel my nipples growing harder by the second, drawing in the heat of his body. I stand up on the wooden box at my feet, exploring his body from above. I put my hands on his shoulders, and turn him to face me. I want his mouth on mine. His eyes trace over me; I can feel his desire in that burning stare. He looks deep into my eyes before finally leaning into me. Our mouths meet in a storm of passion. We kiss each other feverishly, overwhelmed with desire. Each of us moans in delight as our tongues explore one another's hungry mouths. Suddenly I am in his arms, swept off of my perch and getting carried towards the desk in the center of the room.

He steps back from where he sits me, and gives me a long look. He seems to be gathering himself for something as he untucks his shirt. I am getting ready to help when he motions for me to stop. "Wait your turn" he says, smiling at me. He removes his shirt, finally revealing to my eyes what my hands had felt earlier. His skin is tan and smooth, and his carved body is flawless. He removes his socks and shoes, and then unbuttons the top two buttons of his fly. My eyes explore every inch, and I smile in anticipation of my hands on him. We embrace again, and kiss like we have been together before, already comfortable with one another.

"My turn" I say, grower bolder due partly to the wine but mostly to my heightening desire for him. I take his hand and lead him to the chair in front of the fitting mirrors. With one pull of the ties on my dress, it is around my ankles. I step out of it, standing before him as he had done for me. I am wearing only my favorite pink laced-trimmed panties, foregoing the bra in protest of convention. I look into the mirror, surveying the scene from a third person point of view. I walk over to him and make him scoot out to the edge of the chair. I kneel in front of him, reaching up to meet his mouth as we kiss again. My hands travel all over him; feeling his muscular frame under my soft hands. He reaches down and cups my breast in his hand; I think I will melt under his touch. A whimper escapes my lips as he kisses my neck. I am careful to avoid his crotch for now; I want it to be at full mast when I first see it. He begins kissing and gently clamping his teeth down on my neck, and both hands are on my breasts. He plays with my nipples and the shivers of pleasure course through me like flashes of lightning. My desire is growing, and I reach down and feel his swollen member for the first time. He is rock hard alright, ready for action. I slide my hands down to the waistband of his jeans; I rub his cock through his jeans before finding the buttons. I tug them apart, releasing his cock. He is not wearing underwear, and he is now free in front of me. He is thick with desire, and I am unsure if I should be excited or concerned about his size.

I want it in my mouth and waste no time grabbing the bottom of his shaft and opening my mouth to slowly engulf it. The head of his cock is purple with straining desire. I run my tongue around it, moistening it to glide it in my mouth. I work my tongue over it, amazed by how hard it is. It is rock solid, and I can only imagine what it would feel like sliding in and out of me. For now, I enjoy the taste of him; his masculine salty taste fills my senses. I twist the bottom of his cock, my hand slippery from my own saliva. I shoot a glance over to the mirror, finding me kneeling in front of this Greek god of a man, pleasuring him like a servant. The scene is incredible; his head thrown back in pleasure, his hand entangled in my hair. I lift and lower my mouth on him, watching the reflection of my head bobbing up and down as if I am watching someone else through a window.

I can tell he was really getting into the feeling of my mouth on him, and before long he is going to reach the breaking point. After a few more minutes, he grabs my hand from around his cock, and helps me to my feet, signaling his inability to continue and still maintain control. We switch places; I am now sitting in the chair and he is on his knees on the floor. He kisses me again, running his hands over my body as I had just done to his. He pushes my breasts together, straining to get both my aching buds into his mouth at the same time. His tongue runs all over both of them, increasing the sensitivity to new heights. I throw my head back, staring at the ceiling, locked in a silent scream of ecstasy. I am boiling with desire at this point, internally begging for him to touch me and release the fire trapped inside. He lifts my legs, and placing them over the arms of the chair. Oh God yes...please! I scream inside my head. He pulls my panties to the side, revealing my glistening pussy. Thank God I had not cancelled my appointment to get waxed yesterday, I thought to myself. "Surprise!" I exclaim.

Suddenly his fingers pierced my waiting folds and I gasp in delight. I am drenched with anticipation, and touching the walls of my aching pussy felt long overdue. I toss my head back as he twists his fingers in and out of me, arching to meet his gentle intrusion. I am growing close to exploding already. He removes his fingers from me and gently pinches my clit between his thumb and finger. The sensation is incredible, and as I let out a deep moan I begin to come. My orgasm peaks as he gently rubs my swollen clit in his pleasure pinch. It feels like I explode into a thousand pieces as I ride the waves of pleasure induced by his touch. Just as I am starting to come down from the impact of my orgasm, I feel his tongue on me. He returns his fingers inside me, and now rubs my pleasure button with his tongue. It is a stark contrast from his thumb; like silken fire, fluttering over my clit. He is driving me insane with pleasure, and I can feel another one welling up inside me. His timing is impeccable; and I buck my hips into his face throughout the next orgasm. I collapse into the chair, totally spent from the intensity of my explosions.

He lets me catch my breath before leading me to mirrored partition. He turns me to face the mirror, and presses me against it gently but firmly. He grabs my hand and places it on his cock, and leans forward to whisper in my ear. "Put me inside you" he says in a voice raspy with desire. I want his thickness in me, and guide the tip into my entrance. He is big, and I wince a little at the pressure in spite of how wet I am. He understands, and slowly guides himself in and out of me until I grow accustom to his size. Before long, he is stuffing every inch of that cock deep inside me. He occasionally has to pause to collect himself, reveling in the feeling of my tight pussy resisting his cock on every stroke. Soon he is pounding me against the mirror, my hot breath fogging the glass in front of me. My groans grow louder as he continues to impale me with his hardness. I am reaching the top again, and his pace quickens. I feel his hand on my shoulder, and I brace for the impact of his cock buried up inside me as he too reaches his climax. I come first, but he quickly follows, jamming me down on his cock. We shiver and struggle against each other as we ride out the orgasms to completion. I am weak with pleasure, and he has to pin me against the mirror to keep me from crumpling to the floor.

I feel him reach down and put his arm around the back of my legs; he picks me up and carries me towards the desk. I stare into his eyes, glazed over from the sheer pleasure he has induced from deep within me. I am quickly gaining my sobriety as he walks with me in his arms. I want to return the favor, and I have a wickedly naughty idea. I tell him to have a seat in my boss's chair. He does, and I straddle him with a leg

Her Eyes

over each arm of the black leather chair. I put my hands on the top of the chair and settle down onto his cock. I slowly begin to grind into him, feeling every inch of it delve deep into the folds of my pussy. Soon I am lost in a frenzy of pleasure, riding him like a jockey. The chair rocks back and forth in time to my hip undulations, adding to the rhythm we are creating. I am climbing towards another, and can tell this one will be big. It is like diving off a cliff; free falling in anticipation as I grow closer and closer, until I dive into the depths, an ocean of pure ecstasy. I cry out loudly as I come, grinding into him with a fury I have never known.

He lifts me up, and stands me in front of the desk. I lay down on it, my stomach pressing against the cold wood. I look back at him, brushing my hair aside so I can see the eyes that belong to the man who is fucking me like no one ever has before. "That's right, fuck me right here on my boss's desk" I say playfully, knowing full well I am quitting this job anyway. He leans forward to whisper directly into my ear "As you wish, my dear". His gruff words echoing throughout my body. He places his hands on my ass, spreading me open for entry. He guides it in again, that big cock diving into my depths. He goes right to the hilt on the first stroke, and never breaks stride from there. He parts me with full thrusts, banging me into the desk with deep, hard impacts. Pleasure ripples throughout my body; I shudder and wince under every impact of his body into mine. I feel the now familiar aching of my orgasm rising from within. It starts from deep down inside me, fighting its way to the surface at a slow, steady pace. I keep pushing back into him, begging him not to stop, to keep fucking me like this forever. He places his foot on top of the desk, and continues his long, powerful strokes into me. He groans and again I brace myself for his explosion. He drives deep into me, shudders, and releases himself into the very core of my being. The feeling is perfection, and I want this moment to last forever.

He collapses on top of me, spent from his second orgasm and all the work he has done. We look at each other and laugh. We kiss, tenderly this time, and get up to gather our clothing. I grab my clothes, hiding behind them as I leave the room to dress, suddenly not feeling so bold in front of him. I return with his tuxedo in hand and a huge smile on my flushed face. "That will be $125.00 for the tux, and my number is on the receipt" I inform him. He hands me his Visa card, and I laugh, thinking

72

that he will have a great story to tell his friend at the wedding. I am already looking forward to seeing him again.

Thank you for purchasing my book, I hope you have enjoyed it to this point. Please visit my website at www.flipside-erotica.com, and as a thank you for your purchase, view the "internet only bonus story" that I have posted for you. Please type in www.flipside-erotica.com/free to enjoy the bonus story.

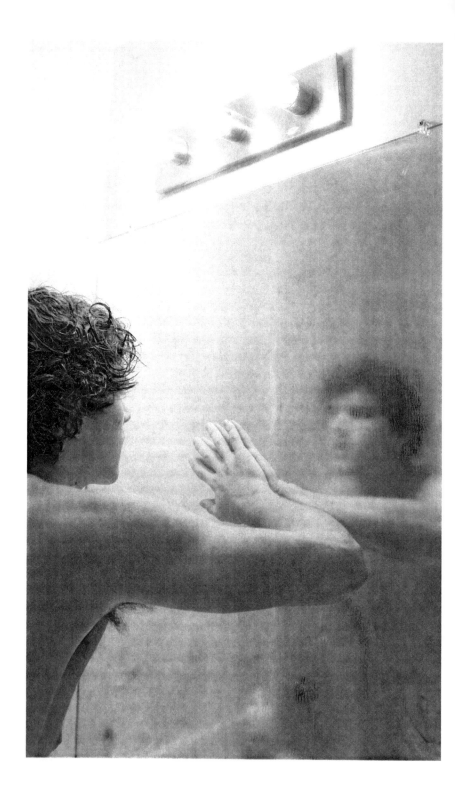

Nicole

God, do I look forward to Tuesday mornings. We have arranged our schedules to allow us several hours of suspended reality together. It is amazing the chemistry the two of us still have after this much time together; even now I still get nervous and excited with anticipation.

My cell phone rings, and I run out of the bathroom to get it. I know I am going to be a sweaty, disheveled mess in less than an hour, but I still go through the trouble of looking good for him when I walk through his door. I love the sound of his voice in the morning; it has the same gruff raspiness that it does halfway through an intense session between us. He told me he wakes up rock hard, and I feel a twinge of excitement every time I think about it. I picture him stroking it as he talks to me on the phone. "Good morning" I purr to him. "Are you ready for me?" he inquires in his sexy voice. "Always. See you in a few minutes" I say, and hang up the phone.

I know he will be waiting for me, door unlocked. Some time ago we began the habit of me walking into his place, sometimes finding him still in bed, waiting for me. He certainly does a good job of mixing things up; never letting me know what would be waiting for me on the other side of that door. Even subtle things like not shaving his face so that his rough beard would redden my skin everywhere it touches let me know that he is a man truly tuned-in to his lover. I got him in the habit of shaving like I do; slick, so I can taste his skin. The feeling is more intense; skin on skin is the only way to go.

Walking up the stairs to his place my heart already racing with excitement. I can feel myself clenching up, as if he was already inside me. Even the motion of walking makes me ache inside. I quietly open the door and then lock it behind me, entering the safe haven of his place. Within these walls there are no rules, no inhibitions, and I am totally free to be whomever I want.

I walk into the bedroom, and hearing water running I turn towards the bathroom. The door is almost shut, and I push it open, peeking inside. The air in the room is still heavy with steam from the shower, and the mirror is fogged over. Standing in front of me clad only in a towel, he is finishing shaving his face. He reaches up with his hand and wipes a spot free of steam to see his reflection. Our eyes meet in the mirror, and I give him a wry smile, approving of today's scenario he's created. "Don't stop on my account" I tell him. My breath quickens as I move forward to touch him. I put my hands on his shoulders, feeling the strength in his frame. I lean in, and kiss his neck. Standing in my heels, I have access to more of him than usual. He continues to finish his task, while I am free to explore him from the unusual position of being behind him. I reach around his waist, and release the towel that is hiding that firm ass of his from me. It hits the floor, and I bite my lip expressing my delight. He finishes shaving, and cleans off his razor. I know he would be almost at full tilt already, and reach around to grab his length. As soon as my hand touches it, he turns to face me.

My hand is still on his cock, and his hardness is visible on both sides of my grip. I squat down in front of him, balancing on my heels. I slide my hand to the base and squeeze him, fighting to make it give under my grip. He is so hard he reminds me of my vibrator, but so…much…better. I open my mouth, preparing to slide it in. I love to go slowly step by step through my routine with him, allowing him to enjoy it and yet making him want me all the more. My problem is that I get so wound up I have to constantly remind myself to maintain my composure and not go too hard too fast. I slide my hand up and down his shaft and begin slowly jerking his stiff rod. My mouth slides all over him, my own saliva runs down into my hand. I use it to glide my hand farther up the shaft, feeling like a porn star as I work over his cock. God I love the way he tastes. I begin to increase my pace as the desire within me builds. In spite of the fact that I know I can't get it all in my mouth, I try over and over anyway.

I slide the towel under my knees so I can focus on his cock in my hand. I am about to burst from the excitement, and I know I am going to have to take matters into my own hands. I am glad I chose to forego the underwear today, and I push my skirt up and out of my way. I quiver under my own touch; squatting in front of him, I begin to rub my throbbing clit. I moan deeply, aching to release the firestorm between my thighs. He reacts to my moan, feeling it reverberate deep in his shaft. I am close already, and I slide my fingers up into my waiting pussy. I am beginning to lose my senses; guided by instinct and desire instead of thought. I finger fuck vigorously myself, and my mouth follows the lead of my fingers, increasing the pace. I am lost in a frenzy of passion; sucking and jerking him while I finger myself into oblivion. I can't take much more, and I am about to explode all over my own hand as I feel him move.

I feel his hand on my wrist, and he pulls my hand away from my melting folds. "Oh God, no…please, please let me come!" I beg, my voice rough with desire. "Ooh, you are sooo close aren't you?" he says. He grabs my wrists and spins me around, my ass pressing against the counter. He lifts me onto the counter and I know relief will soon be mine. My thighs are involuntarily clenched from the maddening desire that possesses me. He pries me apart, and pushes two fingers into me. I throw my head back in pleasure, smacking it into the mirror. I am too far gone into my rising orgasm to even acknowledge the stars I should be seeing from that impact. The suddenness of my orgasm almost catches me off guard, and I revel in the release that I have been longing for. I let out a loud scream, my cries echoing through the bathroom. I can feel him fighting with my pussy; the walls trying to clamp down on him as he continues to corkscrew his fingers in and out of me. I am hiding another orgasm right behind the first, and I want it desperately. I reach down and grab his wrist, taking control of the speed with which his fingers penetrate me. This one comes from deep; I swear it felt like it started in my toes and races through my entire body. I am frozen by it, pressing myself into the mirror as the waves radiate through every inch of me.

After giving me a moment to recover, he helps me slide out of the puddle I am sitting in and places the towel on the counter top. Still woozy, he helps me remove my shirt, pulling it over my extended arms. I feel drunk with pleasure, barely cognizant of what is going on at this point. I unbutton my skirt, letting it fall around my feet. I reach down to unbuckle my shoes, but he tells me to leave them on. I don't know what he has in mind, but I like it. He puts his arm around me and pulls me into his naked body. The firmness of his body restores some sense of sobriety.

The steam has left the room and I can now see myself in the mirror. He is behind me; his body hidden as I stand naked in nothing but my four inch heels. He reaches around and cups my breast, and pulls my hair aside to expose my neck. He bites down on my neck, sending a river of electricity down my body. I tilt my head back onto his shoulder, lost in yet another moment of pleasure under his touch. He turns his head and whispers in my ear "I want to try something." That is good enough for me; I am in, I don't care what it is, I think to myself. He has earned free license to do with me what he wishes. I hop back up onto the countertop, eager to see what he is coming up with this time. He kneels down in front of me, his face between my legs. His eyes smoldering as he looks up at me, and I am ready to come again before he even touches me.

He starts at my knee, kissing the inside of it, far away from his intended target. He is slowly working his way up the inside of my thigh, but his pace is too slow for my growing desire. I put my hand on the back of his head, gently trying to urge him upward. He gives me a moment of hope, only to end up kissing my navel. I have come so hard already, how can I need it this badly still? But I do; I need it, wanting him to taste me, flick his tongue over my pink pearl, to release yet another storm from within. Finally he does; shooting his tongue into my waiting hole. I slam my hands onto the countertop, the sting in my palms barely noticeable compared to the electricity jolting through the center of my body. He is using long strokes of his tongue, going from my soft opening all the way up to my clit. I reach down and spread myself open, giving him even more access to my slippery folds. He looks up at me, his eyes peering over my left hand I slipped between my legs. The look in his eyes and the scene he is creating is almost too much for my brain to take; I close my eyes, burning the image into my mind forever.

My eyes are still shut tightly as I feel him slide one finger inside me. He focuses his tongue strokes on my clit, gently flicking it with quick, short strokes. His finger rubs in and out of me, and my body clenches around him. He slips his finger out of me, and replaces it with something cold and hard...and vibrating??? I look down to see the top half of his battery powered razor sticking out of me. "Oh Jesus that feels good!" I tell him, approving of his idea. His tongue is back on my clit, working me over as the vibrations in my pussy resonate deep in me. He can tell I am getting close again, and the force of his tongue increases accordingly. I grab the back of his head, pulling his face into my crotch, and begin bucking my hips. I am lifting myself off the counter, supported on my heels and right hand, powered by my own desire. I become aware of animal-like growling noises from within the room, only to realize that the noises are coming from me. I scream his name at the top of my lungs, bucking for all I am worth, until I can take no more and fall back to Earth, landing on the countertop from where my climb through the heavens began.

I am paralyzed; unable to move as I sit on the faux marble surface. Now it is his turn, and I can't even help him along, my head spinning from the last orgasm. He removes his razor and replaces it with his hard cock. His thickness stretches me, forcing himself into my sopping wet pussy all the way to the hilt. The most I can do to aid in the frenzy is to wrap my legs around him. I fling them together behind him, my heels clicking loudly against one another as I buck upwards to meet his thrusts. I am not sure where the energy is coming from, but I begin to regain my strength. I reach up and put my arms around his neck. I tuck my chin, looking down to watch his cock slide in and out of me. He slides his hand into my hair, and I brace myself for the oncoming pull. I am now staring at the ceiling while he plows away at me below. I can no longer watch, so I close my eyes and focus on the feeling of him ramming his cock into me. Our bodies make slapping noises as he pounds me relentlessly. I can feel him swelling inside me, and brace myself for the impact of his orgasm. Instead of giving in, he pulls away.

I make a pouting face as soon as his cock is no longer inside me. "Stop pouting and give me a second" he says in a playfully stern voice. I laugh at him squirming in an attempt to regain his composure. So that's what that looks like, I laugh to myself. After a quick few moments, he is in front of me again. I reach down and grabbed his hardness, guiding it into me. He starts slowly this time, easing his cock into me an inch at a time. Soon he is withdrawing completely and then pushing inside me all the way to the bottom. He reaches over and grabs the razor again, flicking it on. He touches the smooth end of it onto my nipple, sending pulses of pleasure through me. "Like that?" he asks. "Mmmhhhmmm" is all I reply. He rolls the tip of it around on my erect nipple for another minute or two before removing it. He arches away from me, and sticks the vibrating tip down on my clit. He continues to make long strokes with his cock as he holds the new toy in place. I feel a deep stirring within me once again, but this one comes from far away. It is similar to when I do it myself; not violent and incapacitating like when he does it to me, but softer and longer. It lasts a long time, and I ride the wave as long as I can. It left me wanting more, and he is more than willing to accommodate. He never breaks form, continuing to take long, steady strokes in and out of me. He does however add one little twist; he touches the vibrating razor to himself. The sensation is amazing; his thick, straining cock is rubbing my walls inside, and now add the sensation of vibrating pleasure into the mix. "I can feel that all through me" I say. Another one is on the way, and he keeps going to draw it out of me. I bury my face in his chest as I start again, similar to the last one. It starts slow, building force as the waves crash down on top of me. He deepens the impact of each stroke as I squish all over his cock one last time. I can give no more; I am empty. He has emptied me. I release my grip on his back, only then realizing that I had been digging my nails into his flesh.

I am fairly certain that will be the last one for me today, and I am glad he made it last. It is time for him to get his, and I am ready to return the favor. I slide down off the counter, and he spins me around, now facing the mirror. He pushes me forward, and I rest on my elbows on the counter where I had been seated. I am still in my heels, and I push them together, squeezing my pussy tight. He guides his cock into me, forcing through my resisting, pouting lips. He places his hands on my hips, and jerks me back and forth onto his cock, my body meeting his thrusts half way. He fucks me from behind, slamming his thighs into my ass. He reaches up and yanks my head back with a forceful jerk. Now I am staring right into my own eyes as he plows into me. I look up at him in the mirror, his eyes wild with desire. His one hand in my hair and one hand on my hip, he is getting what he wants.

I can feel one more wave beginning to crest within me, and I know I am going to come hard one more time. "That's it...fuck me, FUCK ME DARREN!" I command. He grabs his new favorite toy once more, and places it on my most private hole. It makes me jump with surprise, "Don't you...OOOhhh, GOD!" I only made it half way through my protest before I give in to the feeling. He is ready, and so am I. He shoves forward, burying his cock deeper into my depths. He starts to spasm, and it triggers mine. I explode into a frenzy of pleasure, my pussy clenching him, milking every drop of it out of him. We collapse on the counter top in a sweaty, spent heap.

After a few moments, we have the strength to move from our position. We head for the shower, playfully washing one another under the warm water. We savor the last few moments of our time together, and I am already looking forward to next Tuesday.

Stacy

"Maybe I should dye my hair a different color"... I think to myself as I walk down the aisle of hair care products. Maybe that will get me noticed. I spend twice as much time at the grocery store as I need, just to be out of the house. "Hey, isn't that the guy from my condo complex?" my internal dialogue continues as he walks over to me. We chat for a few moments, and I discover that he is new here also. I tell him I moved to Florida for my job about four months ago, and am bored out of my mind while trying not to sound too desperate. He is about an inch taller than I am, great smile and appears to be in really good shape. I don't want to let this chance slip by, so I scribble my number down on a business card and hand it to him. I tell him to call me sometime; we had a nice chat and I walk away hoping he calls me soon. I hope that being this forward will work out for a change.

A couple of days later my phone rings and it's him. He is free tomorrow night, and what a surprise, so am I. We decide to go to a movie together, and he will meet me out in front of the complex. We arrive at the theater, only to find the movie is sold out. Instead of making him see a chick flick, or me sit through a bad action film, I suggest that we go across the street and have a drink. We sit at a back table away from everyone else and spend a good hour or so talking and drinking. After several drinks and lots of laughs, I am ready to really party; I can feel my old wild side returning. I am ready to take things to the next level. "You know what would really kick this buzz into high gear...a Jacuzzi" I state, wishing there was one back at our complex. He mentions that there are several at the resort he works at. Without hesitation I wave at the waitress to get our tab and we're headed for the car as soon as we pay. We are headed to the resort in his car, and the question of what the next step should be has been answered.

We pass the guard station and enter the resort, parking in front of one of the pools on the property. We look around and find the pool deserted. It is almost midnight, and the resort is quiet. I can smell the strong chlorine wafting off of the Jacuzzi, and am dying to tear off my clothes and jump in. We walk around the fence and enter the pool area. "We should get in" I tell him, my mind already made up. I keep walking; he starts to protest, but I have already decided I'm going in. "Suit yourself, but I'm getting in" I inform him as I start shedding clothes and walking to the hot, bubbly water. He seems to be stalling, looking for towels in the cabinets. Better for me; I will be already in the water by the time he gets around to joining me. I will be a lot more comfortable not stripping down in front of him. The cool night air hits my body and I get goose bumps almost instantly. I step into the hot water and it is a stark contrast to the outside temperature. A rush of heat floods upwards through me as I climb down the steps one at a time. My back is to him, hiding the view for now. I hear his footsteps as he approaches, but I don't turn around. I walk to the other side, squat down so I am under water up to my chin, and then turn around to take a seat on the other side. He will get to see me soon enough. He stands at the edge, seemingly realizing the dilemma of having to get naked in the cold air.

He drops the towels on the deck, and slowly begins to unbutton his shirt, pulling it over his head. I sit back, putting my arms over the sides, being careful to not expose my best feature to him just yet. I lean my head back, pretending not to watch him as he undresses in front of me. I cannot resist the urge to glance at him frequently, excited to see his body in the flesh. I can barely sit still as his pace slows. He turns away slightly, as if shy all of the sudden. I can see the waistband from his boxers peek out over the top of his jeans, and I realize it will be a little longer before I get to see what he is packing. He loses the jeans, and walks to the steps in his skin tight boxers. The label on the front reads Everlast...God I hope that's true, I think, giggling to myself. I can see he is growing with excitement, and that is all it takes. I jump from my seat across the hot tub from him, meeting him on the stairs.

I attack him on the stairs, grabbing him and kissing him with my hungry mouth. He meets my lunge halfway, and we embrace on the steps, kissing feverishly. "God I have wanted to do that since the first time I saw you" I confess in a break between kisses. He leans in and kisses me as if echoing my words with his actions. We continue to kiss until he pushes passed me and heads for the other side. He sits where I was seated, on the opposite side of the hot tub from the stairs. He looks at me standing where he left me, a little confused as to why he no longer wants to be kissing me. "Come get me" he says playfully, and the game is on. His eyes travel all over me, and my nipples stiffen in anticipation of us fucking in the Jacuzzi at the resort. I hesitate a moment, loving the look on his face as he drinks in a long, hungry look of me. I go to him, straddling him on the bench seat. The thin fabric of his underwear does little to hide the hardness of his excitement. I rub myself against him as we kiss again. We turn our hands loose, allowing them to roam over one another's skin. I lean into him, arching my back and pressing my heat against his firm cock. He dips me backwards, my hair disappearing into the water. I run my hands through my hair, squeezing the water out of it. I am glad to know I will not be fighting my hair through the rest of this encounter. Now that my neck is exposed he dives in, kissing and biting where my neck joins my shoulder. His hands are on my breasts, lifting and squeezing them. He is working his way down to them, and I ache deep inside to have his mouth on them. Between the cold air and the hot session we are in the midst of, my nipples are so hard they practically hurt.

He continues his journey downward, and I arch to meet his mouth. I close my eyes, waiting for the sweet relief of his mouth on me. He stops, and I open my eyes to see him staring up at me, mouth open, tantalizingly close to my nipple. He breaks into a smile, knowing he is torturing me. "Stop teasing me and do it" I say to him, half pleading and half ordering him. His mouth finds my breasts, and I hold myself there so he can suck my nipples. My hips react involuntarily, and grind my pussy into him as his tongue whips my nipples into submission. After a few luscious moments, he returns his mouth to mine. His hands slide behind me, grabbing my ass and helping my hips do their thing. He pushes me away after a few hard strokes against him, I assume the pressure becoming too much to bear.

My hands dip below the surface, tracing his body lines down to his crotch. I feel his length with my hands for the first time, and moan in anticipation of it inside me. I want to touch it, and try to remove his shorts. He gets the hint, and stands up, removing them himself. He throws them aside, and they splash down on the side near the rest of his clothes. He goes to sit down again, but I push him against the side. The sight of it has increased my desire to another level, and I want my mouth on it immediately. He sits and I go to work, running my mouth all over him. He is so hard, and I love every inch of it. I look up at him, and he watches me intently as I slide my mouth all over it. His eyes are half closed, and he tosses his head back as I go all the way down on it. He moans in delight at my mouth on him.

He is holding true to the label on his boxers and I am impressed that he is enduring the workout I am giving him. Just as I think that, he pushes me away from him. Guess I got to him after all, I laugh inside. "Your turn" he tells me, switching places with me. He kisses me again; his tongue traveling down my neck, to my breasts once again. He lingers at each spot, drinking me in before moving on. I arch my back to meet his mouth again. He sucks one tenderly as he pinches the other firmly, the contrast spellbinding. I am lost in the electric feeling shooting between….Oh God! His finger is deep inside me without warning. No build up, no feeling his way around, straight into me like an arrow. I open my mouth to scream out, but the noise won't leave my body. His hand is on my mouth, preventing me from blowing our cover. I hear him laugh as he realizes I can't scream.

His finger moves in and out of me slowly, and he keeps kissing his way down my stomach to where his finger is. He removes it, and then pushes two inside me. His mouth is right there, but he goes to my thigh instead. He keeps twisting his finger in and out of me, increasing his speed, then slowing once again. His face is close again; he extends his tongue while looking up at me just like with my nipple earlier. I am bursting with desire, insane…and I can't take it any longer. I grab him by the back of his head and yank his face into my pussy. I feel his tongue touch me, and that is all it takes. I close my legs around his head, grinding my hips into his face as I explode. I have never come so hard and so…violently in my entire life. I don't know if it is pent up frustration, the alcohol, or just him driving me crazy but I keep going and going. It feels like I am turning inside out.

I finally let him free from my thigh clamp, but he never leaves me. He continues to flick his tongue over me, softer and more gently now. I shudder uncontrollably at times; I am leaning back on my elbows, watching him work. His tongue is still on me, his fingers in me, and I lean my head back looking into the stars as I come again. This one starts slower, but builds quickly to the force matching the first. My hips go at it again, grinding my pussy into his face. I barely finish before he suddenly stands up out of the water and puts his hands under my knees, lifting my ass off the side slightly. I look up just in time to see him bury himself into me. I throw my head back once again and moan loudly. He repeats the motion over and over and over. He fucks me hard, and I love every stroke. I start again, and wrap my legs around him, holding him deep inside me. I buck my hips once again, fucking him back. I hold myself up on my hands, and fuck him as fast as I can for a moment before I collapse on the concrete, my whole body quivering in pleasure and momentary exhaustion.

He sits down on the bench seat again, warming his skin. He leaves me in a heap on the deck, giving me a moment to recover. I am cold from being out of the water for so long, and I join him in the hot tub. He gets up and goes to the steps, taking a seat on the top one. I know what he wants, and I want it too. I climb to the top step, putting a foot on either side of him. I straddle him, the cool air caressing my flesh once again. I grab the railing for leverage, and put my other hand on his shoulder. I am on top, fucking him in the Jacuzzi at the resort. The thoughts echo through my head as I ride him like a mechanical bull. I am barely aware of my surroundings, lost in the moment. I cry out his name over and over as I ram myself down on him. I come once again, screaming out, slapping my hands down on his chest. I feel the sting in my hands, my rhythm breaking as the electricity runs through me. He takes over, grabbing my hips and moving me back and forth on top of him. It extends the pleasure a little longer before I feel myself go weak against him.

He holds me against him, and then turns to the side, pouring my melted body onto the concrete, face down. I am leaning over the edge on the towels that he dropped earlier. He is close, and ramming himself into me once again as he closes the gap to the finish line. I can feel it growing inside me; he grits his teeth and braces for impact. I have a better idea, and I turn around, pushing him away. I get down in front of him, wanting to feel it. He looks surprised, but quickly catches on. "Come on my tits" I tell him, grabbing his cock and jerking it furiously. He tenses, exhales, and explodes shooting his man juice all over my chest. He falls away from me, submerging his body in the water one more time.

Her Eyes

He comes up out of the water, and sits again. I join him on the seat and we kiss some more, this time more tenderly. I open my eyes, and he saw it too...a light scanning across the pool. We grab our clothes and run for the poolside bathroom. We quickly dress, and then peek out the door looking for the security guard. We run for the car, and squeal out of the parking lot. Heading for home, we drive quickly until he parks in front of his place. He gives me a deep, lingering kiss, and then I turn and walk away. This was a little faster start than I had planned for, but now that we are going I can't wait to see where this leads.

Katherine

It was all arranged; and I have every detail discussed and planned to a tee. I am working late all week, and know that no one will be around the office by 7:00pm. I have found my fascination with this strange, but have finally decided to embrace one of my ultimate fantasies. My boyfriend is a man I am very comfortable with, and who I trust enough to be right for the job. The plans are laid out, all to my design.

I try to focus on the work at hand, but I'm bored with this case and straining for the hours to pass so the office will empty. I know today is the day, and that information is making me twitch with desire. I am wearing my favorite dark blue business suit; conservative and smart. I take delight in the fact that I have such a cold and professional reputation at the office. Cold-heart bitch; ruthless attorney incorporated. I take on the big boys and win; I am one of the most feared defense attorneys in town. The men in the office joke at my expense that I would lighten up if I took the time to get laid once in a while. Heh, if they only knew what a dirty girl I can be.

Finally, six-thirty and my secretary is leaving the office. I have a mountain of papers to review, but can feel myself growing moist with excitement as I watch the minutes tick away. I know he will be coming for me soon, and I try to look busy sitting at my desk. The phone rings, and I pick it up instinctively. The west coast office is still going strong; great I thought, last thing I want right now is a lengthy phone conversation with Bob from our L.A office. We are collaborating on a case, and I know that I cannot ignore him. The conversation takes 25 minutes; elapsed time estimation is a by-product of the job. I hang up the phone, glancing nervously at my watch to confirm the time. Seven-fifteen, where is he?

I barely finish the thought before I feel someone standing behind me. I am aware of his presence before I even turn around. Then it happens; the blindfold goes over my eyes before I can put my hands up. He tightens the cloth behind my head, and clamps his hand over my mouth before I can draw a breath. He jerks the chair backward, the feeling of falling over backwards rushed through my body. I reach back to brace myself, and feel the cold metal hit my wrist. I hear the repetitive click a handcuff makes when it is closing. He forcibly lifts me out of the chair, and I struggle against his grip. Before I know what is happening, he shoves me forward over the desk. I fight back; he tries to hold me down but I struggle free. I am still blindfolded, but because we are struggling, I know where he is. I stomp on his toes and take a swing at him with my free hand. He catches my wrist, and forces my arm behind me. I can feel his body press into mine, his hot breath on my neck as he reaches behind me and pushes the cuff around my other wrist. He forces me forward again, my face pressing into the glossy finish of my mahogany wood desk.

He leans over me, grabbing my hair and tugging firmly. I feel him lay his body on top of mine, his weight pressing me harder into the desk. He holds me there, running his free hand over my body. He whispers in my ear in a gravelly voice "I am going to fuck you, right here in your office, Katherine!" His words ring in my ear, and a chill runs down my spine. I try to get up off the desk, but his weight easily prevents me from moving. My jacket is already off, hanging over the back of my chair. I had kicked off my shoes a couple of hours ago, and I can now feel his hand running up and down my leg. My skirt clings to my shape, leaving little between him and me. I hear something hit the desk; and get a whiff of a pungent and familiar smell. I can't place it, and am searching my mind when I heard the telltale sound that answered my question. The object in question…duct tape. He tears a piece off and lifts me off of the desk by my hair. I am about to yell out when he slaps the tape over my mouth.

I hear him laugh to himself, and he is breathing heavily from the excitement and struggle of the events so far. He sits in my chair; the leather scrunching beneath his weight. I stay still, contemplating my next move. I feel him reaching for me; like he is tracing the outline of my body without touching me. He stands, positioning himself directly behind me. He reaches out and places his hand in the middle of my back. I can feel him exploring me; he takes his time running his hands over me. I tremble beneath his touch. He smoothes the silk of my blouse against my skin, then suddenly jerks it from its tucked position in my skirt. The suddenness makes me jump, and I would have sucked in my breath if it were not for the duct tape over my mouth. He finds the zipper on the back of my skirt, and very, very slowly unzips it. He grabs the skirt by the bottom, pulling it down over my ass. I feel it bunch up at my ankles. I stand there in my heels, exposed in my nylons; bent over my own desk.

His hands cup my ass, squeezing my firm cheeks. He exhales an approving sigh, and then gives me a firm slap on my right side. I jump at the impact, and then wince a little at the sting. I can feel the heat welling up on my cheek, his handprint now glowing on my ass. He goes back to fondling me, taking his time enjoying my gym-hardened curves. I spend a considerable amount of time at the gym; weekly kickboxing classes have put my body in great shape. It appears the training I have been doing may not have served me as well as I thought if this situation were actually real. I am being dominated in my own office, in my place of ultimate power and control; I am at the mercy of another. He slides his hand between my legs, feeling my growing wetness. I recoil from his touch out of instinct, but then settle and begin to accept it. He lingers on my most sensitive spot only for a moment, making me yearn for more.

He stands me up, reaching around me and placing his hand between my breasts. I pretend to continue struggling, and he prevents it by grabbing me and pulling me against his body. He wraps his arms around me, pulling me close against him. I feel the bulge straining through his pants, jamming into my leg. His hands are all over me; squeezing my breasts and brushing over my crotch. I'm not wearing anything but my nylons, and I get a faint whiff of my musky scent. The smell of my own excitement intoxicates me. I want to turn and face him, tear off my gag and kiss him, but he will not let me. He holds me there, teasing, almost torturing me with his hands slowly taking inventory of my entire body. His hot breath is on my neck, and he bites down on the junction between my shoulder and my neck. My knees almost buckle as he times squeezing my nipples with his well-placed bite. It is like lightning shooting through me. I let out a moan of desire; the only indication so far that I am enjoying the game. But I am...far more than I ever thought I would. He continues mauling me, squeezing my breasts inside my bra. Finally he sets them free, unclipping my bra through the front of my shirt. He reaches under my silky blouse, touching them skin on skin. The warmth of his hands sends another ripple of pleasure through my body. My nipples grow hard, jumping to meet his touch.

He reaches up and grabs my hair, yanking my head backward and forcing me to look at the ceiling. His other hand slowly begins to

Her Eyes

unbutton my blouse. *God, he is taking forever!* I think to myself. I want him inside me right now, but he is the one in control, and the frustration just adds to my excitement. I squirm against him, pressing my ass against the rock hard lump in his pants. "I will fuck you when I am good and ready" he says, as if reading my body's thoughts. His hand slides down the front of me, coming to rest over my throbbing pussy. Only the sheer material of my nylons prevent him from touching me directly. He curls his fingers underneath, pressing them into me. The feeling of pressure against my clit is exquisite. I throw my head back onto his shoulder, a flood of heat and pleasure cascade over me.

Suddenly he spins me around and pushes me back on the desk. He presses his thumbs against the seam of my nylons and finds a separation. A little gap is all he needs; he pushes his thumbs through the sheer material and rips a gaping hole in them. His pace increases; he is tearing at my undergarments which separate him from what he wants. He keeps tearing away, tugging at the torn material until my soaked pussy is accessible. I am up on my elbows, peeking under the blindfold, watching him frantically tear my nylons apart. I'm aching to help, wanting to return the favor to him, but my hands are trapped behind me and all I can do is watch.

I am exposed, and he plunges two fingers deep inside me. I slump back on the desk writhing in pleasure as he works his fingers in and out of me. My eyes are shut tightly and I am unaware he moves, but soon his tongue is on me. I let out a loud moan, the force of it tearing the tape away from my upper lip. I keep trying to peek at him from under the blindfold, but have a hard time keeping my eyes open from the intense pleasure radiating up from my thighs. I scream aloud, my mouth finally free. *"Oh God YES!"* I cry out. Ten seconds of this is all I need. All of the anticipation and pent up frustration comes pouring out of me as I explode into an amazing orgasm. I am growing dizzy from the impact of the first one, and he keeps working me over, looking for another. I don't usually come back to back, but tonight is totally different. I'm turned on beyond anything I can recall.

I can't really tell when the first one left off and the next began, but I quickly reload and ready to explode again. My "captor" knows I am close already, and wants it almost as much as I do. I arch my back and lift myself off the desk; I let out a scream of ecstasy that surely anyone left in the building will have heard. I come twice as hard as the first time, exploding all over him. He continues to lap away at me until I finally relax and go limp on top of the desk. I am spinning in a whirlpool of sensation; unable to think, only able to feel my own heartbeat seemingly pounding in my thighs.

He stands in front of me, and lifts me off of the desk. The change in perspective helps me regain my equilibrium, and I'm ready for whatever is next. He forces me to my knees, and tears the tape off of my mouth. I wince in pain, my lips stinging from the adhesive. He grabs the back of my head and pulls my open mouth down over his cock. I can't see it, but I can sure feel it. The smell of his excitement is obvious; that musky, testosterone smell that turns me on more than anything else I know. He makes me suck his hard length, forcing his stiff cock into the back of my throat. I suck him hard, moaning and fighting the urge to gag at the same time. I am on my knees in my office, blindfolded, sucking the cock of my "captor" exposed through his zipper. He moans every time my throat hits the tip of his cock, so I decide to oblige him and try to keep it there. I fight the urge to gag again, coughing and blow my cheeks out. My eyes begin to water and I finally have no choice but to pull away.

He looks down at me and laughs, helping me back to my feet. He spins me around and pushes me over the desk. He tears the remains of my nylons out of the way and buries himself all the way up inside me, taking me from behind. I am so wet he goes right in, and fills me completely. He pulls all the way out, only to shove it back where I want it. He fucks me slow and deep at first, slowly building speed and force. After a minute or two, he is pounding me from behind. I am sure I will have bruises on the front of my thighs from the pressure of him banging me into the desk, but I don't care. The feeling is amazing. He holds the chain between the cuffs in one hand, and brings his other hand down on my ass, HARD. I jump, and draw in a quick breath, only to let it out in pleasured moan. The sting is delicious, and he knows I like it. I am moaning and groaning, lying there and taking it just like the dirty whore I am. He fucks me like he means it, taking what he wants, and I love every second of it.

After another few moments of this, he stops suddenly, commanding me not to move. He has pushed the boundaries again, barely stopping in time to delay his orgasm. Unlike me, he only gets to come once, and neither of us wants this to be over just yet. After about thirty seconds, he is ready to go again. He pulls out of me and walks over to my chair. He sits his sweaty ass on my leather chair, and laughs. He knows that later this will irritate me, but at the moment I don't care. "Get your ass over here" he barks at me. I comply and walk to him, following the sound of his voice. He spins me around and grabs my hips. Then he positions me over his cock, and pushes me down onto it. Having him inside me once again feels so good. He forces me up and down on him, penetrating my depths with his hardness. I am so wet he easily glides in and out of me. My feet barely touch the floor, and I have to stay on my toes to be able to move with him. I love fucking him, sliding that hard cock up into me. I am building towards another orgasm when he moves a little and pushes upwards into me. The feeling is incredible, and the rush of my orgasm surfaces in me like an explosion. I come hard, grinding into him as fast as I can.

He let me rest for a few moments, catching my breath before lifting me off of him and setting me down on the desk again. This time I am facing him. He tears off the blindfold, finally letting me see him. He grabs the back of my head and tilts it downward just in time to see his swollen cock disappear into me. He stuffs it into me, and pulls it out. It glistens with my creamy wetness, and he pulls all the way out and penetrates me again, unimpeded. He is swollen, getting close to his own turn. I love watching him fuck me, and like it even more when he makes me watch him. He holds my head in place firmly with a handful of my hair. He thrusts into me, harder and deeper with each and every stroke. It is building up in me again as well, and I want one more.

He likes it when I talk dirty to him, and what better time than now. *"Fuck me, fuck me hard!"* I growl at him. *"Yes! Harder, Harder!"* He is banging into me with such force the impact sends shock waves of pleasure throughout my body. A few more strokes and I am there..."*Oh God, Yes!*" I repeat over and over. He begins to moan as well, and I know we are both very close. He releases my hair, puts his hands under my ass and lifts me to meet his final thrusts. He pounds into me, and we begin the climb together. I come first, but he follows close behind. I can feel my pussy tighten around him, feeling him swell, ready to explode inside me. I wrap my legs around him, holding him deep inside. He puts a hand on my shoulder and pulls himself into me just a little deeper. He throws his head back and explodes inside of me. Strong hands grip my ass tightly as he pours the last bit of himself into me. His pleasure-contorted face melts back into a spent smile. We collapse on the desk in my office, sweaty and exhausted from the most intense sex I have ever had.

I have struggled with this idea for years, but am so glad I finally scratched the itch I have had all this time. This night was incredible; and I have found a man who can make my fantasies come true. I will have to start making preparations for our next adventure soon. Very soon.

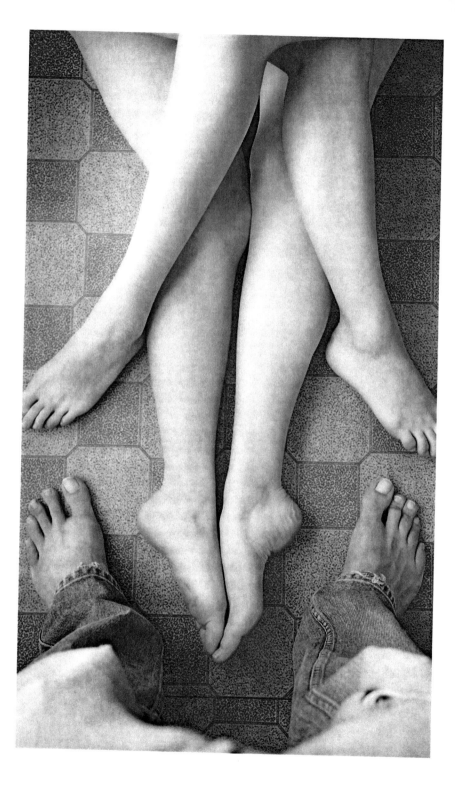

Ashleigh & Hannah

Thank God! A weekend in the mountains. After the week I've just had I can't wait to relax, unwind, and fuck. I can be such a nympho when I want to be, and this particular weekend I am up for anything. Filthy thoughts have been running through my head all week, and I am so revved up I want to climb into the back seat and go for it right now. Lucky for me, he always makes sure I get mine. I can tease and play with him the whole drive up, knowing my satisfaction is never a question.

It is obvious that the clouds are building up in the direction we are headed, and the more we drive the worse it gets. We have been talking the whole time; catching up on each others lives from the past two weeks. We don't get to see each other as often as we would like, so I enjoy our conversations whenever we get together. I am sure part of the plan is to do some fishing this weekend, but I am also sure neither one of us will mind if the weather forces us inside. "Looks like we may be spending the weekend indoors" he says, as if reading my mind. "What on Earth are we going to do to keep ourselves busy?" he adds. I smile, laughing as his cheesy innuendo and also busting him in a lingering glance at everything but my face. We have frightening sexual chemistry, and he can make me shudder with desire just by looking at me that way. It is difficult working together at times; I feel like everyone is always watching us, suspecting what we are up to. He reaches over with his right hand and rubs my breasts through my shirt. I feel my nipples jump to attention under his hand. "You watch where you're driving; we'll get to me later" I tell him. I unclick my seatbelt, freeing myself to gain access to him. I can see him growing under his shorts in anticipation.

I love getting him off, pleasuring him selflessly. Getting a blow job while he is driving is one of his favorite things, and I am more than happy to oblige. I reach over and untie the drawstring in his shorts. The flimsy material is doing nothing to contain his excitement, and I massage his burgeoning hardness through his shorts. "God this turns me on; I want to tear his shorts off and swallow his cock whole" I think to myself. I struggle trying to get his shorts out of my way so I can put my mouth on him, but to no avail. Finally I realize he is playing with me, sitting still and not helping me slide his shorts down. I slap his thigh, feigning

99

my displeasure with his tactics of denial. We both know better; he learned long ago that it only heightens my pleasure anytime he makes me wait. Finally I get what I want; his cock free to do with as I please.

I decide to return the favor of teasing, and start by slowly kissing his stomach and around his thighs, avoiding touching him where he wants. This is the only time I feel like I have any semblance of control with him. It is so frustrating that he completely owns me at times, and I can rarely achieve the same. I know I am getting to him when he forces the issue and grabs me, expediting the process of what I am doing. I keep teasing him for several minutes, stroking it with my hand and occasionally running my tongue over it. He squirms in his seat, trying to guide it into my mouth, but I dodge it. I know I am winning the game, and it feels good. Finally, he's had enough, willing to give in to get what he wants. He grabs a handful of hair and pulls me down on his aching hardness. I am ready and take it all the way down. It touches the back of my throat, and I fight not to pull away. He lets me up, and I go down for more even before I am ready. My own desires begin to override my reflexes, and I cram him into the back of my throat over and over. He grabs a handful of hair and begins to brace himself for the impact of the pending release. I reach down and cup his balls, the skin tightening as he readies himself for an explosion.

I can tell the time is drawing near, and I suck him even harder, ready for it. After a few short moans, he arches upward, driving his stiff rod into the back of my throat. I turn my head slightly to allow deeper access into me, easing the pressure that threatens to make me gag. I can feel the hot streams shoot down my throat as he pushes my nose against his hard stomach. I hold myself there, fighting to not follow my reflexes and pull away as he finishes. He relaxes, and slumps back into his seat. I give him a good once over, and then sit up. I wipe the saliva from my lips and sit back smiling, knowing that was a job well done. "Wow...That was awesome!" he says. I take pride in my work and it shows, I thought to myself. I was so focused on my task that I didn't even notice it had started to rain.

After about an hour, the rain is really coming down, and it is growing dark. We turn off the main highway and begin our journey down the bumpy dirt road that leads to the cabin. As we come around a turn, there is a vehicle sitting half way in the ditch next to the road. Immediately someone jumps out of the car and tries to flag us down. My first thoughts are selfish; concerned about whom the person we may be stopping to help and also the fact that I am dying to get to the cabin and release the pressure that has built up in my thighs. I see him hesitate, and I know we are going to stop and try to help this person. He gets out of the vehicle and walks over to the car as I sit there wondering if this is a good idea. I've seen too many horror movies that start out like this. The next thing I see is them walking to the car. What is he doing? I say aloud. They both climb into the car; him in the front and the stranger in a hooded rain jacket into the back seat. "Oh my gosh, thank you so much for stopping" a woman's voice says. I look into the back seat as she pulls her hood back onto her shoulders. Our eyes meet, and she has a relieved look on her face. She is soaked and dirty from her struggles, and I sympathize a little more with her situation. "Ashleigh, this is Hannah" Darren says, introducing us.

We get to the cabin and unlock the door. I go in first, carrying my bag and other items for the weekend. He goes to make a fire, and I head upstairs to the bedroom to fetch Hannah some dry clothes and a towel to use for a shower. "Everything you need is in there, and here are some dry clothes" I say, handing them to her. She thanks me again, and shuts the door behind her. I walk away wondering if this kind act is going to dampen the plans we have for the weekend. It obviously deviates our usual plan of attacking each other as soon as we walk through the door here at the cabin. I walk back down stairs; he has a roaring fire going. Dinner preparations have begun, and I walk over to help. He is focused on his task as I ask him "what do you think of our guest?" "I think she is lucky we didn't get here earlier and she'd be stuck out in the middle of nowhere. I don't know what..." he stops in mid-sentence when he sees the look on my face. He suddenly realizes that he is not answering the question I had really asked him. The turn of events seem to have distracted him; that and the fact he has already gotten the chance to cool his flames today. The thought of rescuing this woman and adding her into the activities of this weekend is driving me crazy. "Let me do the convincing, and follow my lead" I state. I see the flash of delight in his eyes.

Her Eyes

We make dinner, and I retrieve two bottles of wine that we had stashed here for a rainy day. I open a bottle for us, and pour everyone a glass to accompany dinner. Hannah appears much more comfortable now; out of her wet clothes and knowing she will not be spending the night in her car stranded in the woods. Before long the wine is flowing as well as the conversation. We open another bottle and finish dinner. Darren clears the dishes as I lead Hannah to the couch. We brought the movie <u>Unfaithful</u> with us to watch, and I pop the DVD in. Hannah and I are both a little tipsy, and as I slightly stumble back towards the couch, she laughs at me. I fall onto the couch, and the two of us giggle like school girls. I lay my head in her lap and she strokes my hair as we laugh and laugh. I playfully bite her thigh to see her reaction, and it was one of surprise and intrigue. "Bingo" I thought to myself.

I am barely cognizant that Darren has joined us on the couch, and I sit up to settle in for the movie. The three of us sit in silence as we watch the first steamy sex scene in the movie. Hannah is mesmerized, totally fixated on the action of the movie. When the scene ends, Darren gets up and goes to retrieve the open bottle of wine. He refills our glasses, emptying the bottle before getting to his glass. "No more for me!" Hannah says, waving him off. "I am already drunk...my lips are numb." This is the opening I am waiting for. "Really? Let me feel." I am half way to her mouth as I finish my sentence. I lean into her, kissing her mouth in a deep, soft kiss. She kisses back at first, even flicking her tongue into my mouth, before catching herself and pulling away. She has a stunned look on her face as our eyes meet again. "Oh my God, what are you doing?" she asks quizzically. "Kissing your beautiful mouth," I inform her.

There is an agonizingly long pause as she searches herself for a response. I know we are at a cross roads, and I pray that I haven't jumped the gun too soon. She reaches up and brushes the hair out of my face, tracing the line of my cheek with her delicate fingers. "I've never done anything like this before" she says, obviously considering what is about to happen. I waste no time, considering her answer permission to proceed. I kiss her again, longer and deeper this time. She cradles my face, mirroring the force of my kisses. Our tongues gently slip in and out of one another's mouths. It has been a long time since I kissed another woman. She reminds me why I enjoy a woman so much; everything is tender, slow, and exploring. We never rush; we linger and tease, drinking in every inch before moving on. God I wish I could see the look on his face right now. I'm sure he is aching to dive right in, but he is following my advice and letting me handle the preliminaries. His help will be needed soon enough, and it will be worth the wait.

I reach for him, and signal that he should go sit next to Hannah. In a moment he is on the other side of her, and she is now sitting between us. I tear myself from her mouth, only to meet his. I reach up and pull him into the back of her, sandwiching her between us. He and I kiss now; and it is delightfully different from hers. He is strong and aggressive, jamming his tongue into my mouth, invading me. I pull away from him, and turn to her. "Your turn" I tell her. She turns her head, and he is waiting for her. She slides her hand up around his neck, and beckons him to her. They kiss, but he is looking deep into my eyes. If there was a shred of doubt in my mind which of us he desires more, he erases it with that one look. This is hot as Hell, and I am dripping with anticipation of him ravaging the both of us.

I grab her hand, placing it on my breast. My nipples are hard enough to cut glass, and I am aching for someone to touch them. She allows her hand to explore me, feeling the hardness poking out from the middle of my fleshy mound. They keep kissing as he reaches around her and takes her breasts in his hands. He squeezes them just like he has done to me so many times. I'm not sure if I shudder more from her touch or the act of watching him touch her. I am surprised to find that I am so turned on by watching him touch someone else. I didn't think I would be jealous, just impatient to be the focal point. Instead, watching the two of them only adds to my desires. "Let's go upstairs" I say, my voice roughened with longing already. I help Hannah to her feet, the sudden rush of being vertical makes her sway a little bit. We both laugh again, breaking the little bit of tension that our pending tryst may have caused.

We make it to the bedroom, and I walk in and grab a pack of matches. I light two candles, and turn to find our guest. The room is illuminated with the flickering light, and I find Hannah standing in the middle of the bedroom looking a little unsure of what to do next. I walk over to her, and kiss her again. She is trembling with nerves. I look deep into her eyes and assure her we will go slow and easy. I grab the bottom of her sweatshirt, and slowly lift it over her body. I reveal her perky, small breasts, her nipples pointing at the ceiling in excitement. I moan in approval and lean down to take one in my mouth. The heat from my tongue makes it relax, and I flick and suck it slowly before moving onto the other one. Finally I lift the shirt over her head, tossing it aside. I step back and do the same, throwing my sweatshirt on the floor. I step into her, pressing my body against hers as we kiss again. My breasts engulf hers; mine are larger and softer. My nipples are big and hard, and they press into hers. Her sleek young body melds into mine, and we kiss and explore with hands and lips in the middle of the room. I open my eyes to see him walking over to the window. He opens it, and I can smell the rain I heard start up again a few minutes earlier. I continue to explore Hannah as he walks up behind me.

He removes his shirt on the way, and now I can feel the heat from his body behind me. He kisses my neck and shoulders, putting his hands on me. I love the feeling of both of them touching me at once, being pressed between the two of them. Darren pulls away, and lies down on the bed. Hannah sits down on the edge, and I stand before her. My breasts are right in front of her face, and she caresses them both. She extends her tongue, flicking it back and forth over both before pushing them together and taking both my nipples in her mouth at once. I toss my head back as the ripples of pleasure cascade through me. I reach for her head, grabbing her hair and trapping her face in my bosom. I look at Darren; lying on the bed doing his best to be patient until he is called upon. His jeans are gone, and his hard on is peeking out over the top of the silky boxer briefs he is wearing. God I want him in my mouth again. He moves towards me, settling in behind me. He kisses me, and quickly pushes his hand into my sweatpants. I am dripping wet, and his fingers easily pushing into my waiting folds. I can feel his thickness pressing into my back as he guides his fingers in and out of me. I am close to exploding immediately, but he knows me well enough to make me wait. The denial is sweet torture, and it makes the orgasm that will follow so much more intense.

We decide to turn our attention to our guest. Hannah stands and her eager young mouth meets mine. We kiss and run our hands over one another. I can tell by her intensity of her kisses she is very excited. I untie the knot in her sweatpants, and push her back onto the bed. Her tan body is a stark contrast to mine; a little taller than me, blonde hair and almost ten years younger. I want to run my tongue over every inch of her, but decide to put that off just a little longer so I can have his cock in my mouth. He is still on his knees on the bed, and I practically rip his boxers off of him, freeing his manhood from its silky confines. I gobble his cock down, taking as much of it as I can in one move. Hannah watches for a moment, and then joins Darren on her knees. She kisses him, growing bolder with each passing minute. His hands run over her body; pausing over her young tits and feeling as much of her smooth skin as he can reach. I tilt my head so I can watch him touch her. Since his hands are occupied, I decide that I will take matters into my own hands. I am aching with desire, and I need to release the fire built up inside. My clit is throbbing as I slide my finger down on top of it; I work my finger back and forth over it a few times, and I am ready. I increase the pace, pleasuring myself even though there are two others here with me. I yank him out of my mouth just in time to let out a loud cry. I rub it harder and harder as I come all over my own fingers. My eyes are tightly shut and I am lost in my own world. I come back to my senses; opening my eyes to find the two of them staring down at me.

"Wow that was a good one!" Hannah exclaims. "You haven't seen anything yet" he assures her. "You ready?" he asks, looking at Hannah. She didn't bother to answer. Biting her lip in anticipation, she put her hand on his shoulder as if to brace herself. His fingers find their way down her stomach, tantalizingly slowing his pace as he closes in on his target. Finally his fingers find their way into her moist pussy, and I give him a moment to work her all by himself instead of joining in. The pressure of his touch is perfect; not too hard but just firm enough, and I know from experience what he is making her feel. She turns into him, burying her face into his chest. She is already close, and I can see the skin on his shoulder reddening under her fingernails.

The pace of her breath quickens, and I know what is going to happen; he wants to hear her beg for it. Just as it seems she will explode, he stops. Her eyes open, and she looks up at him, finding the devious smile on his face. The carnal hunger rose within her, and she gives him what he wanted. "Oh God, please...please make me come!" she begs him softly. He relents, and flicks his thumb over her button while he pushes two fingers in and out of her. It comes bubbling up from deep within her, and a low growling sound escapes her lips. Her orgasm burst inside her, and she bucks her hips in an autopilot response. Her orgasm is long and drawn out; not an explosion like mine but more like fanning the flames of a growing fire. It goes on and on, and she writhes under his fingers in total ecstasy. She falls backward into the bed, still quivering from the aftershocks. I stand up and kiss him, raising an inquisitive eyebrow, not even needing to ask. "Go get her" is all he says. I moan in delight, relishing the chance to bury my face between her thighs.

I climb onto the bed towards her, and begin my sensual journey at her knees. I kiss and tongue her sweet young flesh, working my way slowly upward. I can smell her musky scent already, and it excites me as if for the first time. I reach up and part her waiting lips with two fingers, still kissing her thighs. I get the feeling that Hannah is still somewhat immobilized, and couldn't have protested if she would have wanted to. I go to work on her, flicking my tongue over her most sensitive place. She is shaved slick except for a thin little trail right down town. I rub her inside while I lick her outside. I glance up to see the look on her face as she slides up onto her elbows. She looks a bit surprised to see my face looking up at her, but as I suck on her clit she quickly loses any of the last reservations she may have had. Darren is repositioning himself in front of her, his stiff cock beckoning her touch. She puts her mouth on him, slowly sucking his swollen shaft. She runs her tongue all over his length, licking him from top to bottom and back again. She reaches down and brushes my hair back so she can see what I am doing to her. She watches me out of the corner of her eye as she continues to taste him. The sight of her slowly taking him in and out of her mouth while I lick and suck her juicy pussy is possibly the hottest thing I have ever seen.

I reach down between my own legs again, and touch myself once more. I can tell my efforts on her are getting close to paying off. Not only is she slowly moving her hips into my face, but she switches from her mouth to her hand on him. He reaches down and begins tweaking her nipples, which are at full attention. I withdraw my fingers and shove my tongue as far into her as I can. My action is met with an immediate response; she reaches down and grabs the back of my head, pulling my face into her bucking hips. "Fuck that is hot" I think…I rub my own clit faster and harder. I ride Hannah's erratic rhythm as best I can, while

106

conjuring my own release once again. She starts first, but I quickly follow right behind her. My mouth never leaves her, and my cries of delight seem to echo inside of her. She comes just as long and hard as the first time, riding the waves of pleasure my tongue creates for what seemed like minutes. I look up to see the hungriest look on Darren's face I have ever seen. He has been enjoying the show, despite the lack of attention directly to him, but he looks like he has reached his limit.

After having a moment to recover, Hannah seems to sense his dilemma, and she rolls half way over towards him. She starts to suck his cock furiously, intent on relieving him of the pressure inside. He lies down on the bed, careful not to disrupt her rhythm. He reaches over for me, grabbing me under my hip and pulling me his direction. A jolt of electricity shoots through me at the vision of the three of us in a triangle on the bed, all pleasuring someone while receiving the same from someone else. I quickly slide my hips over his face, lowering myself down onto his waiting mouth. He wastes no time diving in; his tongue like silken fire as it slips between my velvety lips. Hannah is working him over good, and I go back to work on her, making the triangle complete. I roll to my back, giving him better access to me and allowing me to slide directly under Hannah. I grab her ass and pull her down on me, her hot sex smothering my face.

Darren is driving me crazy with his usual tactics, and I can feel the vibrations of his moans into my pussy as Hannah is drawing him closer by the second. I reach up and bring my hand down on her ass, the shock wave echoing through the room. She moans in delight, and the vibrations in her throat seem to push him over the edge. I look over to see him grab a fistful of Hannah's hair as he braces himself for what is sure to be a forceful explosion. "Oh fuck, here I come!" he cries out. Hannah is ready for him, and jerks his juice into her waiting mouth. He is so hard she cannot make it budge in any direction, but jerks it furiously towards her as he pumps over and over until he is empty.

The whole scene is overwhelmingly erotic; the smell of the rain through the windows, the candles, and the hot musty smell of the three of us is almost too much to take. I return my fingers to Hannah, and now that she is free to focus on herself is quickly rising to another. I feel the five o'clock shadow on his chin brush over my thigh again, and I know mine will not take long either. I lick my thumb and place in on Hannah's most private place; her own motions making it rub on her back door. Darren sees what I have done and follows suit, and now I am getting exactly what I am giving. This time I go first; I wrap my arm around her waist and hold myself there, burying my face up into her. Darren continues to lap away at me as wave after wave ripple through me. Hannah follows just a moment later, her deep moans echoing through the master bedroom in the cabin. The three of us collapse into a heap in the middle of the huge bed, temporarily spent from our session together.

I am craving him inside me, and I push her aside to get what I want. I climb on top of him, easing it into my slick pussy. "That's right baby, you first" he states. I am sopping wet, and guide it in and out me with ease. He is quickly back at full strength, and I take all of it into my waiting hole. The feeling is incredible, and I although I intended to ride him slowly I find myself increasing my speed already. I plant my hands firmly in his chest, gaining more leverage. I ride him hard, extending the range of my hips as far back and forth as they can go. Hannah lies beside us, watching. I tilt my head back, arching my back and looking at the skylight above. It looks like a mirror with the darkness outside, and I can clearly see the three of us on the bed below. This only adds to the desire within, and my body finds another gear. I am moving faster and faster on top of him, grinding myself into oblivion once again. This orgasm hit me out of nowhere, and the impact is staggering. It catches me off guard, and I let out a loud yell as I ride him like a racehorse. He reaches up and grabs my hips, trying his best to match my moves. I last a few more moments before I collapse forward onto him, my chest heaving in breathlessness.

"Is it my turn?" she inquires, seeking my permission. I look up at her, brushing the hair out of my eyes. I climb off him, and sit down at the head of the bed, and motion for her to join me. I have her lay down on her back, her head against my chest and her arms over my legs. "Give it to her good" I tell him. He smiles back at me, shooting me that sexy grin of his. He moves in front of her, positioning himself between her legs. I reach around and begin to caress her tits, pinching her nipples gently between my fingers. He grabs it and guides about half of his cock inside her. She shudders upon his entry, bracing for more but not getting it. He teases her with it just like he does me; making me want more,

108

raising my desires to maddening heights before finally giving me what I need. He knows how to please, that's for sure. And now she is going to get her dose of it, too. He looks at me while he teases her with his rod, leaning forward to kiss me. As much as I thought his focus would turn toward her, he continues to let me know I am the one. She is here for our delight; to be share and explored, but not to replace.

I can tell by her body's reaction he hits bottom. Her eyes widen in surprise, pain and pleasure coursing through her at once. I can feel the impact of his body right through her, and I settle in behind Hannah to hold our new lover in place as he pounds her into submission. I spread her open for him, and hold her there, waiting for the next thrust. I have felt the brunt of his force many times before, and I wonder if it is too much for her. The impact is reverberating through us both, and I know she is getting what she wants and then some. I look up, remembering the skylight above. I watch him on top of us, and her in my arms. The scene will be burned in my brain forever; watching him hold himself above her as he works his hips up and down. Her moans inspire him, and he pounds her thin frame like he is trying to break her in half. He looks deep into my eyes as his body continues to meet hers, slapping noises bouncing off the walls in the room. I lick my finger, and place it gently onto her swollen clit, his impact presses my finger against her most sensitive spot. I rub it in between his strokes, stopping when his body presses my hand into her. Hannah is growing louder by the minute, and it sounds like she is going to get her wish.

Darren continues to pound into her, slamming his hardness deep into her body. Ecstatic cries of "yes!, Yes!!, YES!!!" come from Hannah, and I clamp down on her to make sure she isn't going anywhere. "Fuck me, FUCK ME!" she screams, seemingly losing control over herself. Darren drives deep into her, holding it there. She bucks her hips in spite of my attempts to restrain her. She fucks him back, stretching her own depths with each motion as he continues to press into her. "Oh God, Oh FUCK!!!!!!" she screams, and he let her have it. He pulls out and drives into her, withdrawing and entering her in a frenzy of speed. She explodes into a huge orgasm, her body convulsing, sandwiched between the two of us. I rub her clit until spasms subside. She slumps to the side, nearly passing out in my arms.

Her Eyes

I am ready for more, especially after witnessing what had to be one of the best orgasms this girl has ever had. I slide out from under Hannah, and Darren motions for me to assume the same position. He loves to fuck me in that position, and apparently the session with her has not quite quenched that desire. I lie down on the bed, and lift one leg. He grabs my ankle, and throws my leg over his shoulder. He entwines his other leg around mine, and begins to rub his hardness over my clit. He is doing it again, and I love it and hate it at the same time. He pushes it into me, only to withdraw. I am ready to beg for it already, but my pride won't let me just yet. I crumple a handful of the comforter and try to fight my own desire. He puts the tip of it in again and I try to scoot towards him, getting what I want without having to ask for it. Finally he has had enough, more interested in the pleasure than power today. Relief and sensation tear through me as he plunges deep. He is splitting me in half with this position; his thrusts lifting me off the bed with their force.

I reach up and put my hands on the wall, and push back into him, taking all of it into me. He is a perfect fit for me; his length stretching me just enough to walk the line between pleasure and pain, and yet his hard abs can still slap into my clit and send wave after wave through me. I am lost in a sea of mixed sensation, struggling to find the surface and break through. I am climbing, short of breath, struggling against an unseen force until finally I explode through the surface, parting the water, gasping for breath. It is as if I regain consciousness again suddenly; I realize the sounds I am hearing are my own cries of ecstasy. I push harder into the wall, not wanting it to end and yet quickly losing the strength to continue on. I give in, going limp under him. He slows his pace, giving me gentle strokes now that I need them. I moan in delight as he reads me perfectly once again.

I lay there, reveling in my own pleasure. Darren is ready to go, and he wants another taste of our guest. Hannah has been watching the two of us, and looks as if she feels the same. He rolls her onto her side, and lies down beside her. She reaches down and grabs him, guiding it into her once again. He put his arm around her waist and rolls onto his back. She is now lying on top of him, facing the ceiling. She arches her back, pressing her shoulder blades into his chest. His hands roam over her body, his hips slowly pushing the two of them upward and then back down again. He reaches over the top of her shoulder with his arm, and presses downward. The action forces her down on his full length, and she squirms in delight. He guides her up and down on it, thrusting to meet her body, relaxing to withdraw. They fuck like this for a few minutes, and I can tell he is growing close once again. I roll over and climb between their legs, gaining access to where they are joined. I lick my thumb, and gently placed it on Hannah's clit once more. I lean down to run my tongue all over his balls. When she rocks back a little, I have access to the base of his cock. I lick what I can reach, the rest of it buried inside her. I decide to do both of them, and extend my range to cover her as well. I lick and suck everything I can get my mouth on. Each of them moans in pleasure as my tongue runs over them.

It is going to be a race to the end, both of them drawing near at a rapid pace. I focus on Hannah for a moment, trying to get her over the top first. I know he will hold out as best he can, diminishing his own release in effort to put her first. He deserves the full affect, and I want him to have it. I carefully force one of my fingers into Hannah's tight pussy. She is so wet I know she can take it, and push forward. It relents and accepts my finger. The added friction is just what she needs, and the process begins. He grabs her hips, holding her as still as possible so I can continue my task. Hannah follows suit and reaches for the wall, and pushes herself down onto him. She holds herself there, impaled on him. I work over her pink softness with my glistening tongue, riding out her long, drawn out orgasm.

Now that she is done, it is his turn. He lifts her up and begins to pound her from below. Hannah is doing her best to help, but appears incapacitated from yet another orgasm. Her continued moans are her only contribution at this point. "Yes...yes let me feel you come" she mumbles almost incoherently. I have different plans. As he reaches his breaking point, I shove her back and grab it, jamming his entire length down my throat. I deny our guest her wishes, but gratify my own desires. "Oh Jesus Christ....yes, oh fuck!" he exclaims, loving the feel of my hot mouth on him. "One last taste" I exclaim. I jerk his cock furiously until he explodes all over Hannah. He falls back into the bed; spent from the performance he just delivered.

The two of them fall into a deep, exhausted sleep. This turned out to be quite an interesting twist to our weekend. As if our sex life wasn't

Her Eyes

already amazing, this encounter just added another dimension to it. And never once did he make me doubt my place in the proceedings. Eventually I drift off to sleep as well, dreaming of what tomorrow will hold for the three of us, and what adventures he and I will have next.

CPSIA information can be obtained at www.ICGtesting.com
Printed in the USA
LVOW051149230712

291153LV00001B/164/P

FLIPSIDE EROTICA
both sides of the story

flip book over ↺

Darren Michaels

ISBN: 978-0-615-27210-8

Printed in USA

www.flipside-erotica.com

This book is dedicated to those who are
smart enough to *dream*, brave enough to *act*,
and confident enough to know that life is all about the
experiences you have along the way.

A special thank you to HyperDonkey.com
for the technical assistance on this book project and the
www.flipside-erotica.com website. Without your help,
this project would not have been possible.

.

Table of Contents — His Eyes

	Page
Introduction	
Leslie	9
Ashleigh	17
Jillian	23
Laura	31
Katie	39
Gina	47
Andrea	61
Lindsay	71
Nicole	79
Stacy	87
Katherine	95
Ashleigh & Hannah	103

Introduction

I hope you enjoy the unique twist this book presents. I have written each and every story; I did "research" with some of the people in the stories, and have certainly asked questions regarding thoughts and feelings to gain a better understanding of both sides of the story. These stories are a mixture of experiences I have had. All are based on fact, at least concerning the person(s) involved. Some are true to the letter, some are the way I wished things worked out, and some of them are total fabrications built around someone I met. As the reader, you will have to decide which is which.

If you are looking for a romance novel, put this book back where you found it. This is a book about classy adults doing erotic things. Take it for what it is worth, pure entertainment. As an advocate for safe sex, I strongly encourage you to take the necessary precautions in your adventures. Although I do not make reference to the use of condoms in every story, I assure you I do my part to protect myself and my partner. You should be sure to do the same.

Please log onto my website at www.flipside-erotica.com and let me know what you think of this project. Enjoy the free preview of the audio download that is offered. Some of the voices in the audio files are the actual people in the stories; some are just friends of mine. Again, you will have to decide for yourself who's who. ☺

Leslie

"Hey, what are you doing tonight?" the voice on the other end of the line asked. "Hmm, I don't know, did you have something in mind?" I ask playfully. "Let's go for a swim...see you around 8pm." I am smiling before I hang up the phone. I know what I am in store for, and I am looking forward to it already.

Leslie is a little older than I am, and has an appetite for sex that is very similar to mine. An executive by day, she has always contended that nothing relieves the stresses of the week like a couple of deep, hard orgasms. A little shorter than I, she likes getting handled a tad on the rough side almost as much as I like tossing her around. You'd never know by looking at her conservative business suit and short, smart hairstyle that she is such an adventurous lover. Divorced for years now, she has her own place, her own money, and wants me for the one thing she really needs from a man.

Later that day I am debating whether or not the wear a pair of shorts that I can swim in, and have to laugh thinking that I am pretty sure I would not really need them. I head for the car and as soon as I walk outside I realize that it is a perfect night out; a warm summer night with no breeze and a nearly full moon rising up over the mountains in our end of town. The pool is sure to be a slightly warmer from the midday heat; a perfect all around scenario for a little fun in the backyard.

I arrive at her place, and the garage door goes up as soon as I hit the driveway. I pull into the garage and turn off the car. She kicks the door open; standing in the kitchen in a sheer nightgown and nothing else. Immediately she comes forward, her mouth hungry for mine. It is quite obvious that I was correct in thinking that I would not need the swimsuit. After a few minutes of warm, deep kisses in the kitchen she pulls away. The nightgown hits the floor as she pulls open the Arcadia-style door to the patio. She turns off the outside lights, allowing the bright moon to illuminate the backyard. It is quite a cool scene walking into the backyard and watching her dive into the pool, her naked body fully visible in the moonlight. She is in great shape for her age, or any age for that matter. She begins each day with a yoga session, and the hard work shows in her slim lines and shapely curves. I walk over to the

9

His Eyes

pool and kick off my sandals. A huge splash of water comes my direction; apparently I am taking too long to get undressed. I turn to protest, only to get hit by another wave. "Alright, alright...I'm coming!" I tell her. I tear off my shirt and toss it aside, followed by the shorts. I am excited already; my cock is half hard as I step into the pool.

She meets me on the stairs, swimming up and taking my cock in her mouth in one quick motion. She loves to get it before it's totally hard, when she can still get all of it into her mouth. She sucks it in, devouring all of me while she has the chance. I am growing harder by the second, and before long I'm at full length. Soon is unable to take all of it in despite her diligent efforts. She settles for clamping her hand around the base, jerking the bottom half while she works over the top half with her mouth. I lean my head back, looking at the stars as she settles in for a good long session of one of her favorite parts of our time together. I can't help but look around, wondering if her neighbors have any idea of what is happening just on the other side of the wall.

The moon is so bright that a very distinct shadow is cast against the deck of the pool. I find myself absolutely lost in the moment. Her mouth devours me while I watch her shadow meld into mine as she moves up and down. The warm night air, the moonlight, the warm water circling my legs, and her knee deep in the pool running her tongue all over my cock is an incredible flood of sensations. She continues to work it, alternating her hands but her mouth doing the majority of the work. She loves it, and the look on her face tells the same story. I revel in how her expressions change from furrowed concentration to total delight. She has told me that in her mouth that it is the only time I let go and she has some control. Once in a while, I like to take a little of that control back.

She is so focused on her job she barely notices as I begin to stroke her hair. I brush it back from her eyes and slide my hand around her head. Before she even sees it coming I grab a handful of hair and pull her away from me. My cock pops out of her mouth but she never breaks focus with it. She leans forward, trying to reach it, but my grip firms and I hold her just out of range. I laugh a little, and the game is on. She reaches back and smacks my bare ass hard. The echo of skin on skin resonates in her back yard. "Say it" I command. We've played this game enough by now that I know the stages; protest, feigned sadness,

10

anger and finally reluctant submittal to my demands. She is a control freak by nature, and secretly loves it when I take control and make her give in. She didn't have to tell me, I know the type. I took a chance and tried this bold move on our first time together, and every once in a while do it just to remind her who's really the boss.

"Say it and you can have it." I inform her. "Oh come on...don't do this to me" she pleads. "You know the rules, and who makes the rules?" "Me" she states with authority. I jerk the handful of hair until she winces a little. "Who makes the rules?" I ask again. "Fuck you!" she snarls, trying to hide the delighted smile. Guess we are skipping right over the sadness part and into stage-three anger, I think to myself. "Do you want to suck my cock or not?" "Yes" she replies sheepishly. She knows she will lose at this game; I am willing to getting into the car and leave if necessary to win. She *has* to give in, and she knows it. The tone of her voice and demeanor changes accordingly; and she relents. "Please?" she asks sheepishly. "That wasn't so bad, was it?" I say, letting go of the handful of hair I have. She practically tackles me as she lunges at my cock. I sit down on the pool deck as she pushes me backwards. She attacks my cock, moaning with desire as she jams it into the back of her throat. Fuck...it feels so good.

She continues to run her mouth over the entire length, hard and fast as if she is making up for the lost time while the power struggle played out. I let her go at it for a few minutes before I finally decide to give her the release she so desires. I lean forward, reaching for her breasts. Her nipples are rock hard already as her level of excitement elevates; I brush my fingertips back and forth gently over them. She moans a little at my touch, so I proceed to pinch her nipples...gently at first. I increase the pressure and send the shockwaves of pleasure rippling through her. "MmmnnnooGggooddddd!" she cries out, pulling my cock from her mouth for the first time in several minutes. She buries her face into my thigh as I continue to roll her nipples around in between my fingers. I lean forward and reach under her, into the wetness between her thighs. "Oh God... Yes...touch me!" she cries out. I oblige, and touch her throbbing, swollen clit. She shudders under the gentle touch of my middle finger, rubbing her clit with small circles. I am stretching to reach her already, and as if she reads my mind she moves forward so I can plunge my fingers into her. She cries out loudly, exploding instantly

11

as my fingers slide into her. She arches her back, looking up at me as I continue to work her over. Shuddering and writhing under my touch, she stares deep into my eyes. By now she knows that the best part of all of this for me is the look on her face when she comes, and she isn't going to deny me what I have earned. She continues to ride the wave as I look deep into her soul.

"Oh fuck that was so good!" she exclaims. "Only the beginning, sweetheart…only the beginning" I remind her. I see the queen-sized inflatable raft floating at the other end of the pool, and tell her to wait here. I walk around the edge, line up my target and jump on. The force of me hitting the raft has me sailing across the pool, and right toward Leslie. She smiles, knowing exactly what I have in mind. She climbs on board, and right on top of me. Positioning her hips over my face, she settles down over my mouth. She grabs my cock again, making me spring back to life instantly. I waste no time and shove my tongue right into her, causing her to moan aloud and arch to meet my mouth. I withdraw, and plunge again, over and over before settling back into rhythmic tongue strokes. In this position she can get my cock all the way into her throat, and continues nearly sucking the life out of me. We float around on the raft, occasionally bumping into the sides. We are adrift in a sea of pleasure, mutual exchange; free of any inhibitions. The raft acts as our own private island, and we are unfettered to revel in our ecstasy.

We continue on until she has come a few more times, and I am teetering on the brink myself. "You're going to have to quit that soon" I inform her. "I don't want to quit…give it to me" she says. I have never done this with her, but apparently the heat of the moment has caught her and she doesn't want to hold anything back. Leslie continues on with her quest, jerking the base of my cock as she sucks hard on the rest. I am drawing near the point of no return, and she can tell. I am swelling in her mouth, and beginning to groan in anticipation of the release of pressure in my core. "Oh fuck, here it comes!" I mutter through gritted teeth. With that she removes her hand and goes all the way down on my cock. I arch and stiffen, hesitating just for a moment before letting go. I empty myself into her mouth as the pleasure crashes through me.

I slump back into the raft, temporarily spent; feeling the pleasure throughout my body until it slowly subsides. "I want you inside me" she

states as she turns around to face me. She climbs on top of me, straddling me in the middle of the raft. Guiding my cock into her, she slowly settles all the way down on it. We begin slowly at first, rebuilding the heat and tension from before. Once again I grow rock hard inside her moist heat. She slowly grinds herself onto me; pressing down and slowly twisting her hips, her hands firmly pressing into my chest. I lie under her, looking up at her incredible body framed by the moonlit sky. My hands trace the lines of her body until they are on her breasts. Gently I settle my hands on them, feeling her nipples jump to attention at my touch. I squeeze them slowly and firmly, building the pressure in my hands based on her encouraging moans. I push them together and separate them, working them in counterclockwise circles as I begin to increase our rhythm on the raft.

The surface of the water reacts accordingly, becoming choppy as our force increases. I can tell she is getting close again, and I grab her hips so I can push her on towards yet another explosion. Her eyes widen as I touch her deep inside, and she meets my change in rhythm with deeper strokes of her hips. She grinds herself into me, pressing down to meet my upward thrusts. Our timing is perfect for several strokes until her orgasm starts. The electric explosions in her head throw off her rhythm as she becomes paralyzed by her own pleasure. She comes hard, moaning loudly. I reach up to put my hand over her mouth as she grows louder. I keep arching into her, lifting her as I drive upward, allowing her to ride it out. She is lost in the moment, total silence in her head as she shudders with pleasure from the inside out.

She collapses forward; limp on top of me. I look around to see where we are, and realize we had come to rest against the wall in the deep end. I put my foot on the side and hold us in this spot as the water slowly returns to calm. We are sweaty from our ride; I wrap my arms around her, holding her tight against me, and promptly roll over into the water. The water is just cool enough against our sweaty bodies to restore our sobriety, and she gasps as she comes up for air. "You bastard!" she yells, splashing me with water as she treads to stay above the surface. I laugh aloud, and start for the shallow end. She quickly follows, the water renewing her energy. I get there first, and stand up on the top step waiting for her. I grab the towels that are waiting for us and lay them on the pool deck. She comes over to me and stands up on the stairs next to

His Eyes

me. She takes a playful swing at me, and in one quick move I grab her wrist and spin her around to face away from me. I pin her arm against the small of her back, freeing my hands to explore her one more time. I squeeze her tits, pressing them into her chest as I chomp down on her neck. She arches back into me, smashing her ass against my cock. I lift my left hand away from her breast and slide it up her neck and over her chin. She opens her mouth instinctively, and I put my two fingers into her mouth. She sucks them feverishly, her desire growing once again. I pull my fingers out of her mouth, tracing them down her body, finally coming to rest between her legs. The pool water has washed her clean, but my slick fingers quickly enter her once again. She throws her head back as I work over her pussy one more time. I pull away from her slightly so I can use both hands. My right hand delves into the growing wetness between her thighs. My left hand goes to her clit as my right index and middle fingers slide into her. I stand beside her, building her up for one more explosion.

I stop suddenly and grab her arms, shoving her forward onto the towels on the deck. I put one foot on the pool deck and I stuff my cock into her all the way to the hilt. The force and suddenness of the move catches her by surprise, and she cries out loudly. At this point I no longer care about the neighbors hearing us, and I proceed to enter her with slow, long and deep strokes. Her thighs are pressed against the side of the pool as I fuck her from behind, water splashing with each thrust. I hold her arms trapped, pressing her down onto the hard surface beneath her. I reach up and grab a handful of wet hair, yanking her head towards the sky. She is helpless underneath me as I pound away at her. I hold her down and fuck her, taking what I want as we near the finish. She starts first and I am mesmerized by the sound of her cries of unbridled ecstasy, the impact of my body into hers and the water splashing all around us echoing through the back yard. I quickly follow her orgasm with my own. Her body meets my thrusts as I begin my release into her. I give one final thrust and hold it deep as I explode inside. Her moans continue as my cock pumps every last drop into her. I release her from my grip, and brace myself over top of her. "Holy shit that was hot" I manage to mutter. I pull away from her, falling backwards into the pool.

When I come up for air, she is sitting on the side of the pool with her face in her hands like she is hiding. Then I hear it too. The neighbors

14

had caught wind of the activity in her backyard, and are cheering and clapping to our efforts. Apparently we were louder than we realized. I am sure that Leslie is far more embarrassed about it, given that those are *her* neighbors. Me, personally...I wanted to take a bow.

Ashleigh

An old friend of mine and I set off on a hike that would take us deep into the mountains of Northern Arizona. We have been friends and lovers for a long time, until she began seeing someone else. For us, the sex was absolutely amazing; mind boggling, bone-charring, porn-star style sex. We tried being a couple, but just couldn't make it work. Obviously, because of the recent development in the relationship department, we have cooled things off. We have been very close for quite a while, and so thought that we could spend the day together just enjoying each other's company. She looked as good as ever, but I tried not to think about it. I loved every inch of her, and cringe at the thought of never being with her again.

We leave early in the morning, and reach our destination in good time. Setting off about nine in the morning. we pass a few people on the trail in the first mile or so. We run into two guys fishing, and ask if they have seen anyone else come through recently. They respond that they had not. It is a hot day, and we are both sweating from the rugged hike to this point. I know the area well, and suggest a shortcut over a ridge to a swimming hole in the creek that is far away from anyone else. She agrees, and off we go. At this point, I am driving myself crazy with thoughts about her and the way things used to be. She has given me no indication that she is feeling the same way, so I keep my thoughts to myself.

We climb through the rough terrain and top out over the ridge, seeing the creek stretch out below. You can see for miles, and it is obvious that no one else is around. We head down the hill and make our way to the creek. By now we are both really hot, and as soon as I get there I take off my shirt and hiking boots and dive in. The water hits me; it is colder than I anticipate. The shock takes my breath away and I surface just in time to see her jumping off the rock ledge. Our eyes meet on her way down, and I know she is in for a shock. She hits the water and comes up quickly, gasping for breath. We both laugh at our over-zealous attitudes, and how apropos it is that we both jumped in without checking the water temperature first.

17

His Eyes

After a short time, we get somewhat used to the water temperature and begin to enjoy the cold contrast to the day's heat. There is a large rock in the middle of the pool that is only under the surface about two feet; I swim to it and sit in the shallow water. I put my hands behind me, lean back, close my eyes and enjoy the sun on my face. I sit there for a few minutes, absorbing the moment until I feel water lapping against my stomach. I open my eyes to find Ashleigh sitting right next to me. She is looking at me the way she used to; I recognize the evil glint in her eyes immediately, but I play it cool. "What do you think you're doing on my rock?" I ask her in a playful tone. She gives me a genuinely surprised look at first, but quickly catches on. "But I like your rock, don't you want to share?" she says. I inform her she will have to pay the toll for spending time on my rock. "I've wanted to suck your cock all day" she replies. I am surprised at her statement given her relationship status. When I question her about it, her only response is "He doesn't do it right."

It's kind of a strange sensation to have a throbbing hard on while sitting in cold water, but I am enjoying it immensely. The thought of being out in the open, sun on our skin and air blowing against our bodies is highly intriguing. She reaches over and pulls the drawstring on my shorts. I stand up on the rock, now only about thigh deep in the water. She gets onto her knees, smiling as she looks up at me. I can see that she is just as excited at the prospect of fucking outdoors as I am. She pulls down my shorts, releasing my manhood from its confines. She goes to work immediately; swirling her tongue around the head and then jamming it as far down her throat as she possibly can. I am able to judge the level of her excitement by the way she does this; somehow the more turned on she is, the better control she has over her gag reflex. She barely flinches as my cock rubs the back of her throat. She is really working it, moaning and slurping away as she reaches around and grabbed my ass. She hungrily continues to work, swallowing as much of my cock as is able to handle.

Before long, I have managed to remove her wet shirt and bra with only minor interruption of her oral pleasures. I see she is squeezing her thighs together in frustration, and I am sympathetic to her desire. I grab her hands and stand her up, and in one swift move have her shorts around her ankles. I waste no time returning the favor of preparing her for sex

18

the way she did me. She slings one of her legs over my shoulder and carefully balances herself on the rock. I am on my knees on the smooth rock, the cold water once again surrounding the lower half of my body. I dive into her crotch with fevered desire. I skip through the usual teasing and slow, gentle build up and start licking her with long strokes of my tongue. She throws her head back and lets out a loud moan, digging her nails into my shoulder. It is almost painful enough for me to protest, but I continue to shoot my hot tongue in and out of her juicy pussy. I move back to her clit, now slowly licking long strokes and short strokes with my tongue. She moans aloud, stiffening and exploding in an orgasm that seems to start in her toes and race upward through her. She arches to meet my mouth as she balances herself over me on the rock in the middle of the stream. I know from past times with her that if I lighten the pressure on her clit just for a moment, and then go back after it, she will come again almost immediately. I did, and then she did, even harder than the first time. She collapses onto me, and I have to hold her up for a minute before she is able to catch her breath.

She bounces back quickly, hungry for more. "God do I miss this" she says. I reach down and grab behind her knees and lift her up. She squeals in delight, knowing what is in store for her. She reaches behind her, guiding me inside. We both moan in delight as her warm pussy envelopes me. Placing her arms around my neck, she begins to slowly buck her hips, grinding into me as I hold her in my arms against my body. She is quickly closing in on another orgasm, and increases the speed of her hips. We are both still wet from the water, and she easily glides over me as I ram her down onto my stiff rod. Her arms tighten around me and I drive deeper into her. She is hit by wave after wave of pleasure as I impale her. Ashleigh comes again and again, growing louder with each one. Before long her cries are literally echoing through the canyon. I am so turned on I have to stop now or be finished before I want to. I set her down gently in the water.

The cold water brought her sobriety back, and she suddenly becomes aware of the fact that we are out in the open. Growing shy, she turns and dives off the rock. I follow right behind her, aching to continue what we started. She reaches the far side and climbs out of the water. Reaching into her pack, she grabs a towel that she brought and places it on the rock. She quickly sits down on it, facing me. Ashleigh wants to tease

19

His Eyes

me, closing her legs and coyly looking up at me. I am not interested in playing games any more; I grab her legs and spread them, plunging myself deep into her pussy. I need to have her right now. She gasps in delight as I shove my hard cock deeper and deeper inside her. My feet are fighting for traction in the sand as I pound her into the rock. I hold her legs at the ankles, and slam myself into her over and over. I love the sounds of our bodies slapping together, the open air, and the noises that we make as we fuck in the wilderness. Before long I am ready to explode. I ask where she wants it, and she replied "right here", squeezing her tits together. This usually isn't her thing, but she seems to be caught up in the moment as well. I pull out of her as she slides down off the rock. Grabbing my cock, I begin jerking it furiously. I last about three seconds before I splatter my load all over her big tits. She leans forward and takes my sensitive cock in her mouth, loving the fact for a brief moment she has total control over me. She looks up and smiles as I shudder at the sensation of her tongue running up and down my spent erection.

We both jump back into the water and cool off before heading back to the car. We have a long hike ahead of us, and now we both have wobbly legs to do it on. We take our time, dragging out a day spent together just a little longer.

Ashleigh

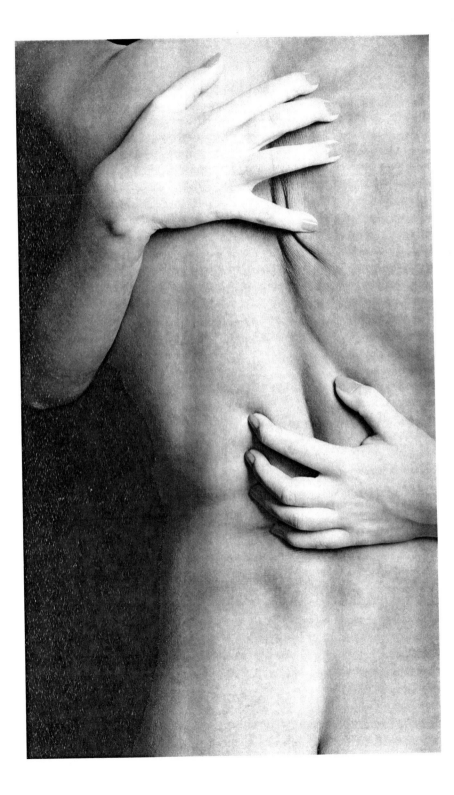

Jillian

I called an old friend the other day, and we met later that week for a drink. Greg and I laughed and joked, reminiscing about old times, especially when he worked at the health club where I was a member. I went through a list of employees, asking if he knew their whereabouts. We of course focused on some of the girls who worked there; ones that either of us dated, and the ones that got away. He brought up someone I hadn't thought about in quite a while. "Do you remember Jillian, the woman from the hotel?" he asked. I laughed aloud at the mention of her name. He looked at me quizzically, asking "what's so funny?" Jillian is a tall blonde, older than the both of us by about eight years, who worked as an event coordinator for the hotel to which the club was attached. "Oh, man; have I got a story for you!" It goes like this...

I am in charge of running an event that utilized both the health club and the hotel, and am scheduled to meet Jillian in her office on a Monday afternoon. Her administrative assistant escorts me into her office. "Anything else?" the assistant asks. "No" she says firmly, and the assistant shuts the door behind her. We speak professionally, pouring over the details of my upcoming event. She's efficient and professional, and never smiles at me. When we finish, she stands and shakes my hand firmly; she's much taller than I expect. She wears a very classy gray business suit; conservative and tasteful. She is a good four inches taller than I am, and wearing heels to make it even more obvious. I left her office thinking she is a cold and calculating bitch, bitter about the male dominated world in which she likely struggles for recognition.

It became a weekly ritual as the time of my event drew near. Jillian and I meet once a week, usually early afternoon. Over the course of time her demeanor towards me very subtlety began to change. She is by no means warm, but the chill seems to have left her office. We decide to meet again late Friday afternoon just to confirm all the details for next week's event. I thank her as usual and head for the bar next door where I am supposed to meet a friend of mine. I take a seat at the bar; I have been there about ten minutes when Jillian walks through the door. The bartender notices her as well, and pours her a glass of the house red before she even finds a seat. Jillian sits down at the end of the bar, away from everyone. She smiles briefly at him, and then notices me sitting at

23

the bar. She waves politely, and I smile back. After a brief awkward moment, she motions me over to a table right behind her. We sit and begin to talk. I tell her it appears my friend is standing me up and that I am probably leaving soon.

She goes quickly through her glass of wine, and waves at the bartender for another. I am still nursing the beer in my hand, but offer to buy the next round if she would like the company. She laughs, saying the drinks are on her because her money is no good here. "I used to date that bartender" she reveals in a low voice. "Really! Isn't he a lot younger than you?" I inquire out loud. "Oh my God, I can't believe I just said that" flashes through my head. Open mouth; insert foot...nice going. I am about halfway through chastising myself with internal dialogue when she breaks into a big smile. "Yes, I like younger guys." she says. "They're the only ones who can keep up with me." I try hard not to flinch upon hearing that, but apparently I didn't do a great job. She laughs as I fumble with something to say; I am so caught off guard by her statement that I end up just laughing nervously. "I'm sorry, I shouldn't have said that. I'm going to scare you off" she says laughing at me.

I laugh again, admitting to her that she has an intimidating presence, and that I am glad to see she has another side to her. She tells me she leaves the "bitch mask" on the door handle at the office. In the last few minutes, she has changed right before my eyes. As we continue to converse, I watch her switch from serious business woman to giggling college girl, and somewhere in between. It is quite interesting to try and keep track of all the different people I am speaking to within Jillian. We have a few more drinks, and the conversation flows between us. We laugh and have a great time together. It is getting late, and I look at my watch. She sees me, and says "it's about that time, isn't it?" I lay a twenty down on the table for the waitress and bartender for keeping us in drinks all night. We head for the door. "Oh, I need something from the office, would you mind walking over there with me?" she says. "Sure." I reply. I think nothing of it, just being polite since it was so late and the hotel is closed sans the front desk attendant.

She opens the door to the office, and turns on the lights as we enter. I stop in the doorway, assuming she is going to grab something from her

desk and we will be off. I am leaning against the door looking towards her office when I hear her call my name. I walk into the office, and find her standing in the middle of the room, unbuttoning her shirt. "I want to suck your cock, and then fuck you on my desk. Any problems with that?" I am stunned; I wasn't sure what to say, but obviously my answer didn't contain the word no. I just nod my head. "Shut the door" she commands, clicking back into her office role. I comply, a little nervous but certainly willing.

I push the door shut and turn around. Jillian is now standing in her nylons and garters, and a sexy push-up bra. She slips off the heels but is still taller than me. She walks over and puts her hands on my shoulders, turning me in a half circle and backing me up against her desk. I am growing hard in a huge hurry; anticipating screwing Jillian on her desk is a very exciting proposition.

She pulls at my shirt and practically yanks it off of me. She grabs me and pulls me into her mouth. Her mouth tastes like the wine she drank and the Altoid she slipped into her mouth on the way over to the office. She is grinding her lingerie-clad body into mine as she kisses me forcefully. She is wasting no time exploring my body and she removes her mouth from mine. Her mouth follows her hands, tracing the lines on my chest muscles. Her hands continue running all over me as she returns to kissing me. She is leaning down just a little bit to kiss me, and I have to laugh a little on the inside. On the outside, I am ready for battle.

Jillian reaches down and grabs my cock through my pants. She seems bent on skipping the preliminaries and getting down to business. I am basically just letting her lead until the time is right. I have a feeling I know what she really wants, she wants to be controlled. She is used to being in charge all the time, but what will really get her off is being truly taken over. But first things first, she mentioned something about sucking my cock. Apparently she meant it, because next thing I know she is on her knees in front of me. She looks up at me, smiling. She takes off my belt and throws it on the floor. Her hands are tugging at my pants, unzipping my fly. My cock pops out in front of her, and she jumps at it. Her hot mouth is all over me, swallowing my entire length and smashing her nose into my stomach. She gags a little, but fights back the urge to stop what she is doing. She continues sliding her tongue all over me,

sucking my hard shaft as she goes. Jillian is good, no doubt. She knows what she wants, and how to go about it. She is sucking the full length on each stroke of her mouth, and the feeling is phenomenal. Once in a while, just to break it up a little she will ram my cock into the side of her mouth making her cheek bulge out. The vibrations of her moans and groans only add to the feelings she is sending down my shaft.

After a few minutes of this, I am ready to pop. She can tell I am getting close, and her pace increases. She is really going at it; and I am loving every slide of her tongue and jerk of her hand. I reach my peak, and promptly grab the back of her head and forcibly yank her away from me. "Not yet, my dear" I inform her. "I am far from done with you."

"My turn" she says. She stands and walks around to the other side of her desk. She moves the chair, and sits down on her desk. She tells me to come to her, and once again I obey. I sit down in the chair, and look up at her, waiting for my command. "Go to work" she says, pulling her panties to the side and exposing her glistening pussy. I reach up and tear her silk panties off with one forceful jerk. The move shocks her, and now it is time for me to turn the tables. I push her back onto the desk and unclip her bra in between her breasts. I smash her tits against her body, kneading them between my hands. I stand between her legs and lean over her to reach her nipples with my mouth. They are rock hard by the time I get there, and I gently but firmly clamp down on them with my teeth. She squirms, moaning in delight as I suck and flick my tongue over her erect nipples.

Because of the position we are in, my cock is poking at her moist pussy lips. I am aching to be inside her, so I enter…just a little bit. She lets out a loud moan, arching her hips to meet me. I tease her by pulling it out; only to push it back in a moment later. She puts her hands on my ass, trying to pull me into her. I stand up and look at her, and firmly state "You'll get fucked when I am good and ready." She looks a little shocked at the turn of events. Just a few minutes ago she was in complete control, and was well on her way to getting what she wants on her timeline. Now I have turned the tables. I try to hide my delight at the look on her face.

I begin working my way down her body, kissing her stomach and

the front of her thighs. Since I moved away my cock is no longer pushing in and out of her, so I replace it with my finger. She is really wet and my finger glides right into her. I stroke the walls inside while I nibble and tease the outside. I want to make sure this is not a one time thing, so I pull out all the stops. I do everything I can think of to that pussy, and am making shit up as I go, too. She comes hard and fast, and then again and again. After about five minutes and I am not sure how many orgasms, she has knocked just about everything off her desk. The phone is on the floor beeping, papers are scattered everywhere. I have rarely seen someone come that hard once, let alone that many times with that kind of force within five minutes. "Holy Fuck!" she exclaims as I stand and look down at her trembling body. "I am ready to fuck you now Jillian. How do you want it?" She stammers for an answer, but by then I am already inside her. Her eyes open wide in surprise.

I make her hang her legs over the desk, and I put my hands on the front of her thighs to hold her in place. The angle is perfect as I slide my hard cock in and out of her. I know I am rubbing her G-spot from this angle, and she reacts accordingly. Jillian begins thrashing around on her desk again; her hands gripping the edge. I fuck her good and hard for a little while, and then decide to up the ante a little more. I lick my thumb, making sure it is good and wet, and then slide it right down onto her clit. She loves it, knowing it will push her over the edge once again. She gets up on her elbows so she can watch me rub her clit and shove my cock in and out of her. I can tell she is getting there once again, so I pay very close attention to the look on her face. Just when she thinks she is going to come again, I stop. And I mean stop completely; no thumb, no cock, nothing. She is instantly frustrated, wanting to come. She reaches down to rub herself, but I grab her wrist and pulled it away. "No!" I scold firmly. "Not until I say so." She is so pissed off she tries to take a swing at me, but I block it before her hand hits my face. I laugh at her, and pull my cock all the way out of her, standing in front of her on the desk. "Please!?!" she says in a desperate voice. "That's better" I say, ramming my cock all the way back inside her. I put my hands on her shoulders and thrust into her as hard as I can. I hammer her for all I am worth as the cries of "OH God, OH FFFFUUUUUCCCKKKKK!!!!!!" echo through the office. It takes about five strokes to start it, and 20 more bone-jarring impacts to ride her orgasm through to the end. It is the best one yet. She collapses on the desk, and I back away on the verge of

His Eyes

coming myself. I sit down in her leather office chair to cool off.

After a little bit, she's ready for more. I can't believe the appetite this woman has. She is quite possibly as insatiable as I am, which is really saying something. It's rare I find a woman that wants and can take the pounding I want to dish out. Apparently she hasn't reached her limit, because she climbs on top of me as I sit in her chair. She straddles me, and I put my hands together against the small of her back. She has her hands on top on the chair, placing her breasts right at face level. She grinds on me, rotating her hips front to back and side to side. It is awesome; the smell of sex and leather, fucking someone new, and factor in our location and you have all the makings of a world class fantasy coming true. She keeps fucking me back and forth, and side to side until she grows close again. "Ready?" I ask her. "Oh yes!" she exclaims. I put my hands onto her hips to help her grind me faster and faster. She goes back and forth on my cock at a high rate of speed, our sweaty bodies easily gliding on one another. I jerk her back and forth on top me until she comes again in one long, drawn out orgasm. It sounded like she punctured the chair with her nails about halfway through, totally lost in pleasure. She slumps against me, gasping for breath.

After a few minutes, she stands up and returns to the desk. I tell her to turn around. She jumps at my command; a far cry from her attitude earlier. "That's better, be a good little slut for me." I coax her. I put my hand on her lower back, and grab my cock with the other. I ease myself into her pussy. No, scratch that, it's *my* pussy now. I put my foot on the desk, and slowly begin to fuck her from behind. Before long I am pounding into her again, my thighs slapping into her legs. I lean back, raise my hand high and I let it drop down onto her ass with a loud smack. She lets out a little gasp, followed by an approving groan. I reach up and grab a handful of her hair, pulling her head back. I spank her ass again as I make her look at the ceiling. I am building up to my own release, and want to make sure she gets one more before I finish. I fuck her like this for a few more minutes, fighting my own orgasm back the whole time. She is getting close, and I cannot hold out much longer. I don't think I can fuck her any harder, so I rely on another trick to expedite her climax. I spank her ass one more time, and then lick my thumb. I gently push the tip of my thumb into her ass. She goes nuts, coming almost instantly. I keep it going, pushing a little more forcefully now. She

seems to either have one orgasm after another, or one long, continuous one, I'm not sure. I am growing ever closer as she growls and thrashes around underneath me.

I can't hold out any longer; I am going to come hard. I shove my thumb into her ass as I take the last few strokes. Mine finally begins and I ram my cock and my thumb as deep into her as possible. I let go of her hair, and slap her ass hard one last time. I shudder and stiffen for a brief second right before I explode into her. It seems that my own orgasm lasts longer than usual; I can feel my cock flexing over and over inside her.

We both slump forward onto the desk. "Wow!" is all I can manage to say for a few minutes. I pull out of her and sit back on the chair. My legs are shaking, my hips hurt, and my foot has a cramp in it; all tell-tale signs of a great fuck session. She peels herself off of the desk, and then kneels down in front of me, laying her head on my lap. "I have conquered Mt. Jillian" I thought to myself. What an incredible night. She looks up at me with kind of a delighted surprise, like she had never considered it would be like that with me. I just smile at her, stroking her hair out of her eyes.

Greg just sat there with his jaw open, he couldn't believe the story I had just told him. I laughed at his reaction, and his disbelief. "How could I make up a story that good" I asked. "Screw that, how could you not have told me until now?" he blurts out.

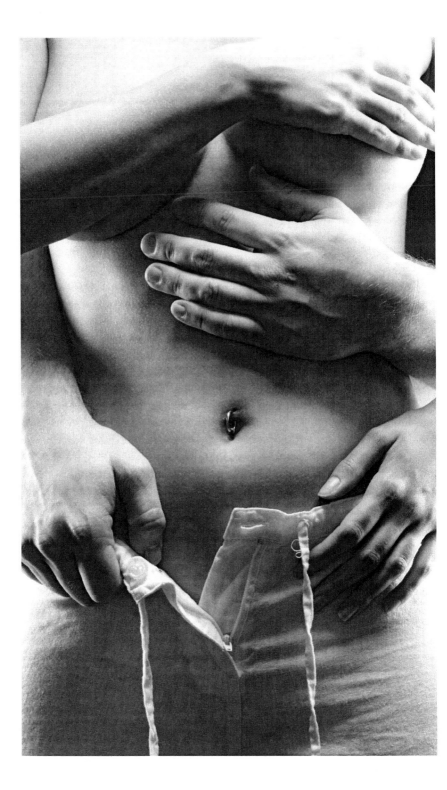

Laura

Its 1:00AM, who the Hell is calling me this late. I am going to Vegas tomorrow for my friend's wedding, I've gotta be up early..."Who is this?" I bark into the phone. "Oh, hey…wait, wait, calm down and tell me what happened. Start walking, I will pick you up in 20 minutes". I hang up the phone, thinking it is strange to hear from her after all this time. But I guess given the situation she's in she is probably just desperate for help.

Laura and I go way back. I have known her since she was about 15. Despite her persistent efforts, I would not lay a hand on her. I always told her that once she turned 18 we could talk about it, but even then I wasn't sure I would be comfortable. Here we are about a year past that landmark birthday and nothing has ever developed, so I figure it isn't going to. I am revisiting all of this in my head as I hop in the car and head out to find her.

"Oh my God am I glad to see you!" she says climbing into my car. "Misty and I were out with some friends, she met a guy and we came back to his place and she disappeared with him, leaving me with his friend. That guy would not take no for an answer, and I didn't know what to do so I just left. I can't thank you enough for coming to get me" she explains breathlessly. I almost feel guilty sneaking a peek at her as she climbs into the car. She is dressed a touch on the provocative side, and I can see why the guy was being so persistent. God she looks hot. Her hair is longer than the last time I saw her, and she added some highlights to her sandy blonde hair. Her eyes are as crystal blue as I remember, and she is still in great shape from playing softball at college. I know her friend is prone to this sort of behavior, so I'm not surprised to hear how this situation occurred.

"Okay, so now what?" I ask. "I can't go home, Misty and I are supposed to be somewhere at 7:30 tomorrow morning, and I used that as the excuse to get out tonight. Can we go to your place?" she asks. I oblige, not thinking this is anything more than just helping a friend. I have to laugh a little inside; her statement refreshes my memory that she still lives at home. I can tell she had been drinking, and figure she would be asleep pretty quickly anyway. I have to drive to Las Vegas in the

morning for my friend's wedding, and don't relish the idea of doing that without sleep. I really don't think anything is going to happen, but it is already 2:00AM, so sleep is looking like less and less of a possibility. We chat the whole way to my place, seemingly picking up where we had left off many months ago. We always did have a great time together; a very easy relationship and this is no different. She seems a lot more relaxed after just a few minutes with me, letting the uncomfortable situation she fled remain behind her.

We get back to my place and I lead her to the door. "Well, where do you want to sleep?" I ask her. "With you, I guess" she says smiling. I head to the bedroom and grab a tee shirt and pair of shorts for her to sleep in. She goes to the bathroom to change as I climb into bed. Rolling over, I set the alarm for 6:45AM, ouch! As I lie back down she comes in, feeling her way around the dark room. She comes into the bedroom, and my heart about stops. I can see her silhouette in the room and I can tell she is not wearing the clothes I had given her. Her perfect, young body looks amazing; better than I had pictured all these years.

She climbs into bed, and snuggles up against me, pressing her firm, large breasts against my back. Her hard nipples relax against the warmth of my skin. I can't believe this is happening; I have wanted this for so long. I roll over to face her, and put my arms around her. The feel of her smooth skin naked beneath my hands is incredible; I run my hands all over her body, exploring every inch of her. She reaches out and touches my face, leaning forward to kiss me. Her touch is gentle at first, stroking my face as her mouth tenderly meets mine. It is soft and warm; a little tentative, and exploring. Pushing her body against mine and I'm sure she can feel my growing hardness against her stomach. It appears this excites her and she begins kissing me harder, shoving her tongue into my mouth. I roll over onto her, taking control. I grab her hands and pin them against the bed above her head. This makes her arch her body slightly, lifting her hips up into me and she kisses me even harder. I slowly start to grind against her, rubbing myself against her lithe young body. I am straining to break free of the shorts I am wearing, which at this point are doing little to hide my excitement about this unanticipated encounter.

After a few moments, I release her hands and start to explore her body a little more. I finally touch those breasts of hers I have coveted the last few years. They are perfect; amazingly firm yet supple, and very responsive. Her nipples are taut from the excitement, and I want to taste them. I lean down and take one in my mouth, much to her delight. She moans slightly, putting her hand on the back of my head, arching to meet my mouth. I reach my hand around her small waist and lift her into me. I can feel her heat against my shorts, and I ache to be inside her. I fight the desire to rip my shorts off and plunge deep into her. I know better, and I want to make this last. So I continue on my slow, deliberate path; sucking one nipple and then the other, squeezing each of them in my hands. I keep going down, tracing the subtle line of her ribcage with the tip of my tongue. I slide my hand down her back and under her ass, squeezing her. She is arching so only her shoulder blades are now on the bed, and I can smell her scent for the first time. She smells like cotton candy, and I can't wait to taste her.

I slide down and position myself between her legs; her shaved young pussy right in front of my face. I tease her at first, biting and nibbling her inner thighs, above her clit, and anywhere but where she really wants me to. I know she is getting frustrated, and she squirms and wriggles, trying to get me to hit the magic button. I finally relent, flicking my tongue over her swollen clit. She gasps, and grabs the back of my head, pulling my face into her. I take this as an obvious sign that she is really into what I am doing, and so I go for it. Without warning I shove two fingers deep into her, and begin kissing, sucking and licking her pussy for all I am worth.

She goes ballistic, bucking her hips furiously into my face. I put both of my arms over her legs and hold her still; partly to protect my nose and partly to make her come as hard as possible. I get the feeling she likes struggling against me, but to no avail. I hold her almost perfectly still and shove my tongue inside her as far as it can go. That does it; she stiffens and cries out my name as she has her first orgasm under my touch. It is awesome, feeling her bucking and squirming underneath me. She rides the wave for about 20 seconds before going completely limp. She trembles underneath me, trying to catch her breath. I laugh, looking up at her from between her legs. God how I wish I could have seen the look on her face when she came.

33

His Eyes

I want to take her, but I also want to have her mouth on my aching hardness. I imagine the look on her face in the darkness, recovering from what appeared to be a brain-melting orgasm. As I deliberate my pleasure dilemma, she reaches down and grabs my cock, making the decision for me. She quickly spins around and has me in her mouth before another thought crosses my mind. "I have always wanted to do this to you." she says. I am so hard it almost hurts. I think I am going to explode as soon as I feel her sweet young mouth wrap around my cock. She starts out with just the top, sucking and running her tongue all over the top half of it.

After a moment, she puts her hand back on me, and slowly begins jerking the base as she continues to suck the rest. Her pace is perfect; not too fast and just enough tongue. It is as if she is reading my mind and doing what I want at each moment. She continues at this for a few more minutes, and just when I am about to warn her that I am ready, she releases my cock and slides her hand between my legs. She grabs my ass and pulls me into her, ramming my cock into the back her throat. She grips my ass, holding me there as she fights the urge to gag. My orgasm comes so quickly it is like a shotgun blast. I empty my juice into her throat as she continues to suck my cock. I shudder heavily, almost feeling as if I am going to fall over. The sensation is incredible. She swallows all of it without losing a drop, sucking me until I am so sensitive I have to push her away.

Now it is my turn to recover, and I lay down next to her on the bed. She is not interested in waiting any longer, and immediately climbs on top of me. She reaches down and grabs my glistening cock, guiding it into her. Impalement is her only goal, and she drives down on me, taking the length of it into her. We both groan at the same time, experiencing both the pleasure and finally getting what we have wanted all these years. She grinds on me slowly, rubbing her clit against me as she slides back and forth. I reach up and cup her breasts, squeezing them together. I sit up under her enough so I can have them in my mouth as she rides me. She holds me there by wrapping her arms around the back of my head. I put my hands behind me on the bed, and lift us off the mattress with a hard thrust. She lets out a gasp, loving the deeper penetration into her depths. I keep doing the same thing every once in a

while, lulling her into a smooth rhythm and then occasionally surprising her by jamming myself deep into her.

We continue to grind like this for several minutes before she shows the signs of another orgasm rising within her. She grinds against me faster and harder; so wet she is easily sliding back and forth on me. I can tell by the increasing frequency of her moans that she is almost there, and I quickly lie down and put my hands on her hips. I thrust upward with everything I have, lifting the two of us off of the bed. The shock and the feeling of it sends her flying over the top, and she comes harder than the first time. She slaps her hands down on my chest as her pussy clamps down on my cock in spasm after spasm. "Oh Jesus! That feels so fucking good!" she cries out. Her speed increasing as she rides out the wave of an intense orgasm to the very end.

"God that was amazing!" she says, collapsing on top on me. "Not the same as the boys you're used to fooling around with, huh?" I say, smiling ear to ear in the darkness. "Not even close" she replies. Every man loves the thought of being the best lover a woman has ever had. I realize that she has a smaller frame of reference than most of the women I have been with, but the words still echoed through my head. I let her lay on me, enjoying the weight of her heaving, sweaty body on top of mine. I stroke her hair aside. I can feel her hot breath on my chest as her breathing eventually slows to her normal rhythm. Remaining motionless, she lays on top of me as if she is so sensitive from the two orgasms that she can't take even a little friction for a few more moments. I do my best to accommodate this unspoken request, but it is difficult. I want more of her; the way she smells, the way she tastes, and all the time spent in unfulfilled desire is almost overwhelming. My head is spinning; a blur of sensory-laden desires rushing through my brain.

I slowly start to move inside of her again, using short strokes to test the waters. She responds with a deep moan, and I figure she is ready for more. She starts to sit up, but I wrapped my arms around her, holding her body against mine. Her knees are on either side of me, as if to trap me underneath her. I reach up and brush her hair out of her face, kissing her again. She moans again, and I can feel the vibrations of it in my face. Our tongues wrestle and our bodies grind into one another, her weight bearing down on me in effort to take my length deeper into her. I

love this position because I get to feel so much of her body at once. I place both hands on her ass, and help her move back and forth on top of me with a greater range of motion. Our bodies are still slick from earlier, and she slides easily in her position on top of me. She put her arms around my neck; her breasts smash against me, and I feel her nipples growing hard against my chest. She is getting close once again, and I relish the chance to get her off one more time. She bucks her hips into me, grinding her wet pussy against me. I continue the process of pushing and pulling, timing her rhythm almost perfectly. She is so tight and so wet, the feeling is incredibly intense. Coupled with the years of longing for her, this is turning out to be one of the most intense experiences I have ever had. I can sense the crest of the orgasmic wave again, and I thrust upward, the force lifting her off of me except for where we connect. She buries her face into my neck, trying to muffle the sounds of her lustful cries. It appears she comes even harder this time, and she gyrates her hips in an erratic rhythm as she draws out her third orgasm as long as she could. She goes limp, signaling the end. I try to move, but she stops me with a barely coherent groan of disapproval. She is panting and shaking like no one I had ever been with; completely overwhelmed with pleasure, incapacitated by her body's explosions.

After a few minutes or so, I roll her off of me and onto her stomach. I get behind her, and position myself between her legs. In spite of her delirium, she wants more. She arches her back like a cat, keeping her upper body on the bed and tilting her hips just enough to allow me straight access into her. She arches her body to meet me, and I guide my cock into her sopping wet pussy. She moans in delight as I lean forward and whisper into her ear "my turn." I am so hard and so close I am amazed I have lasted this long. I start slow, stroking half of my cock in and out of her. I build up speed and intensity, and soon I am ramming my cock into her, slapping my thighs into her ass cheeks as I penetrate her as deeply as her body will allow. She loves it, and put her hands against the wall, pushing back into me, taking every inch of it. I reach up with both hands and hold her hips and pull myself into her, using her body as leverage.

I can tell she is getting close again, I hope she finishes soon because I know I cannot hold out much longer. I let go of her hips and fall on top of her; sliding my free hand underneath the both of us and into her

wetness. I find her clit and rub it gently, pressing it up into her. "Oh Jesus, I'm gonna come again" she cries out. "Fuck me, Fuck me harder!" I comply, and find another gear, spurned on by her cries as I hammer into her. I smash into her ass over and over as I continue to rub her clit. I am so close, but I continue to fight off my own release, waiting for her. Finally she is there, and I shove forward, burying my cock all the way in her. She is trapped underneath me, held in place by my body weight and yet still manages to buck and grind under me. She starts first I think, coming all over my fingers and cock. I quickly follow, louder than I anticipate. I let out a long, low growl as I empty myself into her again. She continues to push back against me, draining every ounce of it out of me. We collapse in a sweaty heap on the sheets, absolutely spent.

After a few moments, I look at the clock. It is 4:30, but I don't care. This was an absolute fantasy come true, and I know my friend will understand when I tell him why I am yawning all through his wedding ceremony. Lying here, I can't help but wonder if she really needed my help, or if she had finally found a way to get me after all these years. Either way, I am glad she called.

Katie

"Good morning Darren" she says in her usual cheery voice. "Hello Katie" I reply, trying to hide my disdain for morning people. "What are you doing this weekend?" It is the typical banter on a Friday from Katie, the receptionist at my office. The usual small talk is about as much as we ever really exchange. "It's a three day weekend...got big plans? What do you do for fun, anyway?" she asks. "Everything but kiss on the mouth" I respond as almost a reflex. I laugh, following hers. "That's funny" she says. "Thanks, I stole that line from the movie Pretty Woman." I glance back to see her watching me leave the room and smiling. I think she is attractive; very short dark hair and glasses framing a cute face. I laugh to myself remembering that my first impression of her was that she doesn't like men, or at the very least didn't like me.

About 10 minutes later the phone at my desk rings and I answer it to find Katie on the other end. "So, were you serious about what you said earlier?" she inquires. I have to stop and think for a second just what I said. I search for something to say, but she beats me to it. "I am going to be alone this weekend for the first time in quite a while, and I was wondering if you wanted to get together. I haven't been with a man in almost four years, and I was hoping you'd want to be the one to...well, I think you get the idea."

I am shocked. I know Katie has a girlfriend; it never really occurred to me that she had been with men before. She has a picture on her desk of her girlfriend, and has never shown any hint of interest in me as far as I could tell. I finally answer her with a surprised "uh, yeah...sure." "Cool, come see me before you leave today" she says and hangs up the phone. I am blown away. Did that really just happen? Four years and she picks me? Needless to say, this was going to be the longest work day of my life. I try to focus and be productive, but it is very tough. I keep thinking about what she said, and that fit body of hers that I think is a shame to "waste" on another woman.

The end of the day finally comes, and I walk to the desk to find out what the plan is. She greets me with a big smile and a look up and down that almost makes me shudder. "God I am so turned on! I've been thinking about you all day" she confesses. "I hope you live close by, I

39

want you right now." "As luck would have it, I do...right down the street. Follow me" I instruct her. We leave separately so we would not raise any suspicions, and she follows me to my house. I drive quickly and she trails behind; we arrive at my house in a few minutes.

I open the door and we walk in. I turn around to shut the door, and she grabs me and shoves me against the wall. Her mouth is on mine before I know it. We are grabbing and groping each other almost forcibly. I kiss her hard, her mouth encouraging mine for more. I run my hands all over her body, feeling her through her clothes. She lets out a deep moan when my hand stops between her thighs. I can feel the heat pulsating between her legs. I decide to be a little playful, and announce "I need a shower." I pull away from her and walk down the hall. I am getting undressed as I go, leaving a trail of clothes for her to follow. I enter the bathroom, turn on the shower and get in. After a moment she appears, completely naked, and slides the shower door back to join me. I shut the door behind us, looking her over. God, her body is amazing! I am really surprised at just how fit she is. And just to further add to the appeal, she has a large tattoo on her thigh. I've never seen it before because she doesn't wear skirts short enough to show it. She looks at me hungrily, and tells me "Come here." "No." I say, smiling and pushing her aside to get under the water. She whacks me hard on the ass at my attempt to ignore her. I spin around quickly and push her against the wall. I see the look of surprise in her eyes at the abruptness and force of my actions.

Now it is on; our naked bodies grinding into each other as I pin her against the shower wall. I grab her leg, pulling it up over my hip and grind my rock hard cock against her. I kiss her hard, shoving my tongue into her mouth. I hook my arm under her leg, spreading her open even further to me. I begin teasing her opening with my cock, brushing it over her throbbing clit and against her wet pussy. I place my other hand behind her head, pushing her mouth into mine even harder. As I finally break away from her mouth, I chomp down on her neck, and at the same time reach up and grab a handful of her wet hair, jerking her head back. She lets out a loud gasp, and then I give her what she really wants...my cock. In one move I am all the way inside her. She comes almost instantly, digging her nails into my back and crying out loudly as she shudders in ecstasy. I smash her against the shower wall, not even

giving her a chance to recover from the first one as I charge towards the second. Our wet bodies slap together as I pound into her. God she feels good and I can tell by her body's response that she has been aching for sex like this for a long time.

After a short while, she is ready to explode again. I increase the speed and force at which I ram into her. Her orgasm starts with loud, deep moans and then into louder and louder screams. She wraps herself around me, pulling me into her as deeply as I can go. I press into her as hard as I can as she grinds herself into me. She explodes into another huge orgasm, shuddering and grinding all the way through it. Finally she relaxes, slumping against me. It feels like I have to hold her up or she will collapse onto the floor.

"That….was fucking amazing" she says looking up at me. I agree, kissing her deeply once again. "Now it's your turn" she tells me with that hungry look in her eyes. I'm not sure what she has in mind as she reaches over and grabs the two wash clothes off the rack. She quickly folds them and places them on the floor of the shower. Now I understand; she gets on her knees in front of me, and places her hands on my hips. She goes right down on it, her nose smashing against my stomach. The feeling is amazing; I am so much more sensitive after being inside her that I think I am not going to last more than ten seconds in her mouth. She pulls back, running her tongue the entire length of my hardness. She cups my balls in one hand as she runs her mouth over me from top to bottom. The feeling is incredible; like every fiber of my being is concentrated into that one area. I lean back away from her, arching to meet her mouth. She puts both hands on my ass as she continues working me in and out of her mouth. The water from the shower splashes over us as she keeps at her task. I run my hands through her wet hair, pulling her into me and guiding my cock into her throat.

I am getting close, and she can tell. She increases her speed, grabbing the base of my cock in her hand and twisting it. I lean back even more, arching into her. "Oh God, Oh my God!" I mumble, biting my lip. My whole body tenses as my own orgasm rises within me. "Oh fuck, here I come." She pulls her mouth off of me and begins to jerk my throbbing cock. She opens her mouth wide, waiting for it. "Come in my mouth" she commands, and boy do I. I explode into her mouth, and she

moans for more. She takes the first few shots on her flattened tongue, and then wraps her lips around me again. She sucks the rest of it out of me before spitting it down her chest. Now it's my turn to slump against the wall, completely spent...for the moment anyway. She stands up, and we shower off again. I turn the water off, and reach for towels for the two of us. We dry off, and head for the bedroom.

We climb into bed, both of us eager to pick up where we left off. She climbs on top of me, pressing her body onto mine. We kiss a little more slowly this time, easing our way back into it. The weight and heat of her body has me back at full attention in a very short time, and she positions herself over me. She grabs my cock at the base and eases herself onto me. She is sitting straight up, and starts slowly grinding into me. She moves her hips up and down, wriggling in pleasure and digging her nails into me. I have my hands on her breasts, squeezing and kneading them against her. I can feel her building up to another orgasm, and I slide my hands down to her hips. I press her down onto my cock, and increase her back and forth pace. She begins to moan louder and louder, and starts to break her own rhythm. I am saving this for just the right time, and that time is now. I arch my back for all I am worth, lifting us off the bed. She throws her head back and screams. I can tell I am hitting bottom, the pressure inside her making her explode with pleasure. I hold us there as long as I can, until I can't take it any more and have to relent. We sink back into the mattress and she collapses forward onto me. She is breathing hard and wants a moment to recover. I let her stay there for a moment, but I am ready for more.

I roll her over, making sure we never separate. Once on her back, she lifts her legs to place her feet on my chest, and I commence sliding in and out of her. I start slow at first, but soon I am building speed. "Oh fuck yes...that's what I want...pound me" she moans. I keep giving her slow, long strokes, occasionally slamming down into her. I love the way her eyes widen with the impact of me into her. I have my hands on the mattress, and her knees pressing together beneath my chest. This provides a great angle into her, and I am selfishly enjoying it for the time being as I penetrate slowly over and over. She wants a little more roughness, and lets me know it. "Fuck me harder" she snarls up at me from below. I oblige and begin slamming into her, slapping our bodies together. I straighten up, and put my hands under her knees for even

more leverage. Spreading her legs open, I smash her into the mattress for all I am worth. She loves every minute of it and begins to buck her hips to meet my thrusts, giving me just a little more access into her. I can feel that I am pressing against her insides, and it's just what she needs. She begins the process again, moaning and writhing under me, digging her nails into my arms. I hammer her for a few more strokes until she comes again. I am glad she does, because I am not sure I can hold out much longer myself. I pull away from her and stand up to regain my composure.

While I am standing there, she rolls over and is staring at my cock. She scoots up to me, and puts it in her mouth again. I know I will not last very long like this, but it feels so good I don't want her to stop. She keeps at it, and I am getting dangerously close to finishing. I decide I don't want to be done just yet, and I pull away from her. "I want your ass before we're done" I tell her. "Oh, you nasty boy, you. Come and get it." I reach into the drawer and remove the warming lube. I don a condom and lube up my cock for a trip into uncharted territory. "Go slow, it's been a long time" she warns. She turns around on the matress and crouches in front of me. I put one foot on the bed and grab my cock, readying myself for something I rarely if ever want to do. I am so caught up in the moment and so turned on by our encounter, I am willing to push my own boundaries as well as hers. I ease into her very slowly as she flips back and forth between pleasure and pain. I slowly work it in and out of her as she grows used to my size inside her most private place. The pleasure overtakes the pain, and I am soon able to start going deeper into her. I reach around and rub her sensitive clit.

She is gripping the sheets and gritting her teeth; her brain wanting more but uncertain her body can handle it. I slide in and out of her at a growing pace, burying about half of my length into her. It is so tight; I know I am going to come soon. She knows it is coming, and braces herself for the impact of my climax. She is getting close, too and I want to get her off one more time before this adventure finally concludes. "Put your fingers inside you" I instruct. I reach up and grab a handful of hair. I fuck her ass as fast as I can, yanking her hair back as she jams three fingers into herself. I am getting so close, but I am determined to hold out until she has one more. She is growing louder, and her hand grows faster as I continue in and out of her. Finally she reaches the edge,

and starts her last orgasm. I am at that point myself and I release the growing force within me. I do my best not to follow the only instinct I have at this moment; thrusting forward would split her in half. I can feel her fingers plunge in and out of her as I reach my breaking point. I explode inside of her as she finishes her own orgasm...both of us feeling the impact of one another's orgasm while enjoying the mutual ecstasy. It is amazing.

We fall forward on the bed, exhausted. I lay on top of her for several minutes before either of us can move. Finally I gather the strength to climb off of her and head to the shower. I come back moments later to find her still face down on the bed, paralyzed by the pleasure of our fuck session. I laugh as I slide into the sweat-soaked sheets beside her. We both fall asleep, and I dream of a future encounter with her.

Katie

Find audio downloads and more fun stuff at:
www.flipside-erotica.com

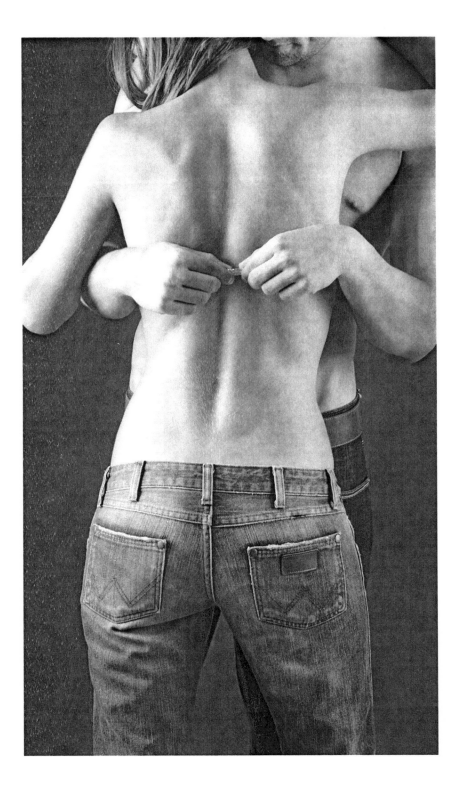

Gina

I see her sitting in the waiting area of my flight, and the first word that pops into my head is: spunky. She is wearing a tight t-shirt that reads I hate NY, jeans with a hole in both knees, and a Red Sox baseball cap. She is girl next door cute; sporting a chestnut brown ponytail that pokes through the back of the hat, no jewelry, and I can see a small tattoo on her ankle. I want to meet this girl, but I don't want to walk straight over to her and try to start a conversation cold. She seems fairly engrossed in the romance novel she is reading, so I didn't think interrupting her would endear me very much.

I notice that she is using her boarding pass as a book marker, and I can see she's in the same boarding group I am. I sit down a few seats away, but she does not seem to notice. After a while, our boarding group is called and we stand to get in line. I time it so I will be right behind her. We work our way down the aisle of the plane, and my chance to strike up a conversation finally arises. I put my bag in the overhead compartment, and then pretend she takes the seat I want. Feigning being mildly put off, I joke with her about stealing the window seat. I sit down in the aisle seat, leaving space between us on purpose. The flight is not that full, and I figure she'll be more comfortable this way. We begin to chat, exchanging pleasantries and spend the next hour discussing a wide variety of topics. She orders a drink, telling me she is always nervous when flying. I decide to join her.

After a while I begin to tease her and have a little fun at her expense, I ask her the month of her birthday. "I was born on June 1st" she replies. "Oh no, not a Gemini!" I exclaim aloud. I begin teasing her about the evil twin she has, and the bipolar nature of her astrological sign. She laughs, and admits she does have a bit of a wild side. I am dying to ask how long it's been since she indulged that side, but I decide not to push too hard just yet. We still have another 45 minutes on the flight, and I think things are heading the right direction. I catch her doing a body scan of me; a clear sign of interest. Couple that with her playfully touching me and leaning over to close the gap between us, I figure I am doing fine so far.

His Eyes

I didn't really have expectations of anything other than a conversation with this woman, but I can't help but explore the vague possibility that there might be a chance for something more. As we approach our destination, the conversation provides an opportunity to talk about one of my hobbies. I choose the topic of the creative writing; erotic stories to be exact. She laughs, not believing me at first. "You don't believe me?" I ask. "What do you write about?" she inquires. I lean over to her, gazing directly into her eyes in attempt to melt her defenses with a penetrating look, and begin to share another one of my fantasies. "Typically I take situations that I have actually been in, and add an erotic encounter to the story, like meeting someone on a plane, for example" I tell her. She laughs at me, seeing right through my thinly veiled pick-up attempt. I can see it in her eyes; she wants to call me on it. "Ok, I am going to need some proof" she states, expecting to hear my verbal back-peddling begin. Instead, I reach into my bag and pulled out my new Dell mini laptop that I carry with me everywhere I go. I have a couple of stories on it; a few I am revising and one that is half finished. "Tell me something that would turn you on, a scenario that you would like" I inquire. "No way! I'm not telling you anything like that!" she states firmly, slapping my arm playfully. "Ok, fine, then we'll go with one I like. Here, read this one" I say while sliding the computer in front of her. I pick the story that I had written a little while ago, involving two people meeting on a plane.

Over the next few minutes, her expressions changes from mild disbelief to total focus. She scrolls down the pages, pouring over the story in front of her. She never looks away from the screen, completely entranced in the story that is unfolding in front of her. Her breath quickens as she soaks in the details of my mind's work. I can see she is really into it; I must have chosen well. The story is about two strangers who meet and end up taking a chance and living out a fantasy. "So what did you think of my story?" I ask her. I can tell by the look on her face that reading it had really turned her on. She looks at me, flushed and slightly embarrassed. I can see her nipples poking through her thin t-shirt, and I doubt it is from the air system on the plane. "Um, yeah…it's good" is all she could manage to say. She sits there quietly for a moment, looking out the window. I am starting to think that maybe I had read her wrong and this has offended her, when she turns to me and asks "Can I buy you a drink when we land?"

The plane touches down and I turn on my cell phone. I receive an email informing me that my meeting had been pushed to tomorrow afternoon, and that I should call the office for more details. My assistant has already booked a room for me at the hotel near the airport. I have to laugh at the good fortune. I was trying to figure out how I am going to juggle having a few drinks with Gina and still getting to my meeting tonight. Apparently fate has smiled on me, and I inform Gina that I would love to hang out with her for a while. I tell her what has occurred, and that I will be staying over tonight, so I was no longer pressed for time. She offers to give me a lift to the hotel. I hint that I would love her company for the rest of the evening, and she blushes at my invitation. She responses with "We'll see how things go".

We go to the hotel and I check in. I do my best to make her comfortable, and I find myself a little nervous as well. We head for the elevator, and I can see her hesitating. She has the look of someone trying to hide the realization that they are making a mistake. We enter the elevator, and I drop my bag onto the floor. "Don't worry, I am nervous about this too" I assure her. "Kiss me" she blurts out. "Kiss me before I change my mind." I put my hand on her face, gently pulling her into me. I kiss her tenderly in a slow, lingering kiss. She kisses me back, allowing herself to relax into it about half way through. "There, the first one is always the toughest" I say. She laughs and pushes me away from her. The doors open on my floor, and we exit the elevator. I swipe the key in the door and walk into the room, throwing my bags onto the bed. She is right behind me, and when I turn she is right in my face. She grabs the back of my head and pulls me into her. This time she kisses me, and I am the one caught off guard. After a moment, she pulls away from me. We both look at each other, and then start laughing. It breaks the tension between us; and I am glad she did it. "You hungry?" I ask. "God yes…but you're buying me dinner first" she playfully shoots back at me. She grabs her bag and heads to the bathroom to change. When she returns, she is wearing a nice dress. We leave the room and head for the restaurant on the first floor.

Over dinner, we really get to know one another. I am glad to see that we have a real connection and not just physical attraction. Since we're on somewhat of an accelerated timeline, it seems a priority for us to get as comfortable as possible with one another. We talk and laugh, drink

and eat as we share details about our lives. I tell her how I travel frequently for business, but rarely find myself in this part of the country. She was visiting her sister back home, and is a paralegal for a large firm here in town. I comment on how her accent has faded; and she agreed that while she didn't speak like someone back home anymore, she still feels a deep connection to her roots. It has been a while since she has been in a relationship, enjoying the freedom to do as she pleases. I tell her I am in the same boat. She reveals she is not due back at work until lunchtime tomorrow; willing to throw caution to the wind and see where this will lead. We start out by sitting apart in the booth, over time inching closer and end up sliding together as we laugh and playfully touch one another. Soon we were practically sitting hip to hip, our arms rubbing into one another as the drinks and the increasing familiarity continue to tear down the walls.

Dessert comes and I grab the one spoon off of the plate. I push her aside to box her out, wedging myself between her and the chocolate dessert on the table. I dig in and take a huge bite while keeping her from even seeing it. She protests at first, and then decides that poking me in the ribs will be a more effective tactic. I jump, and she shoves me over in the booth, prying the spoon from my hand. She carves out a huge bite and a huge chunk of whip cream to boot. She tries to shove it in her mouth, but I accidentally bump her elbow in attempt to regain a sitting position. The melted brown substance and the whipped cream tumble from the spoon, traveling down the front of her dress. I am shocked and a little embarrassed at the mess I caused, and react by grabbing my napkin and trying to wipe the chocolate off of her dress. I am about half way through this when I realize that I was running my hands all over her chest. I stop suddenly, a mortified look on my face. She laughs hysterically at me; I am sure the look on my face is quite funny. Then I start to laugh with her. We are making such a ruckus everyone in the restaurant is looking our direction to see what is going on. The waiter comes to see if we need some sort of help.

He sees the mess we have made, and offers to bring a new dessert to us. "Yes, please, and extra whipped cream this time if you would be so kind. And can we get that to go?" she asks. I look at her, trying to confirm if she is thinking what I hope she is thinking. The glint in her eye tells me I am correct. I ache at the thought of licking whipped cream

off of her upstairs in the room. The waiter returns; I charge the bill to the room and grab the bag he delivers.

We stand up to leave the table and the room tilts just a little bit. I'm not sure about her, but the affect of the drinks we put away hit me a little harder than I anticipated. I catch myself and focus on walking one foot in front of the other until we make it to the elevator. "Wow, I am toasted" she proclaims. "Me too" I inform her. "I am not sure I can feel my feet anymore" I add. "Can you feel this?" she asks and with that she hits her knees and promptly bites into my thigh. My loud yell echoes through the tiny little chamber we are in. I jump in surprise, just as the elevator stops. As the doors slide open she jumps back to her feet, swaying into an upright position before the people entering the elevator notice. I attempt to suppress a laugh, and so does she. Luckily my floor is the next one, and we hold off bursting out laughing until we exit the elevator. We are hanging all over one another; stumbling down the hallway, half from the alcohol and half from the inability to stop laughing. I reach into my pocket and grab the room key. I swipe it through the lock, and pretend to open the door. She anticipates me opening it and takes a step forward, running right into the door. I literally fall down I am laughing so hard. I am on the floor looking up at her as she rubs the mark in the middle of her forehead.

She does not think this is as funny as I do, and decides to take action. She drops down on top of me, pinning my arms to the floor as she sits on top of me. I am still laughing so hard I am practically crying, the noise reverberating down the hallway. I look up at her on top of me, chocolate cake and whipped cream smeared down the front of her dress and realize suddenly that play time is over. The look on her face is now a hungry, almost serious look. I stop in mid laugh; catching myself before breaking into another round of giggling. I buck my hips a little to catch her off balance, and roll her over onto the floor. I am on top of her instantly, pressing her into the floor. I grab her arms and pin them above her head, kissing her long and hard. It is what she was waiting for; her hungry mouth meeting mine for the first time since in the elevator when we arrived.

After a few moments of heated kisses and grinding, I realize that we are in fact rolling around on the floor outside of our room. I break from

her mouth and stand up. I help her back to her feet and I pin her against the door this time to kiss her. I open the door slowly and we walk backwards into the room, still kissing one another. I kick the bag that has our dessert into the room, not terribly concerned about the contents at the moment. The door shuts behind us with a loud thud. The pace of our kisses increase, and I start to run my hands over her for the first time. She whimpers under my touch, desiring more. I reach behind her and undo the two buttons on the back of her dress. I grab the straps and slide the material off of her shoulders, and the dress hits the floor. She is standing in front of me in a matching set of bra and panties, silky and red.

Her skin is soft and lily white, and I step back to drink it all in. I stand there looking at her from head to toe and give her an approving grin. If she had a moment of uncertainty, I am hoping to kill it with my smile. She moves forward and grabs my shirt, untucking it from my pants. I respond accordingly, pulling the shirt over my head and tossing it aside. She feels me with her hands, touching my warm skin. She fumbles with my belt, pulling the wrong direction at first. I assist her, as I quickly step out of my shoes. I pull the belt off and toss it onto the bed. We are moving pretty fast at this point, quickly removing clothing and rushing toward our goal, so I decide to slow things down a little. "What happened to that dessert?" I think to myself.

I grab her hand and spin her around, pulling her in against me. I feel the heat from her skin as my arms wrap around her. I run my fingers through her hair, and brush it aside, exposing the back of her neck. I begin to kiss her neck, feeling her skin prickle under my lips. I open my mouth and gently nibble her neck. I open wide and chomp down on her, feeling her shudder and push into me, wanting more. My hands are all over her, running over her stomach, across her breasts and up through her hair. My hands travel freely, loving the feel of every inch of her. Her skin is so soft and creamy white; she appears to glow in the semi-darkness of the room. She throws her head back onto my shoulder, and begins to press her body into me. The hardness in my pants is becoming uncomfortable, and I reach down to adjust and gain some relief. The grinding of her ass against me now feels good. I continue to bite her neck, changing spots frequently to assure I won't leave a mark. I let my hands settle onto her breasts, squeezing them firmly. She lets out a moan

in reaction. I reach down and unhook her bra, pulling it out from between us without actually separating from her. She is pushing into me hard enough that I am fighting to hold my ground. I drop one foot back to be able to push back into her.

I touch her nipples directly for the first time; skin on skin. They jump to attention, ready for more. I run my fingers over them; the staccato rhythm of my fingers dragging back and forth over them seems to send shivers of pleasure all through her. A deep moan escapes her lips as she responds to my touch. Her breasts are small and perky, defying gravity as she arches her body to meet my hands. Her hard nipples point to the ceiling as I continue to alternate between pinching and rubbing them. I slide my hands to the bottom of her breasts, pushing them up and into her. She reaches up with her left hand and grabs the back of my head. I switch to nibbling on her ear, much to her delight. She takes her other hand and slides it between us, wanting to feel the hardness that is pressing into her through my pants. She lets out an approving moan, feeling my solid erection with her hand. I run my hands down her stomach, both of them reaching into her red silk panties. She is moist with excitement and begins to tremble at the promise of me touching her there. I explore her, caressing every inch of her body. I gently rub her clit, it swollen with anticipation. She removes her hand from my neck, placing it on top of mine. She is feeling me touch her, enjoying my hand. I think to myself that this is one of the hottest things I have ever done.

To my surprise, she pulls away from me. "What's wrong?" I ask. "Not a thing" she replies. I thought she was getting close to coming, and am curious as to why she wants to interrupt that. Meanwhile, she turns to face me, and is lowering herself onto her knees in front of me. She continues running her hand over the bulge in my pants, but obviously has more in mind. I decide to help, and grab the top button on my pants, slowly pulling apart the two sides. The top of my cock is visible right away, and I yank the rest of the buttons open, revealing myself to her in one quick motion. She grabs my cock, jerking it a few times before settling her hot mouth over me. The feeling is exquisite; her warm, soft mouth on me while her tongue explores every ridge and texture. "You are so hard. God I love how you taste!" she says between mouthfuls. She gets down to business, jerking and twisting with her hand while she

sucks away. She seems rather skilled at her task. I can tell she likes doing it, enjoying pleasing me in addition to just enjoying the act herself. She slides her hands around back and squeezes my ass, pulling me towards her. She takes as much of me in her mouth as she can, holding it there before having to withdrawal from it. She repeats the process over and over, taking me deep into her mouth and sliding my cock all the way back out, only to do it again.

I stand there just inside the doorway, leaning against the wall for support. Watching her below me, she is looking up at me while she continues to suck my cock. My head is spinning from the alcohol and the dizzying array of sensations she is producing. I push her away from me, fighting the desire to have her continue until my rising orgasm releases. I help her to her feet, stepping out of my pants that are now down around my ankles. I search the floor and find the bag containing the dessert, grab it and head for the bed across the room. She is already there, stripping off the red silk panties she wore. She pulls back the covers and hops into bed. I stand in front of her, bag in hand. "What do you intend to do with that?" she asks, looking at the bag. "I am going to smear what's left of the whipped cream on your thighs and lick it off of you" I state. "And I don't get any?" she queries. "We can share if you insist" I inform her, smiling as I climb into bed. I open the bag and pop the lid off of the container. The impact of the bag hitting the floor has smeared whipped cream all over the inside of the lid. I dig two fingers into the creamy soft topping, and get a good scoop of it. I reach over to her, touching each of her breasts with a dab of whipped cream, but saving the majority of it for somewhere else. I push her legs apart, and gently spread the whipped cream over her entire lap.

I start out by licking her nipple, slowly removing the whipped cream one tongue stroke at a time. I suck it clean, flicking my tongue over it before moving on to the other one. I do the same thing before kissing my way down her stomach to her waiting pussy. I reposition myself so I am laying on my stomach, propped up on my elbows, my face between her thighs. I look up at her; she bites her lip in anticipation of what I am about to do. I waste no time; I plunge in…face first into the whipped cream. I lick some of it away, cleaning it from her clit. I flick my tongue over her, loving the contrast in tastes. She grabs the back of my head, pulling me into her. I am smearing whipped cream all over my

face as I continue to lap away at her. She writhes under the pressure of my tongue, wrapping her legs around me, securing my position. I am locked in placed, and she seems Hell bent on me making her finish this time. I have my hands on the inside of her legs, squeezing her flesh slippery with cream. I reach up and placed my hand just above her neatly shaved pussy. I grab the small tuft of hair she has there, and pull the skin back. I expose her clit even more, and am now able to run my tongue over its entirety. I slide one of my fingers into her; it glides in aided by her wetness and the combination of whipped cream and my saliva. I add another, filling her further. I slowly stroke them in and out of her while I alternate between sucking and licking her clit.

She moans and writhes under my touches, her orgasm seeming to take a long time to finally arrive. When it does, it is well worth it. She gyrates her hips into my face, cream dripping off of her as she lifts herself off the bed. I continue, trying to stay within her movements as best I can. I take my fingers out and add a third, twisting them as I reenter her. That did it; I feel her clamp down around my fingers as she presses her hips towards the ceiling. I slide up onto my knees, putting my free hand under her lower back to lift her even further. She is bridging herself off of the bed, powered by the fury of her explosion. She comes in one long, hard, intense orgasm. I keep twisting and turning my fingers inside her, rubbing my tongue on her clit until she can give no more and collapses on the bed in a sticky, spent mess.

Still on my knees, I look down at her. "Boy, she's really a mess now" I chuckle to myself. In fact, most of the bed is a mess. There are remnants of dessert on the bed, and she tore the sheets loose during the fray. I wipe my face clean, and lean forward to kiss her. She is still recovering from the impact of her orgasm. I settle in on top of her, and reach up to brush the hair out of her eyes. I kiss her gently, enjoying the calm after the storm. As she begins to recover, she kisses me back with a little more force. My hard cock is pressing against her wet pussy, teasing her with the threat of entry. I am rubbing it on her clit, still hyper-sensitive from her orgasm. After a moment or two, she can't take it any more. She pulls me into her, wrapping her legs around me and granting access into her waiting pussy. I enter her, penetrating her with my full length in one stroke. I plunge into her, burying my cock balls deep. She jumps as I hit bottom, not quite ready for that much of me yet. I couldn't

help it; my desire had grown to virtually uncontrollable heights, and I had to be inside her. All the way inside her. "Does that hurt?" I ask, catching myself. "Almost" she groans. She arches away from me, gaining a little space inside. She wraps her legs tightly around me, wanting me to know I am where she wants me. I start to take very short strokes inside her; her legs around me limiting my motion. She wraps her arms around me as the kisses begin to grow harder and deeper. I slide my hand under her ass, lifting her to meet my growing thrusts. Her pussy has sealed itself around me, and the wet friction feels amazing.

I lift myself above her, freeing myself to pull all the way out and then drive it back into her. She lifts her legs, tilting her hips to meet my thrusts. I pound into her, each stroke ending with a firm impact of my body into hers. The slapping noise of our bodies grows as I continue to hammer away at her. Loud moans escape from her mouth, seemingly coming from deep inside her. She keeps her eyes tightly shut, enjoying the moment inside and out. I straighten up so that I am perpendicular to her, and push her knees together between us. I resume stuffing my cock into her, but this time I am going even deeper. This position makes her pussy tighter, and I can tell I am hitting a different and better spot inside of her. Each time I pound down into her, a loud vocal response is offered. Her cries of pleasure encourage me, and I begin hammering into her like I am trying to smash her through the floor. Each thrust is rewarded with loud cries of my name. I can feel my own orgasm building inside me, and I know it is decision time again. I have to let go and finish now, or stop and regroup so we can continue. I figure we probably will have another chance tomorrow morning, but for tonight this might be it. I decide I want more right now, and slow my pace so I can collect myself.

I pull away from her, and flop down on the bed beside her. She knows what my plan is, and likes it. She climbs on top of me, guiding my cock into her. I lift myself up onto my elbows, and she leans down to meet my mouth. She holds my face in her hands, running her fingers through my hair. As we kiss, she pulls me up until I am sitting, and she is sitting on top of me. She begins to rock her hips back and forth, grinding her clit against me as she goes. I balance myself and use my hands for better things. I push her breasts against her, pinching her nipples between my fingers. I withdraw from her mouth, and begin

kissing her neck. "Oh fuck that's good" she growls. My range of motion is limited underneath her, so she takes over and starts to grind into me harder. Our bodies are slick with sweat, and she easily slides against my skin.

I run my fingers through her hair, and all the way down her back, leaving no spot untouched. I lean back, putting my hands on the bed behind me and freeing her range of motion a little more. She accepts the invitation and really starts going fast. Her pace is impressive, and the look on her face is sexy as hell. She is so intense; her eyes burning right through me as she rides me like a horse. She throws her arms around my neck and slides her body up and down on mine. My cock goes deep into her, and she is grinding her clit into my hard stomach. "Oh, God...Oh God you're gonna make me come again!" she cries out. She is in a frenzy of her own pleasure, bucking her hips and grinding on my cock like there is no tomorrow. "Oh my God, I'm coming...I'm coming." She repeats the phrase over and over, never breaking stride. She digs her nails into my shoulder as she explodes inside in her second intense climax. She slumps forward on to me, exhausted from the ride.

I lay back, and she follows me, lying on top on me seemingly paralyzed from the orgasm she just had. I am throbbing inside her; aching for my own release, but I wait, giving her a few minutes to recover. After a short while, she lifts her head and says "Don't worry, you're next. Did you use all the whipped cream?" She has a sexy glint in her eyes, and I know what she has in mind. I reach over to the nightstand and retrieve the lid from the dessert dish. I am glad to see there is a little bit left, and I hand it to her. She runs two fingers inside the perimeter of the plastic lid, and scrapes off what is left of the dessert topping. "Stand up" she commands. I comply, putting my feet on the bed and resting my ass on the headboard. She gets on her knees in front of me once again, and proceeds to smear all the whipped cream all over my cock. I am twice as sensitive at this point; having had to fight off my orgasm a few times thus far. I am ready to burst before she even gets her mouth around me. Her palm is slick from the cream, and she uses it to glide her hand over my length. She slides her firm grip over me several times before finally putting her lips on it. I am aching for her hot mouth on me, and when she finally does I let out a loud moan.

His Eyes

My reaction excites her, and she increases the pace of her mouth. She is sucking the whipped cream off of me, building her pace as she goes. I am getting close already, and she can tell. My moans deepen, and I begin tensing up, bracing myself for the release I so desire. She looks up at me, "I want it....come for me" that's all it takes. It's as if her words uncork me and within seconds I explode. She opens her mouth, flattening her tongue to be sure to claim her prize. I shoot several streams of it into her mouth, some of it ricocheting off of her lips and onto her chin. She resumes sucking it again, draining every drop. Finally, I have to push her away I am so sensitive that it becomes too much for me to take. "OK, OK...I surrender!" I say laughing. We collapse on the bed, both of us now a sticky, sweet mess.

We spent the night together, exhausted from our encounter and dreaming of what the morning hours will hold for us. Well, at least I am. "Oh my God what a night" I think, as I drift off to sleep.

Andrea

It is a day just like most others; I'm heading to the gym after work. I enjoy leaving the rigors of my daily life behind in the form of sweat on the gym floor. I look to the snack bar on my way in, seeing Andrea working behind the counter once again. Poor girl, she always seemed to be working. She looks up from the blender, blowing her bangs from her eyes. She gives me a quick smile and exasperated look. I wave, and continue walking to the locker room to change for my workout.

I hit the bike for a good warm-up, and head downstairs to the weight room. I work quickly through my usual routine, getting a good pump going as I bounce from one exercise to another. After about an hour, I feel the day's stress melt away. I stretch a little and then retire to the shower. Heading to the locker room, I glance at the clock. It is almost 8pm, and I know the snack bar will be closing soon and decide I'd better hurry.

I put my dress clothes back on and head to the snack bar to visit with Andrea. She is waiting for me; making my usual post work out protein shake. Yes, I am a creature of habit that is for sure. She half-smiles as I sit down at the bar in front of her. The health club is open 24 hours, but she is off at 8:00pm. A few other people come to the bar to grab something from her before she closes for the day. After a few minutes, she flips the sign to read CLOSED, and begins to count the drawer of the day's money. Andrea is a very cute young girl, barely 23 and I'm sure gets hit on by every guy who walks up to the snack bar. I have done my best to never give the hint of interest beyond cordialness, hoping that this would somehow separate me from the others. I am about 12 years older than her, but we seem to get along just fine. I find her very attractive, but often wonder what she thinks of me.

"So, how are you doing today Andrea?" I ask. "Shitty!" she snarls. Wow! That wasn't the usual polite banter we have about this time every day, I thought. She begins to run through the list of things that she needs to do, has half finished, or dreads the thought of doing over the next week. I listen to her ramble and bitch about everything on her mind. After about five minutes straight of her speaking and me just nodding my head, she finally catches herself and begins to laugh. "I'm sorry, but boy

61

did I need that!" she says, laughing. "Hey, that's what I am here for" I reply. I sense an opening. "How about if I do something to take your mind off of all this?"

She looks at me sideways, questioning exactly what I am going to say next. I am at a crossroads with her, the next few moments are critical to where this is headed. "Well, you have your choice, we can go to dinner and out for drinks afterwards, or we can skip dinner...and go right to the drinks." She laughs, and looks me over. "I don't have time for dinner and drinks. Look, you've been coming here how long now, and you're just finally getting the balls to ask me out? How about if we skip the formalities and just go back to your place and have pissed-off, dirty sex?" I do my best to not let my jaw hit the counter. I am blown away that this young girl, who appears fairly innocent, just said that to me. I of course am very turned on by the idea of letting Andrea work out her aggressions on me. "Alright, let's go" is about all I can spit out at this point. She smiles and finishes closing down the snack bar.

She follows me outside, keeping a safe-looking distance away from me as we leave. I am sure a large part of this invitation is the implied discretion. I walk to my car and back out of my parking space, waiting for her car to appear from the back parking lot. I see the headlights of her Jeep and start the short trip to my place. My mind is racing, and the pit of my stomach grows tight. I have been hoping for this to someday occur, but this situation wasn't exactly how I had planned it out. Realistically given our age difference, I doubt that a relationship is in the cards anyway, so a quick fling or a friend with benefits deal is probably the most I can hope for. She follows closely behind, trailing me to my place right down the street.

We pull into the driveway; I park and hop out of the car. I am trying to remember if I have any wine or something to help take the edge off the moment. I'm not sure the right path to take with this impromptu situation. I am leaning against the car thinking when she suddenly appears in front of me. I look up from the ground and smile at her. She stands in front of me, biting her lower lip and I assume waiting for me to make a suggestion. I get about halfway through the sentence of "Well, do you want to come inside?" when I decide to just take control of this situation. I reach out and put my arm around her waist, pulling her body

into mine. I grab a handful of hair, pulling her head back and exposing her sweet young mouth to mine. She moans a little as we kiss. I start out slow and light; feeling her hand on the back of my head I take it as a sign she likes my bold move. I kiss her deeper now. Pulling her tighter against me I feel her firm, young body against mine. I release her hair, now holding her face as we kiss and tongue wrestle. I spin her around, and push her against the car. Lost in the moment, we envelop one another, pressing and grinding into each others' body. She lets out a few sexy whimpers once in a while, as she begins to run her hands over my upper body.

I reach up and grab the back of her hair again, pulling her mouth away from mine. We finally break, staring at each others eyes for a second. I can see the hunger growing inside her. I grab her hand and lead her toward the house. I am trembling with excitement and anticipation as I fumble with the keys. "Hurry up!" she says playfully, smacking my ass. "Patience my dear, patience!" I retort. As I swing the door open she states "quit stalling and kiss me" and practically shoves me against the wall. She basically attacks me, kissing me and shooting her hot tongue into my mouth. I let her enjoy her little illusion of control, knowing that will soon change. We had never talked about it, but I would imagine that most of the guys that she has been with are quick to the task, rushing through the exquisite pleasures of teasing and foreplay. I made up my mind on the way over here that I am going to prolong this experience as much as possible. There is nothing more ego-gratifying than hearing a woman beg me to fuck her.

I drop my keys and pull away from her again; she seems mildly annoyed that I keep doing that. It is the first of several reminders to come that I am the one in control. Shutting the door behind us I turn back to her, look deep into her eyes and tell her to follow me. She obeys, following me to the kitchen. I turn the lights on in the hallway, but leave the kitchen light off. I grab her waist, pulling that ugly tan work shirt of hers free from her shorts. She moves to take off the shirt, but I tell her to wait. "I'll tell you when." I said in a slightly deeper voice. I remove my shirt instead, and allow her to touch me with nothing between her hands and my skin. She runs her hands over me, tracing the muscles in my shoulders, chest, and down my hard stomach. The look on her face let me know that the hard work I am putting into my workouts is paying off.

His Eyes

She leans forward, kissing my chest. She works her way down my stomach. She put her hands on my ass, squeezing me as she kisses and licks at my stomach. I am growing harder by the second, and my cock pressing through the thin fabric of my pants. She notices, and slides her hand to the front of my pants, stroking my throbbing cock through the fabric. "May I?" she says looking up at me from her knees. She is already in position, and I almost agree. "Not yet" I reply, trying to keep my voice from quivering with the anticipation of my cock in her mouth.

I walk to the cupboard and grab a glass. Next I go to the freezer, removing several ice cubes and placing them in the glass. "What are you doing with those?" she inquires. "You'll see" is all I say. I walk over to her and pull her shirt over her head, tossing it onto the floor. I put my hands on her hips, and lift her up onto the marble counter top. I begin kissing her again, and push her down on the counter top so she is parallel to the floor. I stand next to her as she lay there in her bra and shorts. I start to run my hands all over her, brushing over her breasts, lightly tracing my fingers over her nipples. They spring to attention at my touch, poking through the sheer material of her bra; I lightly pinch them as I start to kiss her neck. She moans aloud, pulling me into her. I start to really chomp on her neck on the spot she reacts to the most on my first trip through this area of her. She loves it; and moans louder. I unhook her front latch bra, releasing her firm, young breasts from their captors. I remove my face from her neck, and slide my tongue down between her tits. My hands move to her breasts, squeezing them and smashing them into her body. Her nipples are rock hard now; I pinch and twist them between my fingers.

I begin to gently flick my tongue over her nipples, going back and forth between the two. I look up to be sure her eyes are closed, and I reach for the glass. I remove one ice cube, and squeeze it to melt it just a little more. I hold the ice cube over her stomach, and let one drop hit her skin. She jumps at the sensation; she was nothing but hot up until a second ago. The contrast is quite a shock, but not nearly as much as when I rub the ice cube over her nipples. She gasps in surprise, looking at me in surprise. I laugh, savoring the control I now have over her. I enjoy the power almost as much as the sex itself. Almost.

It is now time to reverse the affects of the ice. I place my mouth over her nipples and suck the water off of them. I toss the ice cube into the sink, and immediately start to remove her shorts. She lifts herself off of the counter so I can pull them down. She has on those bun-hugger briefs that I find so sexy. They are light green in color, except for the dark green area over her pussy; she is soaked with excitement. I remove her underwear as well, and now she lay completely naked on the counter top. I pause a second, enjoying the scene of the naked girl in my dimly light kitchen. I move so I am at the end of the counter, standing between her legs. Placing my hands on her knees I slowly spread her legs apart. I stare into her eyes as I open her to me. I run my hands over her legs, sliding them down into her moist inner thighs, but purposely avoid touching her there just yet.

I want to hear her say it, I want her to beg. I put my hands everywhere but directly onto her pussy. She begins to squirm on the counter top, and I am getting close to what I want. Finally she gives in, and says in a raspy voice "Please, please touch me!" Victory is mine, I thought, and with that shove my middle finger as far into her as I can reach. As soon as I bury my finger, I begin to rub her clit with my thumb. She immediately arches her back and slams her palms down onto the counter top, gasping for breath as I finally give her what she wants. I rub and slide, quickly then slowly, for about thirty seconds before she explodes in a hard orgasm all over my fingers. I can feel her juices run out of her, but I keep going, teasing her for a moment more.

I let her recover from the impact of her orgasm, and quietly grab another ice cube out of the glass. I start at her knees, kissing her smooth skin. I go back and forth between her legs, slowly working my way down her thighs. I again push a finger into her steaming hot pussy, working it in and out slowly at first, then building up speed. Just when I think she is getting close to coming again, I stop. She starts laughing; frustrated, yet still enjoying the teasing I am putting her through. It must be great to be a woman; totally losing yourself in the moment of pleasure like this. As a man, I am always monitoring what I am doing to her, am I getting too close to finishing myself, etc. The abandonment and blankness of mind must be incredible. She pries her eyes open, and looks at me, panting with excitement. "I think you are getting too hot." and shove the ice cube as far up inside her as I can get it. She cries out

loudly from the sensation of cold deep inside her. I laugh out loud, enjoying her reactions and the control I have over her. "Cold, huh?" I say smiling at her. "Let me see if I can warm you back up" and with that go down on her.

I start at the top of her shaved-slick pussy, licking and rubbing my tongue over her hood and then directly on her clit. I alternate back and forth between long and short strokes of my tongue for a few moments. I slide down just a little farther, and shoved my tongue into her cold canal. She is beginning to heat up again, but still had some lingering effects from her adventure with the ice cube. I push the bridge of my nose into her clit and shoot my tongue in and out of her pussy. Her moans turn into muffled screams as she puts the back of her hand over her mouth. She arches her back and lifts her hips off the counter to meet my mouth. I move with her, and soon she is on her heels and shoulder-blades, stiffening in another orgasm. She bucks her hips and I do my best to match her rhythm to draw out her orgasm as long as possible. She flops back down on the counter, temporarily exhausted. Unlike her, I am aching for some attention myself.

After a moment Andrea climbs off the counter, her knees hitting the floor almost as soon as her feet do. She unzips my pants as I remove my belt, tossing it aside. Undoing the button has my pants sliding down my legs; my cock springs to life, standing at attention in front of her face. She quickly grabs it at the base, her other hand running across my abs and the front of my hips. She runs her hand over the neatly trimmed hair in my groin area. She cups the smooth skin of my cleanly shaved balls, holding them in her hand as she readies herself to suck my cock. Andrea leans into me, slowly allowing my cock to enter her mouth. God, the feeling I get when a woman first does this is unparalleled by anything else. I am just aching to be sucked, and when she finally does, the feeling is phenomenal. She closes her lips around me, and I think I am going to explode. I lean back, arching my body to meet her mouth, moaning in delight as she goes to work. She begins using her hand, stroking the bottom half as she sucks and licks the top half of my cock. She removes her hand, and slightly extends her tongue as she swallows as much of me as she can handle. She gets about two-thirds of the way down the shaft and has to stop. She begins to pick up the pace a little, sucking me with more enthusiasm. I have to make her quit before long.

As much as I love having her mouth on me, I have to make her stop before getting me to the point of no return. I grab her hair and pull my cock from her mouth.

I pick up her lithe body and carry her to the chair in my living room. Gently I lay her on the chair, her ass just barely on the edge. I get down on my knees in front of her, and spread her legs once again. My plans to tease her with my cock continue, rubbing and poking it into her hot mound. I keep it up, pretending I am going to enter her, only to pull away once again. With some difficulty I hold back my own desire to just take her. This is an absolute fantasy come true, so I am holding out for what I truly love. After a few moments of this teasing, she looks up at me and says in a husky voice "Dammit, FUCK ME NOW!" and with that I finally grab my cock and guide myself inside her. The sensation is incredible, her tight young pussy almost resisting my cock as I try to enter her.

I start slow, gently pushing only about half of me inside. I fight back the urge to ram my cock all the way inside, keeping it slow for now. I wait for her, pacing myself based on her moans and groans. The louder she gets, the deeper and faster I go. This in turn makes her cry out even more, and I follow her lead, going deeper into her. After a few minutes I am sinking my cock all the way inside her, hitting bottom on every stroke. We must be just the right size for one another because instead of bringing pain, the impact appears to send ripples of pleasure through her entire body. She comes again and again, loving every single stroke of my cock. I am not sure how long we stay in this position before my knees can no longer take it. I decide it is time to relinquish a little control and relieve the pressure on my kneecaps.

I pull out of her, and slide into the chair. She knows exactly what I am thinking, and she wastes no time climbing on top of me. She reaches down and grabs my cock, positioning herself over top of me. With one swift move she takes me all the way inside her, burying my cock in her depths. She moans, arching her back and tossing her head back in pure ecstasy. "I love being on top!" she whispers, riding me harder and faster. I grab her hips, increasing the speed at which she is grinding me even more. We fuck like animals, grinding and groaning together as one. "Oh, my God...I'm gonna come again!" she yells out. She begins

bucking her hips harder and harder into me. I try to hang on, and keep my cock buried deep inside her. Just as she starts, I thrust my hips up, lifting us both off of the chair. She screams so loud as she comes I think for sure I'll have the police banging on my door soon. The force of her orgasm is too much for me to take, and I follow right behind her. I empty myself inside her, stiffening momentarily until we both collapse onto the chair. We lay there reeling from the pleasure and trying to catch our breath. She lays on top of me for several minutes before either one of us can move.

She looks at the clock, it reads 9:45. We had been at it for about an hour and a half, and I know she has to leave just by the look on her face. "I know." I tell her. "It's alright." We both get up and dress again, and I walk her outside to her Jeep. When we get to the driveway, I grab her and kiss her long and deep once more. "That was incredible" she states. "You feel better?" I say with a wry smile. She laughs and says "Yes, but next week looks pretty rough, too!" I just smile at her and say "Remember, that's what I'm here for." I watch as she drives away, laughing to myself at the way this worked out. I am amazed, to say the least.

Andrea

Find audio downloads and more fun stuff at:
www.flipside-erotica.com

Lindsay

It is late in the day, and I am hoping for a little luck that the tuxedo shop will still be open. My friend Alex had a last minute cancellation in his wedding party, and I am now saddled with the responsibility of getting fitted for a tux and filling in for his cousin who can't make it to Phoenix. I need a tux, and fast; the wedding is tomorrow. As I walk in the door, I am hit with the wonderful smell of a woman's perfume. It is light, soft, and has a playful quality to it. I stop to enjoy one of life's little pleasures. A gruff man who appears to be the manager mumbles as he hurries past me that the store is closing, and that I will have to come back Monday. He dims the lights and then locks the door behind him, quickly scurrying to his car parked right outside. Obviously he wouldn't lock me in the store by myself so I go looking for whoever is still here, hoping that I can talk them into helping me.

Suddenly a woman appears, holding a glass of red wine. She is surprised to see me; I can tell by the look on her face that she is not expecting to find anyone else in the store. I quickly apologize for surprising her; and begin a hasty explanation of my situation, pleading for her help. She says the store is closing for inventory, but she will make an exception given my situation. Since my first concern is getting a tuxedo for the wedding on such short notice, I barely notice what the saleswoman looks like. When she reappears from the back of the store, I am pleasantly surprised to see how beautiful she actually is. She is wearing a floral sundress, conservatively cut in the front, and about mid-thigh length. She is the one responsible for the wonderful aroma of perfume in the store. I compliment her on it. She blushes a little, and tells me it's something she picked out some time ago. I am becoming more attracted to her by the minute; her laugh, her piercing brown eyes, and the way her whole face lights up when she smiles. She catches me looking at her left hand, and asks "What did you expect to find, a ring?" She smiles, and says she was married once, but it ended several years ago. She admitted that she ran away with her high school sweetheart and eloped. They tried to make it work, but they were just kids. It was too much for them to handle, and eventually went their separate ways.

"No one likes to drink alone, would you like a glass of wine?" she offers, and pours herself another. I realize that I have been at the store

71

for almost half an hour and we have gotten distracted from the task at hand. The conversation flowed easily, and we talk about many different subjects. I have this strange feeling of closeness and familiarity even though we just met. I mention that we haven't gotten around to fitting me yet, and she gives a somewhat embarrassed laugh and hurries into the back to get the wedding party information. I am looking through some of the styles of tuxedos hanging on the rack in front of me when she returns. As I turned around, I notice that she has to look up to meet my eyes. She says this will be a piece of cake; the tuxes are already picked out, and she needs only to take measurements to see what size I am and we will be finished. I am about to make a joke about her choice of words, but I think better of it. I got that quick drop of the stomach feeling when she said that we will be finished soon. I want to stay.

We go into the next room, full of mirrors and partitioned off into several little sections. She fumbles around for a measuring tape, and I remove my jacket. She comes over to me, pausing to look into my eyes before she begins. She lets her fingers run over my shoulders, searching for the correct spot to measure from. Almost imperceptibly, I hear her breathe a little heavier with her hands on my shoulders. I don't want to ruin the moment, or be wrong for that matter, so I just pretend that I don't notice. Soon she has her hands around my waist. She is behind me now, and I can feel her breathe on my neck. It gives me chills, and creates a serious ache in my jeans. My mind is racing, and then it happens. She makes me a believer; I am not imagining this. Her lips gently brush the back of my neck. She makes it seem like an accident, but is fishing for a reaction. I turn my head and smile, giving her a look that easily says I know that was no accident. She whispers in my ear that I should try to hold still while she goes to work. I have a fleeting thought that is quickly confirmed when I see the tape measure lying at my feet. Slowly and tenderly she begins to kiss the back of my neck, running her hands over my chest. I moan out-loud; I love having a woman kiss the back of my neck. I am not sure why the back of my neck is more sensitive than anywhere else, but it gives me chills all the way down my arms.

She continues; pulling me closer, smashing her breasts against my back. The heat from her body is pervasive. She goes on exploring me, running her hands over my hard stomach, my shoulders and my chest as

she playfully kisses the back of my neck and ears. Standing up on the wooden box that is behind my feet, she is now taller than I. She put her hands on my shoulders, and spins me around. I turn, looking directly into those deep brown eyes. I break my gaze into those smoldering eyes of hers, and let my eyes drift downward over her body. My eyes trace every curve; the smell of her perfume is intoxicating. I look up into her eyes again, and then put my arms around her. I kiss her long, hard and deep. Our tongues play, gently at first, and then the intensity grows. Soon we are passionately kissing, really getting lost in the moment. I pick her up off of her perch, and carry her to the desk at the center of the room. I sit her down on it, and pull away from her.

I am not terribly bold when it comes to things like this, but she makes me feel secure in what we are doing. I step back, and undo my shirt. She makes a move to help, but I push her back down onto the desk. "Wait your turn" I tell her with a smile. She smiles back, and lets me continue. I remove my shirt. I stand in front of her for a moment, searching her eyes for a reaction. Her eyes explore me, and she smiles with approval. I reach down and pull off my shoes and socks, and release the top buttons of my jeans. I return to her waiting mouth. We kiss like lovers long familiar with one another. This woman and I are amazingly comfortable together.

"My turn" she says. She leads me to a chair in front of the largest bank of mirrors in the room. I sit down, aching for her to hurry, and yet wanting the thrill of this moment to last forever. The anticipation of what is going on is mind-bending. I can hardly contain myself. With one pull of each of the ties on her dress it falls to the floor. She stands before me, wearing only a pair of pink lace-trimmed panties. Her perfect breasts defy gravity, her nipples slightly curving towards the ceiling. I can see that they are rock hard with excitement. I want my mouth on them, but I wait. She comes over to me, watching herself in the mirror as she walks. She scoots me out to the edge of the chair, and gives me the sexiest look I have ever seen as she falls to her knees. We kiss again for several minutes, like two people who have all the time in the world. Her hands explore my bare chest, and all over my body, carefully avoiding my now throbbing hardness. She is teasing me, making me ache even more for her to touch me. Finally, she put her hands on my button fly, until she realizes that she can feel my hardness through my jeans. She

73

strokes me gently at first, familiarizing herself with the length and feeling of it. She tugs at the jeans, opening the rest of the buttons, and out it comes. I never wear underwear, so there is nothing holding my rock hard manhood back.

She wastes no time; she wants it in her mouth, and that is exactly where she puts it. Her small hands grasp the bottom of my shaft, as her tongue works over the top of my cock. Her mouth feels so hot as she wraps her lips around me. Slowly she works me deeper, until she has two-thirds of my swollen, aching member in her mouth. She slides up and down on it, gently twisting her hands in opposite directions on the bottom of it. I moan in pleasure, fighting to keep my eyes open so I can watch her in action. I look to my left, seeing her in the mirror kneeling in front of me; her head slowly bobbing up and down; the sight and sensation burns into my mind.

After a few more minutes, I have to make her stop. I'm not going to last much longer and I wanted this to *last*. We switch places, and I playfully push her down into the chair. She knows what is in store for her. I kiss her mouth and her neck, and then after much teasing, put her erect nipples in my mouth. Her breasts are just big enough that when I push them together I can get my tongue on both her nipples at the same time. She throws her head back in the middle of a loud moan. She squirms in the chair, her body aching for my mouth to continue its downward path. I lift one of her legs, and then the other, placing them over the arms of the chair. I pull her panties to the side, revealing a fresh wax job. "Surprise!" she says, with a wry little smile. I plunge my two fingers deep inside her sopping wet pussy, and the expression on her face quickly changes. She gasps with surprise at the suddenness, and the incredible pleasure coursing through the center of her body. I look up, and all I can see of her face is the bottom of her chin. She arches forward on the chair, her body curving to meet my fingers. I pull them out of her, and begin to rub her clit between my thumb and finger. She lets out another moan, and that is all it takes…Blast-off! She comes HARD.

I quickly stuff two fingers inside her creamy pussy and work them back and forth. I want to taste her. I start rubbing my tongue lightly up and down, from the top of her down to my fingers. As I slowly work my

fingers in and out of her, I apply more pressure with my tongue. When she gets close again I remove my fingers and grab her legs, trying to minimize the bucking of her hips. My timing is flawless; just as she is coming down from the first one; I bring her back up to the crest of the wave for a second and third, back to back. She collapses, slumping back into the chair.

I let her catch her breath, and then lead her to the mirrored partition. I turn her so she is facing the mirror, and push her feet apart like a cop frisking someone. Reaching for her hand, I place it on my throbbing hard cock and whisper in her ear "put me inside you". She doesn't hesitate, aching for me to be inside her. I start out slowly, pushing my cock in and out of her wet pussy. She is so tight around my cock; I have to stop again to keep from blowing my cork too soon. Quickly I gain control, and begin to increase the pace and depth of my strokes. The faster and deeper I go, the more she loves it. I press her into the mirror; seeing the look on her face and her breath on the mirror may be the most erotic thing I have ever seen. She moans louder and louder with each thrust. After a few more tantalizing strokes, I am ready to burst. I reach up and grab her shoulder, burying my cock deep inside her. I am not sure who comes first, but we sail into the heavens together. We wrestle against one another as we ride out each other's climax to completion. I have to brace the two of us against the mirror as our shaky legs can barely hold us upright.

I pick her up and carry her to the desk. She has that glazed over look that every man longs for in his lover, and I expect her to need a minute to recover from the recent proceedings. Instead, she tells me to sit in her boss's chair. It is one of those big, high-back leather chairs, black in color and still smells strongly of leather. I sit, and she climbs on top of me, throwing her legs over either side of the chair. Lindsay grabs the back of the chair, giving her even more range of motion up and down my hard cock. She rides me, slowly at first, and then harder and faster. She uses the rocking motion of the chair with perfect timing, well on her way to reaching yet another orgasm. She screams very loudly this time, her voice echoing through the empty store.

I pick her up one last time, and we walk over to the desk. She lies down on the desk on her stomach, her ass in the air. She looks back at

me, brushing her hair to the side and said "That's right; fuck me right here on my boss's desk." I just smile at her. "As you wish, my dear", I whisper in her ear. I place my hands on her ass, spreading her open as I part her waiting lips with my cock. I want to go crazy and just smash into her as deep as I can go, but I control my desire, sort of. I drive my cock deep into in one stroke, pushing until I feel bottom. I start slow, but soon I am pounding her deeper and harder than before. She comes again; this one a long, drawn out affair that seems to last a full minute. She keeps pushing back into me, begging me not to stop. No worries there, as I grow closer and closer to my own orgasm. I keep pounding into her with long and deep strokes. I build up until I can hold out no more. I put one foot up on top of the desk and shove forward for all I am worth, exploding inside of her in an amazing orgasm of my own. I spasm erratically inside her as I pour every ounce of what I have into her. I keep pumping into her until I am sure that one more stroke would make me shatter with over-sensitivity.

After a moment, we look at each other and laugh. I kiss her tenderly, and we get up to gather our clothes. I quickly slip my jeans on, suddenly not feeling quite as comfortable being naked in front of her anymore. She covers herself with her clothes as she goes into the next room to get dressed. When she returns, she has my tuxedo in hand and a big smile on her face. She looks at me, smiles and says "That will be $125.00 for the tux, and my phone number is on the receipt. I reach into my wallet, pull out my Visa card and think to myself.....wow, thanks Alex!

Thank you for purchasing my book, I hope you have enjoyed it to this point. Please visit my website at www.flipside-erotica.com, and as a thank you for your purchase, view the "internet only bonus story" that I have posted for you. Please type in www.flipside-erotica.com/free to enjoy the bonus story.

Nicole

Man, do I look forward to Tuesday mornings. We have arranged our schedules to allow us several hours of suspended reality together. It is amazing the chemistry the two of us still have after all this time, and even now I still get a little nervous and excited in anticipation.

As is the usual routine, I wake to the alarm and call her cell phone. I love to fuck with her a little even before she gets here, just to make sure she is good and ready when she walks up those stairs. There is nothing like waking up rock hard with the anticipation; she loves it when I roll over with my cock in one hand and my cell phone in the other. "Good morning" she purrs. "You ready for me?" I ask in my rough, sleepy voice. "Always." she replies, "See you in a few minutes."

I hang up the phone and head for the door. I unlocked it, and then walk to the bathroom. I look in the mirror, and realize that I am in need of a shave. I jump in the shower and rinse off, and do a little shaving. I believe that in returning the favor of taking care of things down there; after all, I know she shaved it slick this morning for me. I figure it's only right.

I dry off, and wrap the damp towel around my waist and pull the stopper up in the sink. I run some hot water into the sink, and wipe the steam away from the mirror so I can see my face. In the reflection I see Nicole standing behind me. I turn around, razor in hand, surprised to see her there. "Don't stop on my account." she says. I obey, and continue with my routine of shaving. I am almost finished when I feel her standing directly behind me. She places her hands on my shoulders, leans forward and kisses my back. I am not sure what exactly she wants me to do, so I just continue finishing my task. She reaches around and releases the towel from my waist. My cock begins swelling in anticipation and being freed from the towel springs me to life.

She spins me around and places her mouth on me, not wasting any time to get my hard cock in her one way or another. The feeling of her tongue sliding down me nearly takes my breath away as she eases her mouth over my length. She always starts slowly as usual; I wonder if she is aware that she follows the same routine almost every time she does

79

this. Not that I mind, but I am trying to make my thoughts wander so I don't blow the back of her head out two minutes into our morning together. After slowly increasing speed, she adds her hand into the mix, squeezing the base of my cock firmly at first. Her grip makes it swell and redden, then she releases her death grip and slowly starts to jerk the bottom half while she fucks her mouth with the top half. She is very good at it, but the best part is that she loves doing it. There is no substitute for enthusiasm, and she certainly looks forward to having me in her mouth.

She moves the towel under her knees, indicating she has no plans of leaving this position any time soon. Sitting back on her heels, she pulls her skirt up around her waist to reveal her shaved pussy to her own fingers. She knows it turns me on to watch her rub and finger herself while she sucks my cock. Moaning deeply, she touches her sopping wet pussy. The vibrations emanating from her throat tickling my cock all the way down the shaft. Increasing her pace, she rubs harder and shoots her fingers in and out of herself. The faster she sucks me, the faster she rubs herself. Or maybe it's the other way around, but her brain has shut off and pure desire has taken over. She is on autopilot, and ecstasy is the only goal. She continues to increase the pace, growing closer to her own orgasm. She moans louder and deeper as she draws nearer the goal. Just as she is ready to peak, I reach down and grab her hand, making her stop.

"Oh God, no…please, please let me come!" she pleads in a rough, sexy voice. "Ooh, you are so close, aren't you" I say. I grab her wrists and lift her to her feet. I put my hands on her waist and spin her, so now I am facing the mirror. I lift her by her hips, and sit her on the counter. She is still squirming, clenching her thighs together trying to get over the edge of her orgasm. I push her skirt back, and shove my two fingers deep into her. She throws her head back, smacking it loudly into the mirror. I can't believe it didn't crack from the force of the impact. The look of shock on her face from my fingers jamming into her, and the sudden rush of her orgasm negate the near concussion she almost gave herself. She screams loudly; one of my favorite things about Nicole is her unbridled passion. Her orgasmic cries echo through the bathroom as I feel her pussy spasm around my fingers. I work them in and out of her; twisting and turning them as I insert and withdrawal. She continues to moan and groan; grabbing my wrist and fucking herself with my hand.

She reaches the peak again, this time coming harder than the first. She rides the wave for what seems like a full thirty seconds, wedged between the countertop and the mirror until she collapses in temporary exhaustion.

I want so badly to just ram my cock inside of her, but I resist. We have plenty of time this morning, so I need to exercise more control than that today. I let her recover her breath, sitting there still fully clothed with her skirt scrunched up around her waist. She came so hard so she is now sitting in a puddle of her own juices, and I help her down from the counter. I lay the towel down on the counter, and turn to address the issue of her still being dressed. I pull her form-fitting shirt over her head, and then turn her around to unhook her bra, tossing it onto the floor. Details like wrinkled clothing always seem to escape us at moments like this. She unbuttons her skirt and let it fall to the floor; but I have her leave her shoes on. She is shorter than I am, so the added height of the heels may come in handy in the immediate future. I pull her naked body into mine, feeling the warmth of her skin for the first time today. I love having her body press against me; it is truly an exquisite sensation.

Something on the counter catches my attention, and my eyes lit up with a devilishly erotic idea. "I want to try something." I tell her. She smiles, not knowing what I am thinking, but trusting that she will enjoy almost anything I want to do to her. She hops back onto the countertop, and I reach for my new Mach 3 razor that I had been using. The advertising says that the vibrations make the hair on your face stand up for a closer shave. At the moment, I am only interested in the first part of that statement. I have a better idea for that little piece of technology this morning. I kneel down in front of her, face level with her pink softness.

I kiss her knee, and then the inside of her leg, slowly working my way upward. She puts her hand on the back of my head, gently trying to expedite the progress to my destination. I resist her, making my pace agonizingly slower yet. I nibble and tease her thighs, her stomach, and everywhere but where she really wants. I decide to grant Nicole her wish, finally lowering my aim and shooting my tongue into her. She arches her body to meet me, slamming her hands on the countertop. I flick my tongue over her clit only at first, and then slowly expand the

81

range of my tongue strokes to include sliding the tip of it inside her wet opening. She loves my tongue, and reaches down with her left hand to expose herself to me even more. I love the expression on her face when I look up at her right after shooting my tongue into hot pussy. Her expression morphs from eyes shut tightly to wide open with pleasured surprise. Certainly one of my greatest thrills in life is pleasuring her to this level.

I return to focusing my tongue only on her clit, and slowly push one of my fingers into her. I alternate back and forth between rubbing her swollen clit soft and gently, to hard and firmly with my tongue. She moans and growls at my touch, and I reach for my razor without her even noticing. I push the button and release the blades, and click the razor on. The vibrations reverberate through my hand, even though there is no noise from the razor. I remove my finger from her, and replace it with the razor. "Oh Jesus that feels good." she exclaims. I laugh, my tongue still all over her clit. I leave the vibrating razor handle inside her, and focus on rubbing my tongue on her clit. I can tell she is getting close again, and so I push even harder with my tongue. She grabs the back of my head, pulling my face into her bucking hips. She is lifting herself off the counter, balanced only on her heels and poised by her orgasm-induced strength. She comes loudly again, growling and groaning like an animal. I am always afraid she is going to break my nose when she comes this hard. I guess the risk is worth the reward, though. And my reward is her echoing my name throughout my bathroom at the top of her lungs. She finally releases my head from her grip, and drops back down onto the counter.

It is time, I must have her. I remove the vibrating razor from her pussy, and replace it with my cock. I am aching to be inside her, and the feeling of penetrating her with my throbbing cock is incredible. I can't even describe just how good it feels to slide inside her on that first stroke. I lay the razor on the counter beside her, and plunge my cock into her, burying it to the hilt. She leans forward into me, wrapping her legs around my back, clapping her heels together behind me. She put her hands around my neck, pulling her body up to meet my thrusts. I fuck her hard and deep, watching us in the mirror. She has her head tilted back again, conscious not to yell her cries of ecstasy directly into my ear. I slide my hand up the back of her head, and give a firm tug with a

Nicole

handful of hair. I make her look at the ceiling while I plow away at her pussy. She loves me fucking her like this; hard and rough. I continue pounding her, slapping my body against hers. I am getting close to coming, and have to stop.

I hit the brakes, knowing one or two more strokes would do it. I step back from her, withdrawing my cock much to her dismay. "Stop pouting and give me a second", I say in a mockingly stern voice. She just laughs, not wanting to stop, but certainly not wanting to be finished either. I only needed a few moments and some thoughts about algebra to regain my composure. I am quickly ready to go again, and position myself in front of her to do just that. She reaches down and grabs my cock, easing me inside of her. We both groan in pleasure, happy to have me back inside her. I begin slowly this time, withdrawing all the way out of her, and then slowly plunging her depths again. I reach over and pick up the razor again, flicking the switch. I touch the rounded tip of it to her nipple. They both quickly spring to attention. "Like that?" I inquire. "Mmmhhhmmm" she purrs. I tease her with the vibrations a little more, and then put it where she really wants it....down south.

I touch it down right above her clit, onto her pink hood. "Better?" I ask. "Oh yes...much better!" she says. I figure from the look on her face that is the case. I continue to stroke her insides with my cock, and hold the rounded end of the razor on her clit. She comes again, this time a more subtle orgasm. It slowly builds up, not violent like most, but steady. A different flavor from her usual, but not any less exciting. It lasts a long time, but doesn't leave her spent; she wants more. Never one to deny her pleasure, I oblige. I continue to pump into her, but this time I put the razor on the base of my cock. I enjoy the sensation, as does she. "I can feel that all through me" she lets me know. The sensation is awesome, being inside her snug pussy, and feeling the vibrations all through my hardness. I keep my pace, stroking in and out of her while pressing the razor into the base of my cock. I continue on; I can tell another one is on the way. Sure enough, she comes again. Similar to before, but harder this time as I begin to fuck her with more force as she grows closer. She explodes in an intense orgasm, digging her nails into my back and biting my chest, muffling her orgasmic cries.

His Eyes

After that last orgasm I can tell she is reaching the point where she is tapped out for today. We've done this enough for me to know how to read her really well, and she has had her fill. I withdraw from her and have her stand, bending over the counter. The heels she wears make her and I the same height, and I can easily enter her from behind. She keeps her feet together, making her pussy tighter still. I guide my cock into her from behind, forcing myself through her resisting pussy lips. I want mine, and quickly build up pace to a pounding force. I fuck her hard, banging into her ass from behind. She has her head down, resting her forehead on her arm as I plow away. I reach up and grab a handful of hair, yanking her head up so she can see us in the mirror. She loves to watch me fuck her, and I hold her firmly in that position while I pound my way towards my own orgasm.

The sight of me fucking her from behind excites her enough to have one more. She can tell I am getting close too, and she begins to encourage my climax. "That's it, fuck me, FUCK ME DARREN!" she commands. I am aware of her routine by now, and know she is getting close as well. I grab the razor and touch it to her forbidden hole, making her jump in surprise. "Don't you...oooohhhhhh, GOD!" The combo of my cock and the vibrations on her most private spot is too much. I shove forward into her, burying my cock into her depths. I hold it there and push into her even more, hitting bottom and stretching her limits. She starts to come, and I quickly follow. She clenches her pussy around me, milking every last drop out of it. I quiver and spasm, filling her with my seed. She has another violently intense orgasm, and together we collapse on the counter.

After a few moments, we finally regain the strength to stand and I lead her to the shower. We wash one another playfully, enjoying the warm water dancing over our bodies. We savor the last few moments of our morning together. Soon our respective days would begin, but for now we are content to relish a few more moments with one another.

Stacy

I was walking around the grocery store when I ran into a woman that I had met at my condo complex awhile ago. We would pass in the parking lot once in a while and exchange pleasantries. Stacy recognized me, and we stop and chat for a while. As it turns out, she is just as bored as I am in my new home here in Florida. Like me, she had moved here for a job not too long ago and didn't really know anyone. It's been a little while since I've even talked to a woman other than for work, let alone anything else. She is just my type too; about my height, curly shoulder-length blonde hair and is not super skinny. Stacy sports a big rack on her athletic looking frame and is a total smart ass. After talking for a while, we decide it might be fun to hang out sometime. I told her I would like to call her to go out sometime, and she hands me her number.

I call Stacy a few days later, and neither of us has plans for the following evening. We decide to go to a movie together; but the one we wanted to see is sold out. Instead of settling for another movie, we decide to go across the street to a local tavern and have a drink. I am glad she suggests it, and we sit and talk for a good long while. We really have a lot in common, and have a great conversation. I can feel things are going well, but wonder what the next step should be. "You know what will really kick this buzz into high gear...a Jacuzzi." She makes the comment that she wishes there was a Jacuzzi at our condo complex, but there is not. I casually mentioned that there are several at the resort where I work and the next thing I know, we are in the car headed that direction.

We pass the guard house and enter the resort; parking near one of the pool areas. I give a quick glance around, and then open the gate to the pool area. We walk around the decking, smelling the chlorine mixed with the cool tropical night air. It is about midnight, and the place is deserted. "We should get in." she says. I laugh at the idea at first; it is a cool night, we have no towels, and technically we are trespassing. I begin to protest, but I think she has just enough alcohol in her to push the envelope. She looks at me and smiles, saying "Suit yourself, but I'm getting in!" I look around to see if anyone is watching, and before I know it, she is shedding clothes and walking toward the Jacuzzi.

87

His Eyes

"Alright, I guess we are going in" I think to myself. I look around and find some towels in a cabinet near the entrance gate, and grab a couple of them. I head back around the corner, and find that Stacy has already dropped her clothes and is in the Jacuzzi up to her waist. She has her back to me, and the scene is sexy as Hell. She slowly sinks into the water, and then sits on the opposite side of the hot tub. The bubbles are on, obscuring all but the outline of her body. I have to laugh, thinking she was smart to get in ahead of me; now she gets to watch me undress and join her.

I thought that we clicked sitting back in the tavern, but this is certainly moving along a lot faster than I expected. I drop the towels onto the pool deck next to the water, and begin removing my shirt. She sits back, arms extended over the sides but just keeping her ample breasts below the water line. I am very turned on by the entire situation; the cool night, the smell of the water, the thought of us screwing in the Jacuzzi, and the threat of getting caught all are causing me to practically tremble with excitement. I drop the shirt at my feet, and remove my belt. I kick off my shoes and begin to unbutton my pants. She pretends not to be watching, but I catch her shooting glances in my direction. I slowly unbuttoned my jeans, thinking I was wise to wear underwear for a change. I have on my favorite ones; the label on the front reads Everlast. I always joke that I had my nickname sewn on the front. I remove the jeans and drop them onto the accumulating pile of clothing. My boxer briefs cling to me like they are painted on, leaving little to the imagination. I climb down the stairs, easing myself into the hot water.

She meets me halfway down the stairs, grabbing the back of my head and pulling me into her waiting mouth. I am surprised, but delighted to see that she is as ready as I am. "God I have wanted to do that since the first time I saw you" she says pulling away from me. We kiss some more on the stairs, hungrily exploring each others mouths. Our tongues wrestle as we press our bodies against one another's. This delightful scene continues for a few more minutes until I walk around her, and sit down in the water on the side opposite the stairs. "Come get me." I tell her. She stands on the steps for a few seconds, a wry smile on her face. Her nipples are hard from the cold air hitting them, and she is starting to get goosebumps from standing halfway out of the water. She finally obliges, and comes across the Jacuzzi to take a seat on my lap. She

straddles me, and we go at it again. We begin kissing even harder this time; our hands exploring each other's bodies as we grind into one another. I lean her backwards, dunking her hair into the water. She sits up, running her hands thru her wet hair and brushing it all backwards. As much as I like her long, curly hair, it will now be out of the way for the rest of this little adventure. I kiss her neck, roughly biting and chomping on her flesh. I work down her neck and towards her breasts, cupping them in my hands. I stick my tongue out to touch her erect nipple, but stop. I look up at her without moving my face, positioned right in front of her breasts.

"Stop teasing me and do it" she orders, glaring down at me. I laugh, and swiftly take it into my waiting mouth. She throws her head back in pleasure, the exquisite torture of waiting finally over. Her nipples are so hard from the excitement and the cold air; I nibble and suck them, alternating back and forth between her breasts. She loves it, and in a few moments is grinding herself hard against my crotch. I go back to kissing her, sliding my hands around her lower back and down to her ass. We continue to kiss and grind, lingering to enjoy the moment before moving on towards our goal. I mash her breasts between my hands and against her body, loving the feeling of her soft flesh in my hands. She begins to run her hands over me, exploring the rest of me that is below the water.

She traces the outline of my hard cock through the briefs I am still wearing. Her mouth is on mine as she let out a moan of approval at the hardness she is feeling. She slides her fingers into the waistband, and starts tugging at the shorts, trying to remove them. Since I am still seated, it is going to be difficult to get them off. I push her away from me gently and then stand up and remove the underwear, slinging them onto the pool decking with a wet, splashing sound. I am about to sit down again when she pushes me back against the side of the Jacuzzi. She urges me up onto the edge, and I sit in front of her. She immediately has my hard cock in her mouth. Oh my God, the feeling is amazing as she slides her hot mouth up and down the shaft of my cock. The mix of sensations is incredible; the cool night air hitting my back, the warm, wet steam from the Jacuzzi, and her hot mouth on me is almost too much to process. She hungrily sucks and slurps my cock as I look towards the stars. After a few minutes of her sucking it from top to bottom, I have to

89

make her stop. I can usually last as long as I want, but the entire situation is turning me on so much I can barely contain myself.

"Your turn," I say as I switch places with her. I lift her up onto the side and quickly start kissing her again. She leans back on her hands, arching her back so her breasts would meet my mouth. I suck one as I pinch the other nipple, switching back and forth between them. I am seemingly focused on her breasts when I sink my middle finger as far up inside her as it could go. She never sees it coming, but she is soaking wet and it goes in all the way to the hilt with ease. It catches her off guard, and she nearly jumps in reaction to it. Her mouth is open in shock, and I think she is going to scream out. Instinctively I put my hand over her mouth to cover the noise, and then laugh as she settles back down onto my finger and moans loudly. I slowly move my finger in and out of her, enjoying the look of sheer delight on her face. I start kissing my way down her stomach, purposely going slower and slower as I get close to my finger. I trade one for two, and detour my way around her dripping wet pussy to her thighs. I increase the pace of my fingers as I go, fucking her in and out with small twists of my hand. She grabs the back of my head and shoves my face into her pussy. She bursts almost as soon as I touch my tongue to her, clamping me in place with her legs around my head. She spasms hard a couple of times, then finally relaxes and slumps back onto her elbows. I never let up; I keep lapping away at her as she quickly recovers from the first one and begins building towards the next.

The next one comes almost as quickly; and it is just as hard as the first one. She bucks her hips and squishes all over my fingers as I try my best to match her movements and keep my tongue right on her. Suddenly I stand up, placing my hands under her knees. I lift her ass slightly off the side of the Jacuzzi, lining her up with my aching cock. I shove it inside of her all the way in one move. She throws her head back and lets out a deep, animal-like moan. I withdraw my cock all the way out, and plunge it into her again. I repeat the process over and over until I can tell she is ready. I release her legs, and put my hands just above her hips. I hammer into her, jarring her entire body. I fuck her really hard for three or four strokes before she locks her legs around my back and holds me deep inside her. She gyrates and squirms in front of me, her

90

pussy spasming around my hard cock. She releases me after a few moments, collapsing back onto the concrete decking.

I sit down into the steaming hot water again, feeling the rush of heat into my upper body. She sits up, looking down at me hungry for more. I am ready as well. I move to the steps, sitting on the top one. She quickly joins me on the stairs, and straddles me as before, but this time with nothing to separate us. She puts my cock back inside her, and slowly begins riding me up and down. She grabs the railing beside us with one hand and digs her nails into my shoulder with the other. Her pace increases, and we grow louder as we fuck. For someone who was worried about getting caught earlier, I am certainly throwing caution to the wind now, totally caught up in the amazing experience we are having. She rides me faster and faster and soon begins saying my name over and over. I ram myself as deep into her as I can, and send her over the edge of ecstasy again. She slams both of her hands down on my chest with a loud slap. The sting is painful, yet exquisite. Her rhythm breaks down, so I keep up the movement for both of us as best I can for the next few moments.

I am glad she is getting hers, but I am ready for my own release. I lift her off me, turning her to lean over the edge of the Jacuzzi onto the towels I dropped earlier. I slide into her easily, burying myself to the absolute hilt once again. I ram into her hard and fast, fucking her as hard as I think she can take. I can feel it building inside of me, my own pleasure becoming too much to contain any longer. I grit my teeth, and keep going. The last few seconds seem to take forever as I slowly rise to the top, and finally, the relief comes. I jam my cock into her as far as it will go, grabbing her shoulder and pulling her into me. She has something else in mind, and shoves me away from her. "Come on my tits" she says, grabbing my cock and jerking it furiously. The sudden change takes me by surprise, but I quickly recover and am ready to go. I tense, stiffening for the impact of my hard earned orgasm. I arch my back, and she tilts her head back as I empty myself onto her tits. She releases me from her grip, and I sink back into the water, my legs shaking.

After a moment or two she comes over to join me. We kiss one another more gently this time, the blinding passion spent but the

91

connection still apparent. I notice a beam of light scan across the pool area, and know it has to be one of the resort security guards. We grab our clothes and run for the poolside bathroom. We dress as quickly as we can, and about half way through we look at one another and start laughing out loud. We peek outside and run to the car, peeling out of the parking lot and laughing all the way back to our condo complex. I walk her home, and give her one more deep, lingering kiss. She turns and walks into her place, and I walk away wondering how we are going to top this experience. I look forward to trying.

Find audio downloads and more fun stuff at:
www.flipside-erotica.com

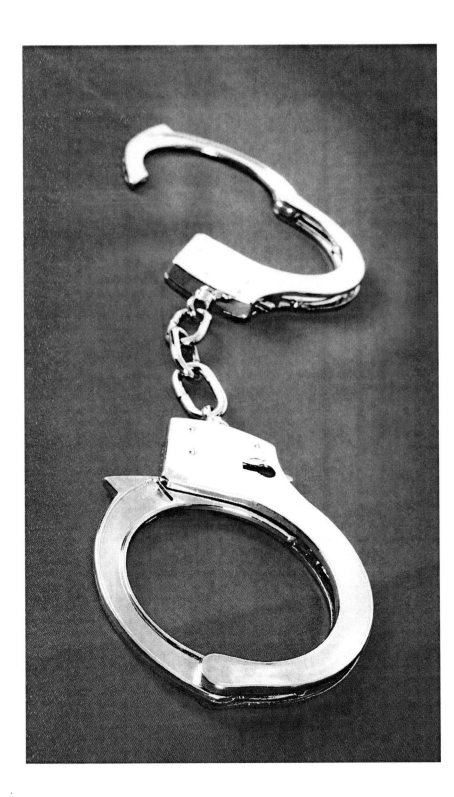

Katherine

It is all arranged; she has planned almost every detail of his wild fantasy of hers, and I am more than happy to oblige. I know she thinks that I think it is strange, but she's wrong...I get it. I am a big proponent of stretching ones own boundaries, and this is just one more area in which to do it. My girlfriend doesn't do anything small; she is very successful at work, in phenomenal shape, and is an absolute animal in bed. I never admit that she is the best, having fun with her competitive nature to do it longer, better or hotter than anyone ever before. Her tall, fit frame is a perfect match to her attitude.

Its six forty five, and I'm late. I sit in the car in the empty parking lot, waiting for her assistant to drive off, leaving only Katherine in the office. I feel a little creepy at the moment, almost like this is real. But I am also turned on by this scenario, and even more so that she is so into it. Who would have guessed that my girlfriend Katherine, the ruthless bitch defense attorney by day, is such a filthy whore at night. And her deepest, darkest secret is to be completely controlled, helpless and taken. Finally her assistant drives off, and I wait another few minutes just to be sure.

I walk to the building, pulling the front door. Locked...shit, now what? It was supposed to be open until 7:00, and its only 5 minutes of. Obviously calling her is going to ruin the moment, so I've got to figure out another way into the building. I walk around back, looking for another door. The receiving department door is open, and I sneak in. Someone is in the office, jingling keys in his hand. I hide behind a pallet of boxes until he leaves, locking that door behind him. I was lucky I got in the building when I did, or I would have some serious explaining to do for ruining her plans. I start to find my way out of the dark warehouse towards the door when I hear a voice, and its coming my way. I run back to my hiding spot just as the door swings open. It's the same guy, arguing with someone on his cell phone. He flicks on the lights in his office, taking a seat behind the computer. Crap, I am trapped here; I'd have to walk right by his office to get out of here. I look at my watch, it reads 7:05. I sit down on the floor, hoping he won't be long.

95

His Eyes

I hear him get up once again, turning off the lights and shutting the office door. I need to move fast. I practically follow him out the door, sneaking right behind him and waiting only a few seconds to open the door he just shut. I gently close the door and move quickly to the stairs. She's on the fourth floor, and I run up every step to the door at the fourth floor. I take a moment to catch my breath, and then open the door quietly. Sneaking down the hall, I hear her voice. I catch her reflection in the glass and see she is talking on the phone. She is facing away from me, rustling through paperwork. I sneak into her office, standing behind her chair. I reach into my pocket and pull out the blindfold, ready to pounce at my first opportunity. She wraps up the call and leans forward to hang up the phone.

As soon as she leans back I lunge at her, catching her off guard. I cover her eyes with the blindfold, tying it tightly behind her head. I clamp one hand over her mouth in effort to keep her from crying out instinctively. I reach into my pocket, pulling out the handcuffs. I jerk her chair backwards, and she reaches back to catch herself, exposing a wrist to me. I slam the metal cuff down on her wrist, the cuff clicking tight against her skin. I lift her up out of the chair, and she begins to struggle. I do my best to restrain her, but she struggles free. Next thing I know she stomps on my foot and is winding up to take a swing at me. I catch her free hand, thinking I was lucky to see that coming. She is making this seem even more real, and it excites me that much more. I force her free hand behind her, and clap the other cuff around her wrist. I spin her around, and push her forcibly down onto the desk.

I lean over her, pressing my weight onto her, and grab a handful of hair. I let my other hand explore her, caressing her ass, running slowly up and down her legs. I pull her hair, bringing her ear to my mouth. "I am going to fuck you right here in your office, Katherine!" I inform her. The words make her struggle again, but I know better. My hand is still over her mouth as I reach into my jacket pocket, removing the roll of duct tape. I drop it down on the desk next to her. I added this little prop into the mix myself, and I want her to know it, to think about it and wonder what little twist I have come up with. I tear a piece off, the noise certainly revealing the new prop to her if she had not already figured it out. I lift her by her hair again, and slap a piece of duct tape across her mouth before she can cry for help. She is now handcuffed, blind folded

and gagged, lying over the desk in her office. I sit back in her chair, surveying the scene. I laugh to myself; my foot is killing me and I am breathing heavily from struggling with her. Time to give her what she wants.

I stand behind her once again, and place my hand in the middle of her back. I hold her in place, unsure if she is going to submit to me or continue to struggle. I run my other hand over her, slowly tracing the curves and contours of her body. I rub the silk of her blouse against her skin, and then yank it, untucking it from her skirt. Next I grab the zipper in the back of her skirt, and very slowly unzip it. I take my time, enjoying the rare treat of complete and total control over her. I grab the bottom of the skirt, and begin to pull it down. Once it clears her hips, it falls to the floor. She is wearing nylons, and I decide they will have to be torn from her. I squeeze her ass, sighing in approval of just how good it looks in this position. I raise my hand high, and drop it down on her ass, making her jump. The impact stings my hand a little, and I am sure she feels the full affect of that. I slide my hand between her legs, feeling just how wet she is. It solidifies in my mind that she is loving every minute of this, and that I should proceed as planned.

I pull her up to a standing position again, reach around, feeling her breasts in my hands. She starts to struggle, and I pull her against me. I wrap my arms around her, pulling her tight against me. I reach around and let my hand linger over her breasts for a moment. I am really hard already, and gain a little relief by rubbing it against her leg. It's as if my body accepts the action as a deposit on more friction soon to come. My hands continue to run all over her, pausing at the spots I enjoy the most. Her reaction tells me her body feels the same way. I slide my hand around her chin, pulling her back into me even more. My breath is on her neck, and I feel her shiver in excitement. I bite her, burrowing my teeth into her flesh. I reach up and pinch her nipples through her bra, fairly convinced that she has given up on the idea of breaking free from me. The combination of sensations seems to make her knees buckle, and I push her against the desk to keep her upright. I want my hands on her breasts, and I reach inside her shirt and unclip her bra, freeing them. I reach under her shirt, and lift them as I squeeze. Her nipples are rock hard, just like always when I touch her.

His Eyes

I reach up, grabbing her hair once more. I yank her head backwards in an act of control once again. I slowly begin to unbutton her silky blouse, taking way longer than I'm sure she wants me to. She squirms against me, not fighting me this time, but rubbing her ass against the bulge in my pants. I know how impatient she gets when she is turned on, and I usually don't make her wait. But today is different, so she will have to wait. "I will fuck you when I am good and ready" I tell her. I reach down between her thighs, feeling her slick pussy through the wet nylon material. I push my hand up into her, unable to feel exactly where I am touching. She throws her head back onto my shoulder, and I continue to tease her a little more.

I spin Katherine around, pushing her back onto the surface of her desk. I can smell her excitement, and I want to taste it. I push my thumb against her again, and this time notice a small hole in the material. I push my thumb into it, and it gives. I press through, and get a grip on the nylon material from the inside. I force my other thumb in as well, and soon I am tearing the material apart in a frenzy. I am like a madman ripping the material away from my target. I shove two fingers deep into her, and she arches her back in response. I hear a muffled moan, the duct tape doing its job so far. I keep working my fingers in and out of her as I lean forward and place my tongue directly on her clit. "Oh God YES!" I hear her scream, meaning she has torn the tape loose. I know she is close, and I'm expecting an orgasm of epic proportion due to the length of time I have made her wait. I work her over, licking and sucking her clit while I twist my fingers in and out of her. She explodes, convulsing on the top of her desk as I move with her. My tongue never leaves her, and I ravage her clit with it. She goes limp, but I know there is more. I lighten the pressure a little, but keep going. Within a minute she is ready again, and this time screams so loud I am sure if anyone is here they would hear and come running. I don't care; I keep at it until she is jelly on top of the desk, completely spent from two great orgasms.

I am ready to burst, and unzip my pants, pulling my cock free. I lift her off the desk, and push her to her knees. Grabbing the top of the tape that she has torn loose from her mouth, I yank the rest of it off. Her lips redden, making me realize that is was not as loose as I first thought. I grab the back of her head and force my cock into her mouth. The wet heat of her mouth temporarily provides some relief, and I fuck her mouth

with my cock. I moan aloud, and she loves it too. Soon she is sucking the full length, ramming me into the back of her throat. I hold still, letting her swallow as much of it as she wants. She is so turned on she is moaning as she sucks it, driving it deep into her throat. She keeps making herself gag, but appears undeterred as she comes back for more. She takes as much as she can, holding it deep, against the back of her throat. Her eyes are watering from under the blindfold and she blows her cheeks out in attempt to hold her position. Finally she is forced to give in, pulling away from me, coughing. I look down at her, laughing a satisfied laugh at the level I have raised her excitement to. I help her to her feet, and spin her to face away from me.

I push her forward, leaning her over the desk once again. Reaching down and tearing the nylons some more, I expose her back side to me. Lining up my target I lunge forward, burying myself as deep in her as I can go in one stroke. I pull out, and repeat the process, shoving all of it into her in slow, deep strokes. I try to keep fucking her slow, but after a minute or two I am conscious that I am now banging into her with quite a bit more speed and force. I hold onto her by grabbing the links of chain between the handcuffs, and I fuck her like I am punishing her. I bring my hand down on her ass again, refreshing the mark from before. I am pounding her into the desk, making it shift slightly with each thrust. I am so into it I'm losing track of just how close I am getting, and all of the sudden I realize that a few more strokes will push me over the edge. I stop suddenly, telling her not to move. She knows the drill, as I have done this before. After about thirty seconds I am ready to go again, but another few moments wouldn't hurt. I pull out of her, and walk to the leather chair.

I sit my sweaty ass on her pristine leather chair, and I know that later she will be mad about it. At the moment, however, it is the farthest thing from her mind. "Get your ass over here" I command, enjoying my liberties once again. I know she can see under the blindfold, and she finds her way over to me. I grab her hips, and spin her around to face away from me, pulling her down onto my stiff cock. I force her up and down on it; the feeling is so intense after not being inside her for a moment. Her feet barely reach the floor as I bounce her up and down on my cock. She comes quickly once again, pushing herself downward as I

lift to meet her. I feel her juices run out of her and down my leg, right on to her leather chair.

I give her a moment, but am ready to conclude this adventure with an epic orgasm of my own. I lift her off of me, and walk her to the desk. I push her back onto it one more time, this time facing me. Removing the blindfold, I look her in the eyes for the first time tonight. I grab the back of her head, forcing her eyes downward just in time to see my cock disappear inside of her. I bury it once again, loving the feeling of her. I pull all the way out, teasing it in front of her, and then drive it home once more. I hold her head in that position, making her watch me pound that pussy of hers. My pants are covered with her juices, and each thrust squishes more creamy wetness out of her. She is getting close once again, and starts encouraging mine by talking dirty to me. "Fuck me, Fuck Me Hard!" she growls into my ear "Yes...Harder! Harder!" she moans loudly as I continue to slam my body into hers. I can tell she is on the verge, repeating "Oh God, Yes!" over and over. I release her hair, and place both hands under her ass, lifting her to meet my final thrusts. I am going to break apart if I don't come soon, and flip my switch, releasing the mental hold on my body's desire. I explode inside her as her pussy clamps down on me in spasm after spasm. She wraps her legs around my back, holding me deep inside her as I erupt in my own epic orgasm, even better than I was hoping for.

We lie still; collapsed right in place on top of her desk. This night was amazing, and I am glad she trusts me enough to let go like this. I can't wait to see what else Katherine has locked deep in that little room in her mind, to which I now have a key.

Katherine

Find audio downloads and more fun stuff at:
www.flipside-erotica.com

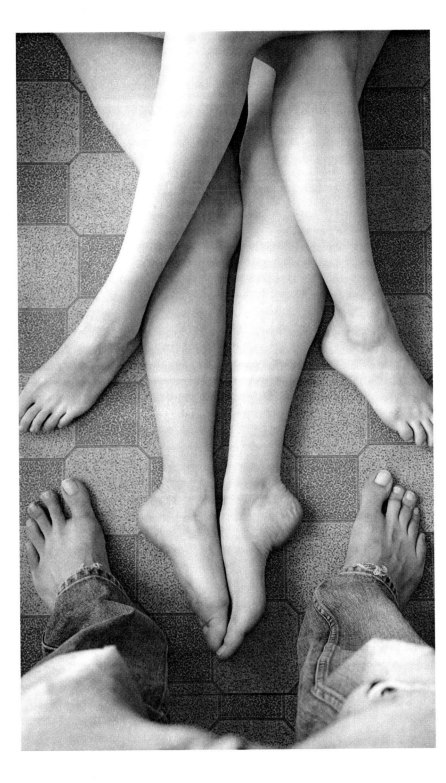

Ashleigh & Hannah

Alright, packed up and ready to go! We jump in my X-Terra and head for the mountains, anticipating a weekend of peace, quiet, and a lot of sex. Ashleigh certainly has an appetite for fun, and spending the weekend at my friends' cabin is sure to get her going. We hadn't seen each other in a little while, and we are both looking forward to this time together.

As we leave town, the clouds over the mountains seem to thicken as we draw closer. We have plans to doing a little fishing at some point during the weekend, so I am hoping the weather will cooperate. But, to no avail; the further north we go, the worse it becomes. "Looks like we'll be spending the weekend indoors" I say. "What on Earth are we going to do to keep ourselves busy?" She smiles, partly at my innuendo and partly because she catches me taking a sweeping glance over her body. The sexual chemistry between the two of us is stuff of legend at the office where we both used to work. The whole staff knew we could barely keep our hands off of each other, and spent many a lunch hour speculating about our activities. And I know one look is all it would take to get things started. She smiles, and the look in her eyes lets me know she is game. I reach over with my right hand and rub her breasts through her shirt. Her nipples become hard immediately, and she shudders under my touch. "You watch where you're driving; we'll get to me later" she tells me. With that, she undoes her seatbelt and slides over in her seat. I know what she is going to do, and I begin to ache at the thought of her hot mouth on me while I drive down the highway.

She reaches over and feels the already stiffening hardness of my cock. The flimsy material of my shorts is doing little to hide my enthusiasm for one of the greatest sexual favors a man receives. Not just getting head, but road-head. That coveted and rarely often achieved total self indulgent pleasure that must be experienced and not described. She unties the drawstring in my shorts and tugs at the material around my waist. She is just as antsy as I am, and I play with her by sitting still and not allowing her to pull my shorts down to a workable level. She slaps my thigh hard, mock-glaring at me for making her wait. She wants me in her mouth, and I love teasing her. I allow her to continue, straining to

103

not shudder with excitement myself. She pulls the shorts down, and begins a task which she absolutely loves.

She starts slowly at first, just teasing me by kissing my stomach and all around my throbbing hard-on. She knows that drives me nuts, and enjoys the little bit of control she has when she is dictating the pace. Finally, I can't take it anymore; I grab the back of her head and shove her mouth down over my cock--all the way down. I know she'll be ready for it; she loves to try and handle the whole thing all at once. She can take it for only a second or two, and I feel her whole body convulse as she fights not to gag. I let her up, and she quickly recovers and goes down for more. Before long she is really into it; she is sliding her tongue all over me; sucking it hard, and cupping my balls in her hand. There is no better feeling in the world, and I have to keep reminding myself to watch the road.

After a few miles of road pass by, I know I am getting close. She can tell as well, feeling my balls tightening as I prepare to empty my gun. Rain begins to hit the windshield, and I crack the window just enough to smell the rain and feel the coolness on my face. I have a handful of her hair in my right hand again, and she knows it is time. I arch into her, driving my cock deep into her mouth as I shoot my load right down her throat. She fights her gag reflex to keep me where I am. I groan in pleasure, thankful for the release, and then disappointed that it is so fleeting. I settle back into my seat, not realizing until then that I had being holding myself up off the seat of my X-Terra. "Wow" I say, "That was awesome!" She smiles that satisfied look of a job well done.

After about an hour the rain begins to come down much harder, and it is growing dark. We turn off the main highway and onto the dirt road towards the cabin. The road is very wet, and puddles are everywhere. It obviously has rained quite a bit up here in the mountains over the past few days. As we come around a turn, there is a vehicle sitting half way in a ditch right along side of the road. Upon seeing the lights of my vehicle, the person in the car jumps out and waves us down for help. I am hesitant at first; you hear so many stories these days about crazy people in situations just like this, but I also hate the thought of leaving someone stranded out in this weather. The odds of someone else coming along any time soon are not good. So, I stop my vehicle and get out to

see what is wrong. The car's front end is buried in the ditch, worse than I originally thought from my first glance at it. The person comes towards me, hunching over in a hooded rain jacket and shorts. It is a woman, and she seems very relieved to see me. I point my flashlight in her direction, and she begins a string of "thank you's" because I stopped to help her. She says she has been stuck there for a couple of hours, and thought for sure she was going to have to spend the night in the car. I tell her that I do not have a tow strap or anything to pull her out of the ditch with, so she should come with us to the cabin. "Us?" she asks. I tell her Ashleigh is in the car, and she seems a little more at ease with the prospect of not being alone with just me. "Alright, thanks." she agrees, and walks towards the X-Terra. She climbs in, and I follow. I introduce myself and Ashleigh, and tell her she is welcome to stay the night with us and we will help her in the morning. She removes her rain jacket, and thanks the two of us for stopping to help her. For the first time I see her face; she is not stunning, but is attractive in that "girl next door" kind of way. Her blonde hair is hanging half out of her ponytail, framing her pretty face. She is soaked to the bone and muddy from her off road adventure; her white t-shirt clings to her body and reveals a flat stomach and a rather firm set of breasts. She catches me looking at her, and covers herself up again. We drive to the cabin in silence.

We get to the cabin and I unlock the door. Ashleigh goes in first, followed by Hannah and then me. I immediately set out to make a fire, and Ashleigh goes upstairs to put things in the bedroom. I turn to Hannah, and ask what she was doing back this road all by herself. She explains that she is on a cross country road trip, and wanted to explore the high country before she goes to start her new job. She has a car full of backpacking equipment and is all set to go, but decided to wait out the rain. An elk ran out in front of her and when she swerved to miss it, she ran off the road. Ashleigh returns with a towel, sweatshirt, and a pair of sweatpants for Hannah. She shows her where the bathroom is, and tells her she can shower and get out of the wet clothes. I now have the fire going, and am really starting to get hungry. I rustle through the cooler, looking for the steaks that I brought along. Ashleigh comes into the kitchen, and starts to help with dinner. "What do you think of our guest?" she asks. "I think she is lucky we didn't get here earlier or she'd be stuck out in the rain in the middle of nowhere. I don't know what..." I look at Ashleigh and realize that I had not answered the question she is

really asking. The look on her face makes me realize that she has something else in mind. I have gotten a little distracted from our encounter with Hannah, and now realize that Ashleigh did not have the luxury of the orgasm I did earlier. She is still revved up. I know that she likes other women; she has told me stories from her past. "Let me do the convincing, and follow my lead" she says boldly. "Ok", I respond, thinking that she never ceases to amaze me. But I really wasn't getting my hopes up just yet; pulling off a threesome is no easy task.

We make dinner, and find two bottles of wine that had been stashed here for some time. Ashleigh opens one, and pours each of us a glass. Hannah appears much more comfortable now; out of her wet clothes, and having a roof over her head for the night. Conversation flows almost as easily as the wine does, and we all talk and exchange stories throughout dinner. I clear the dishes and the girls go to the couch. We brought the movie Unfaithful along to watch, and I had to laugh thinking it might help I know it is a very sensual movie, and the sex scenes with Diane Lane are definitely hot. I think the wine is taking affect; the girls are sitting very closely on the couch, and giggling like 12 year olds at camp. I flop onto the couch on the other side of Ashleigh, and try to make it look like I am not paying attention to them. Ashleigh has taken the lead as she said, and I am trying to follow along. We watch the TV in silence for a few moments. I get up and retrieve the second bottle of wine, pouring each of them yet another glass. "No more for me!" Hannah says. "I am already drunk...my lips are numb." "Really?" Ashleigh asks. "Let me feel" and with that Ashleigh grabs Hannah and kisses her. Hannah looks stunned as she pulls away. "Oh my God! What are you doing?" she exclaims. "Kissing your beautiful mouth." Ashleigh replies.

There is what seems like a long moment of silence, and I figure that the jig is up. But then Hannah put her hand on Ashleigh's leg and brushed the hair back from Ashleigh's eyes. "I've never done anything like this before." From her answer, it sounds as if she is game to try. Ashleigh leans in and kissed her again, and this time Hannah decides to kiss her back. Watching two beautiful women kiss is an awesome sight. I feel a familiar aching in my cock, and want to jump right in between them, but hold off knowing that this ultimate fantasy could vanish right in front of me if I am not careful. The kissing continues, and they take turns shooting their tongues into one another's mouths. Ashleigh finally

decides to introduce me into the mix, and signals to me to go sit next to Hannah. Ashleigh leans over to kiss me. We have Hannah sandwiched between us, and I can feel her warm body press against mine. I kiss Ashleigh deeply, and then look at Hannah. She seems to be waiting for me, and grabs me, pulling me towards her waiting mouth. She has used some of Ashleigh's body lotion after her shower, and the smell of Ashleigh and the taste of the wine in her mouth is a total turn-on. I reach over and begin to rub Ashleigh's breasts, finding already hardened nipples poking through her shirt. "Let's go upstairs" she says, and grabs Hannah by the hand. Our lovely guest grabs my hand and the three of us make off for the bedroom.

We arrive at the bedroom, and Ashleigh grabs a pack of matches off the nightstand and lights two candles, one on either side of the bed. I reach for the dimmer switch, and turn down the lights just a little. I shut the door behind us, and turn to find Hannah and Ashleigh already kissing in the middle of the room. Ashleigh reaches under Hannah's sweatshirt and slides her hands up her sleek body. I don't know if it is the lighting, the wine, the situation, or all three, but she looks phenomenal. Ashleigh pulls the sweatshirt over her head, and tosses it aside. She runs her hands all over Hannah's tan body. She takes her time, as women do, and enjoys every subtle change and curve of her. The rain starts again, and I walk over and open the windows so we can listen. I take off my shirt and walk up behind Ashleigh, pressing against her. I kiss her shoulders and then the back of her neck, before pulling away to ready the bed. I lie down on the sheets, and look up to see my reflection in the skylight. It is almost as clear as a mirror! I don't know if Ashleigh actually knew this in advance, or if the lighting just happened to create this affect.

Ashleigh takes off her sweatshirt, releasing her ample breasts for Hannah to explore. Now it is her turn to be touched. She kisses her neck, gently cupping one of Ashleigh's breasts. Hannah sits down on the bed in front of her, and put her mouth on Ashleigh's aching nipples. She moans and tosses her head back. I get off the bed and move in behind her; I reach around slid my hand down into the moist crevice between her legs. Ashleigh continues to moan, enjoying the attention of both of us. I rub and tease while Hannah sucks and licks her breasts. I begin grinding my hard cock into Ashleigh's ass. She reaches back and starts to rub me. I grab the string on her sweatpants, pulling to release the

His Eyes

knot. She gasps as I shoot my hand down her pants, wanting me to plunge my finger inside her. I achieve my goal, diving my fingers into her wet depths. Hannah didn't let up, and continued to kiss and suck Ashleigh's boobs. It seems she is going to come already, so I stop what I am doing. Needless to say, this did not meet with Ashleigh's approval, but I also know she loves it when I delay her orgasms, especially the first one of the session.

We turn our attention back to our guest. Hannah's eager mouth meets mine. I kiss her very deeply, and caress her entire body. Ashleigh goes to work on the knot in her sweatpants, and very soon has them off of her. I pull back from her, looking deep into her eyes. She is beautiful, and a perfect contrast to Ashleigh. She is my height, blonde, very tan, and very firm; in her mid-twenties prime. Ashleigh is a stunning brunette, white skin and ample breasts that live to be touched. A little older and shorter than Hannah, she shows the comfort in her own skin by displaying the confidence she is tonight. Hannah and I are following her. Ashleigh manages to wrestle my shorts down over my cock, which by now is at full attention. The cool night air hits it, shortly after that Ashleigh's mouth. She is jerking me with one hand, and sucking my cock furiously. I can tell the tension in her thighs is building to the boiling point.

As Ashleigh kneels in front of me, Hannah gets on her knees on the bed and begins to kiss me again. I grab her ass, and explore her entire body with my hands. Ashleigh is hard at work, and knowing that she is out of my reach, takes matters into her own hands. The excitement is becoming too much, and she can no longer wait. Sexual patience has never Ashleigh's strong suit, but to her credit has lasted much longer than I expected. In less than a minute, she removes my cock from her mouth just in time to cry out in ecstasy. She comes all over her fingers, bucking her hips, her eyes shut tightly with a look of total pleasure on her face. Hannah and I both stop to watch her. "Wow, that was a good one!" she says. "You haven't seen anything yet." I inform her. "You ready?" I look at her and smile.

She bites her lip in anticipation, but her mouth quickly reopens as I finally touch her clit. I was being careful to avoid it earlier, and the sensation of finally being touched there appears almost overwhelming to

108

her. I lightly rub her pleasure button, gradually building up pressure. She is getting close, very close to coming. She puts her hands on my shoulders, closes her eyes, and arching her body to meet my fingers. Just as she reaches the top, I stop. She bucks and squirms, and looks desperately at me and cries out "Please!" I smile at her. "OK" I relent, shoving my fingers deep inside her. She goes through the roof! She comes all over my hand, her creaminess squishing out around my fingers. Ashleigh, hearing her orgasm begin turns around from sucking my cock and pushes Hannah backwards and onto the bed. She collapses on the comforter, writhing in pleasure and crying out with abandon. I keep my fingers inside her; I can feel her muscles spasming around them. Ashleigh keeps rubbing until she thinks Hannah's had enough, and then finally stops. Her orgasms are different than Ashleigh's short, violent explosions; hers are long and drawn out, and she needs a break to compose herself. I stand up and kick off my shorts, and then rip Ashleigh's sweats off of her. Ashleigh and I meet in a deep kiss as our guest lies twitching on the bed in front of us.

My hands journey all over her, squeezing those breasts that I love so much, and grabbing her ass. "Go get her" I whisper into Ashleigh's ear. She moans in delight, loving the prospect of shoving her face between Hannah's legs. She slides down to the foot of the bed, and positions herself between Hannah's thighs. She starts at the knees, slowly kissing her way towards her neatly trimmed pussy. Hannah shaves the sides and trims the top into a happy trail, and Ashleigh gives an approving grin. I move forward on the bed, and give Hannah access to my cock for the first time. She touches it lightly at first, petting and stroking it like it is new to her. She wraps her hands around it, feeling my hard cock pulsating under her touch. She becomes distracted as Ashleigh starts to run her hot tongue over her. She manages to concentrate enough to continue jerking me while Ashleigh increases the pace and pressure down below.

The candles, the smell of the rain, and the scent of sex hangs in the room; it is a sensory overload. Soon she is rising again, as Ashleigh expertly flicked her tongue all over Hannah's sopping wet pussy. She does a half roll towards me, and begins to furiously suck my cock. Hannah moans with her mouth full of my cock. She reaches behind me and grabbed my ass, pulling me deeper into her mouth. She explodes

into another long orgasm, pulling my cock out of her mouth and crying out loudly, just as Ashleigh had done herself. Ashleigh is unrelenting down south, wanting to bring another orgasm out of her. I lie down on the bed, and grab Ashleigh's hips, pulling her on top of me. The three of us make a triangle on the bed, each deeply engrossed in pleasuring someone while enjoying someone pleasuring them. I am really rubbing Ashleigh hard with my tongue, and she comes first, bucking her hips into my face. She never pulls away from Hannah, and her cries of ecstasy are muffled in Hannah's pussy. I am trying to hold off, but can't take it any more, and shoot my second load of the day, this time into Hannah's hungry mouth. She follows me closely, pushed over the edge of her own orgasm by the impact of mine. Ashleigh stays with her no matter how hard she bucks her hips. I roll over and help to hold her down while Ashleigh laps away at her.

I lay down on the bed, and Ashleigh practically pushes Hannah aside to get to me. She grabs my cock and stuffs it inside her. The look on her face says it all, total ecstasy. She bites her lip, and rides me like a Triple Crown jockey. We have fucked like this many times before, and I know she loves being on top. Her pace quickly increases, and I put my hands on her hips. I do this in an attempt to control her pace, and the length of her "stride", but usually to no avail. I just hang on and try to ride it out when the orgasm comes. Hannah is lying beside us, watching Ashleigh fuck herself senseless on top of me. She starts the familiar bucking of her hips, and I know it is coming. I arch my back and lift her off the bed, supporting her weight and mine on only my shoulder blades and my heels. I shove my cock right through her, and her slick pussy grips my cock as she drains her juices all over me. She rolls off of me, spent from getting hers.

"Is it my turn?" Hannah asks. Ashleigh gets up and crawls in behind Hannah, lifting her limp body up to a sitting position, and wraps her legs around her waist. She looks at me and commands me to fuck her. "Give it to her good." She reaches down and hooks Hannah's leg, lifting it and giving me access to her glistening pussy. I scoot forward and am on my knees in front of her, ready to feel her around my cock. I can't believe I am still this hard, but then again this sort of opportunity does not happen every day. Ashleigh strokes her fingers through Hannah's hair, and turns her head to kiss her. I ease my cock into her, giving her a few inches,

and then pulling all the way out, only to re-enter her again. Ashleigh is sitting behind her, holding her legs open for me to plow away. And I do just that. I arch my back and then shove forward, driving my cock all the way inside her. She arches to meet me, taking all my length. I pull out until just the tip is left inside her, and drive in again. Hannah whimpers and groans in delight. She loves the feeling of my stiff cock penetrating her, and wraps a leg around me to pull me in just a little more. I quicken the pace, stroking her deeply each time. Ashleigh lets go of her leg, and I take over the job of opening her to me. Ashleigh's hands are busy squeezing Hannah's breasts, and running all over her body. It is obvious she is going to come after only a few minutes of this, and Ashleigh decides to help by rubbing her clit while I pound her pussy. She explodes again, screaming even louder than before. She falls back into Ashleigh's arms, collapsing from the intensity of yet another orgasm.

Ashleigh decides she wants a good hard pounding as well, and assumes the position on her back to receive it. I lift her leg over my shoulder, and entwine her other leg in mine, making sure she can't slide away from me. I begin the same way I did with Hannah, slowly easing in and out, teasing her with it. She wants it hard, and looks like she is ready to burst. I know how prideful she is, and getting her to break down and beg for it is an exquisite victory each and every time it happens. She is right on the edge of giving in, crumpling the comforter in her hands. She squirms and wriggles, trying to get more of it into her. I have had enough power plays for today, and decide to give in before she does. I withdrawal, and hammer into her in one long, hard stroke. She loves it, and wraps around me aching for more. And I give it to her; pounding down into her and splitting her in half in this position. I am slapping my body into hers, jamming myself as deep into her as I can. She struggles to breath, turning red for a second until she erupts into another deep orgasm. It is intense, and I can feel the impact myself. She goes limp underneath me, melting.

I want one more run with Hannah, and tell her to lie on the bed next to me. She laughs and she says she isn't sure she can take any more. I assure her she can. She reaches down to put me inside her; and I roll onto my back with her on top of me, both of us facing the ceiling. I love this position because I can touch every part of her. I look up, watching her writhing on top of me in the skylight. "Look" I say, pointing to the

ceiling. She is shy about it at first, but warms quickly to the idea of watching herself ride me like this. She reaches back over us, and pushes her hands into the wall. This brings her all the way down on my cock, much to her delight. I fondle her tits, and kiss her ears and neck while she rides me. Soon Ashleigh is recovered enough to join in again.

She assumes a position at the foot of the bed, this time with both me and Hannah in front of her. She begins licking my balls, and running her tongue over the base of my cock that Hannah exposes on an upward stroke. She starts to lengthen the strokes of her tongue, hitting Hannah's pussy as well. Soon she is licking the both of us, her tongue running from the bottom of my balls to the top of Hannah's pussy. I feel Ashleigh's finger press into Hannah's soft pink flesh, squeezing into the tight space that my cock occupies. I can feel it too, and it only heightens my desire to explode in Hannah.

The weight of Hannah's body on me, Ashleigh's tongue on my balls, and Hannah's pussy sliding over my cock is too much. Apparently it is the same for Hannah, as she begins to howl in a most unfeminine sounding growl. Her orgasm begins, and seems to trigger mine as well. I begin to moan, and Hannah pushes hard into the wall, wanting to feel the force of my release inside her this time. "Yes, yes…let me feel you come" she mumbles, but she is denied. Ashleigh pulls her off of me and swallows my cock all the way to the base. "Oh Jesus Christ…yes, oh fuck!" I hear myself grunting. "One last taste" she says, and jerks my cock until I explode all of Hannah's stomach, showering her in my jizz. I fall back into the sheets, exhausted from the incredible experience the three of us just had.

The three of us collapse on each other, absolutely spent from the sex. We sleep like that until morning, knowing we would need our rest for the next day. The last conscious thought through my mind was just how amazing Ashleigh is, and what a lucky man I am to have her in my life.